To Bob:

with my best regards

Dan Snow

EYE
TO
EYE

EYE
TO
EYE

DON MORSE

CRYPTIC PRESS
AMBLER, PENNSYLVANIA

Published by
Cryptic Press, Inc.,
P.O. Box 503, Ambler, PA 19002
Copyright © 1991 by Don Morse

ISBN 1-878869-01-9
Manufactured in the United States of America
First printing: June, 1991
10 9 8 7 6 5 4 3 2 1

ACKNOWLEDGMENTS

S pecial thanks to: Dr. Louis Dubin, for hypnosis information; Dr. Howard Hall, for details about psychosomatic interrelationships; Jack Rieur, for information about Haiti, Barbara Esposito, Susan Rieur, and Robert Benowitz, for proofing and suggestions; and Joan Bettendorf, for her careful and thorough editorial treatment.

To my mother-in-law, Betty:
for her implacable will to live.

Death is, to a certain extent, an impossibility which suddenly becomes a reality.

GOETHE

AUTHOR'S NOTE

This is a work of fiction. Many of the events described occur in existing places in real cities. For some places, such as large hotels, universities, and museums, because of the prominence in the particular city, the real names have been used. For others, such as all the places in Pompano Beach, North Miami Beach, New Orleans, and Tokyo, and some of the Haitian cities and towns, locations, names, and times of events have been changed. All names and characters are purely fictional and bear no relationship to any person living or dead. Nevertheless, all the scientific, historical, and cultural materials are either factual or based on evidence from leading authorities. There are two exceptions. The personal characteristics and some of the activities attributed to the houngans and the bokors are not necessarily those of practitioners of these professions. In addition, some of the mind-and physiological-altering effects of hypnosis have not been definitely documented or proven, even though they are hypothetically possible.

"Eye to Eye" was written to be read and understood in its own right. However, in it, mention is made of certain information that would divulge the identity of the killer from the first book of this series, "Deadly Reaction." Therefore, for those of you who plan on reading the previous book, you may prefer to read it first. At any rate, I thank everyone for allowing me to bring forth the further adventures of Meltzer & Meltzer, Private Investigators.

PROLOGUE

Monday, January 9, 1989

The seeds of destruction which bore fruit today were planted a long time ago. Situated in a mountainous region of the Caribbean, this West Indies island had been the home of the Arawak Indians for centuries. In the 1500s, the island was invaded, conquered, and colonized by Spain. It was named Hispaniola. The English and French entered the western region in the 1600s, and by 1650, the English had been driven out. The Arawaks were decimated by the invaders, and African slaves — by the droves — were imported to take their place. The Spanish continued to fight the French, but by 1795, Spain retained the eastern two-thirds as Santa Domingo and ceded the western third — Santa Domingue — to France. Simultaneously, a slave-led rebellion took place in Santa Domingue, and in 1804, the Africans drove out the Frenchmen and established an independent republic. And in this steamy location, an ancient mystic religion and tradition germinated.

This night was dark and starless; the air was thick and motionless. Loud and intense drum beats disrupted the silence sending shock waves through the ground. Oblivious

9

to everything except the sound, the dancers pounded the turf while simultaneously making obscene gestures with their buttocks.   Flickering flames, coming from the candles perched on the drums, provided the only light for the surrealistic celebration. The hypnotic tempo quickened the dancers' pace.   Surrounding the dancers was a group of spectators. They alternately chanted and drank a revolting brew.

Emanating from the depths of the darkness, an apparition unfolded. It materialized into human form as a tall, dark man, featuring a high hat and black robe. He picked up a thin, jagged bone, recently extracted from the flesh of a giant lizard. The earth shook violently as he pointed the bone in a predetermined direction, while simultaneously uttering an arcane incantation.   The recipient was a hapless individual who stared glassy-eyed at the nefarious pointer. The victim suddenly raised his hands as if to ward off the evil fluid which he could feel streaming into his body. His cheeks blanched as if he had just seen a ghost, and his face became contorted into an ape-like configuration. Out of the depths of his lungs a shriek began, but the sound muffled in his throat, and the only discharge was frothy saliva.   He trembled uncontrollably and swayed backward. From the background of the loud drum reverberations, a dull thud was heard as the lifeless body fell to the ground.

1

Tuesday, January 10, 1989

The great-grandchildren hadn't seen their great-grandpop for six months. The last time they saw him, he was playing tennis on one of the soft clay courts at the North Miami Beach Tennis Condominium. He had been an athlete all of his 79 years, and there weren't too many people approaching 80 who could still play singles tennis. But that was six months ago. Today, he was in bed in his Florida condo apartment—wheezing and coughing badly.

"Hi, pop-pop; you no feel good?"

"Hi, grampy; you sick?"

"Hi, Jason, hi, Darlene; I'm not feeling too well. I just can't get rid of this cold."

"Your throat hurt you, pop-pop?"

"It does, Jason; my nose and my chest also bother me."

"Take your medicine, grampy; then you'll get all better."

"You're right, Darlene; I just have to take my medicine, and then I'll be fine."

The great-grandchildren came with their parents to visit their great-grandfather because he was ill. Jason Robert Bonowitz, age two years, two months, came from Moores-

11

town, New Jersey. Darlene Lois Marsch, age two years
seven months, came from Chicago. This was their second
trip to Florida, but their first one as talkers.

Great-grandpop, David Robert Marsch, was thrilled to
hear them talk, but he had been taking his medicine, and the
results weren't good.   His doctors didn't know why.
Although he was an asthmatic all his life, he had compensated
for his weakened lungs as well as any one. Being
happily married for 44 years, having a few good friends, not
smoking, taking vitamins, eating a low-fat diet, exercising
daily, meditating regularly, and having a low-stress life — all
of the ingredients to insure a healthy and happy life. And it
worked, that is, until two weeks ago. At that time, he came
down with a cold. It started out as the sniffles, progressed
into a sinusitis, transformed into a dry, hacking, cough, and
finally worked its way into his lungs as a deep-seated
bronchitis. Once it developed into a severe chest cold with its
thick, yellow, mucus — that was seven days ago — he made
an appointment with his allergist, Harlan Werner, M.D. The
doctor prescribed erythromycin for the infection, added Theo-
Dur to help open the bronchioles, and maintained him on his
other asthma medications: Maxair, Intal, and Beclovent.
After three days of treatment, he showed no sign of
improvement.   Dr. Werner then checked him into the North
Miami Beach General Hospital. He was examined by the
internist, Arnold Banks, M.D., who ordered a series of tests
including microbial analyses, antibiotic susceptibility, lung
function tests, a chest x-ray, a stress EKG, and a blood
work-up. To get a sample of the bronchial exudate, he was
given intravenous sedation by anesthesiologist, Dr. Ralph
Blackmore. Then with the use of a bronchoscope, material
was removed from the deep recesses of his lungs. With all of
these tests, aside from the finding of a minor strep infection,
everything came out normal. His heart was strong; his blood
pressure was excellent (135/72); and his cholesterol level was
exceptional (158 mg/dl). Even though he was still coughing,
the expectorate was much clearer, and the asthma was under

control. To make sure it wasn't all in his head, he had a consultation with the psychologist, Dr. Ronald Fielding. The psychologist's report stated that he was not under undue stress and was mentally stable. David's next encounter was with the physical therapist, Dr. Sidney Largent, who taught him some breathing exercises. After that session, he had sessions with a volunteer, a nurse, and a couple of aides. Following that, he had dinner, watched TV, and went to bed. This morning, he was discharged and told to drink plenty of juices, take the prescribed medications, and just rest in bed. Before he left, he found a place in his overnight bag for the bright-eyed doll — the one he found at the side of his bed. He thought, *"It would be perfect for Darlene."*

Dorothy Frieda Marsch, a sprightly, attractive 70-year old, did all she could to cheer up her husband, David. She was upset that he was still sick, but she was excited to see the grandchildren and great-grandchildren. After greeting her granddaughter, Kathy and husband, Richard, and her grandson, Barth, and wife, Shirley, she spoke to her two great-grandchildren.

"I'm so happy to see you, Jason. It's great seeing you, Darlene."

"Hi, grammy."

"Hi, nanny."

After the customary hugs and kisses, she took them and their parents into the kitchen for milk and cookies (for the kids) and tea and danish (for the adults). Great-grandpop, David, was left alone to rest.

* * * *

The same afternoon, in the picturesque town of Pompano Beach, Florida, ruggedly handsome, Hank Meltzer, a retired Philadelphia police captain and vivacious, Marilyn, the widow of attorney, Jerome Arnetz, were married in a simple ceremony. They had been responsible for the arrest of Dr. Mitchell Turner, the alleged perpetrator of the puffer fish

poisoning series of murders.   At this very moment, Dr.
Turner was sitting in a prison cell in the Miami municipal jail,
while in a northern suburb of Miami, another doctor, from
the basement of his home, was considering life and death
matters.

Unlike many other Florida professionals, this doctor was
not a transplanted northerner, having spent his entire 68 years
in the tropical warmth of the greater Miami area. Although he
had many interests and several fields of competence, he was
recognized as an expert on rats (of all things). Today, he was
ready to conduct a major experiment with these universally-
hated creatures. The previous findings corroborated his
hypotheses on mind-body interactions; this experiment was
to have an added twist. His new, part-time, lab assistant,
Jack Albus, knew very little about rodents. He was about to
get a lesson.   Jack was thin, scrawny, and according to
some, not unlike a rodent in appearance. Unfortunately, Jack
could do little about his genetic endowment: an alcoholic
mother and a drug-addicted father. The environmental
contributions to his maturation (poor diet, filthy living
quarters, inadequate education) didn't do anything to improve
his physical appearance. Nevertheless, he tried to make
something out of his life. At the age of 22, he was tackling
his first real job.

The doctor began his well-prepared discourse: "Rats
have had a bad reputation throughout history. The mouse,
the rat's smaller cousin, is also not too well-liked, but there
are good mice, you know, Walt Disney's Mickey and Minnie
Mouse. Even when we use the word 'mouse' in a negative
way, we are describing a timid or weak person. However,
the rat and the rat designation is only considered to be evil.
The term 'rat' is used to degrade a person. I know you're too
young to have seen the original, but maybe, you caught him
on video. I'm talking about James Cagney in his famous
gangster role where he made that familiar statement: 'You
dirty rat.' That type of rat describes either a contemptible
person, such as someone who betrays his or her friends,

associates, or an organization; you know, a scab or an informer.

Both the mouse and the rat are small rodents; they belong to the class of mammals. That's right, they're our cousins. The mouse's scientific name is *Mus musculis*, but it's better known as a house mouse. House mice came from central Europe. They crossed the Atlantic Ocean hidden in cargo aboard transatlantic ships. By the time of the Revolutionary War, they were well established in the United States. The rats quickly spread all over the populated areas of the country.

As you must know, mice live in our homes and depend on the crumbs from our dining tables. Mice are mainly seed and nut eaters, but they'll eat anything."

"Yeah," Jack added, "Back home in the Bronx, we had a few of those slimy buggers. They were worse than the cockroaches."

The doctor wasn't too thrilled with Jack's reminiscences, but he continued his scientific description. "The average mouse measures six inches long, including its three-inch slender, scaly tail. The entire animal typically weighs less than an ounce."

"No kidding, we must've had some mutants 'cause the ones in our kitchen weighed way more than an ounce."

"Be that as it may, the average mouse is really quite small. Most mice, as you have so vividly described, are household pests, but some domesticated forms, including albino— you know, white — varieties, have been trained as pets, and many are used extensively in biological and medical research.

Now, let me tell you a bit about their cousins, the rats. They're much bigger than mice, and that's probably why they bring forth such terror. All rats belong to the *Rattus group*. The most well-known rat is the Norway or house rat. Like its mouse cousin, this species of rat traveled to the United States hidden in cargo aboard transatlantic ships. Also like mice, house rats can eat anything. Although they can live in the field, these rats prefer to live in or near our homes.

So, they don't have to compete with native rodents for food but can exist on human scraps."

"I bet we had rats, and I just thought they were mice; yeah those ugly things in our kitchen must've been rats."

"Well, you might be right. Anyway, just as is found with mice, there is an albino variety of rats. It is a mutant form of the Norway rat, and has been kept as a house-hold pet, and more importantly, has been used extensively for medical research.

Because of the universal fear of mice and rats, most of the anti-vivisectionists don't object to the use of these creatures in medical research — even when they're beautiful, like the albino varieties. And Jack, my boy, today's experiment is with several of these lovely white creatures."

The Panasonic Camcorder with its 8-hour tape was ready. Placed on a stand, it was focused on the laboratory bench. The doctor turned on the unit. Two huge oblong-shaped jars filled with water were sitting on the bench. After donning a pair of gloves, with the use of silver tongs, the doctor removed three albino rats from their cage and placed them into the first oblong jar. They began to swim vigorously. The doctor checked his watch; it was 11:35 A.M.

"Jack, we're going to leave the lab now. I want you to observe that I'm shutting off the light, locking the door, and we're both leaving the premises. So that neither of us will return without the other, we'll spend the next few hours together. It's an experiment and there's money available for research. So, let's live it up a little. First, we'll have a nice relaxing lunch. Do you like Chinese food?"

"I love all kinds, doc; Chinese, Italian, Japanese, Greek, American; you name it, I'm game."

"Good. After lunch, we'll catch a 2:00 matinee at the Ritz. They've got the latest James Bond movie."

"Doc, you're great. I wanted to see it but haven't had the chance, yet. That'll be perfect because my girl, Barbara, doesn't like 007 thrillers. Now I won't have to bug her to go." (Barbara, who was no beauty herself, liked Jack. Even a rat-like appearance doesn't have to prevent affection.)

"Fine," said the doctor, "then it's decided. First the lunch, then the movie, and we'll take a leisurely walk back to the lab. Let's plan on being back here about 5:00."

"That's swell, doc. Wait till I tell the guys about my hard day at the lab."

"Oh I'm sorry, Jack; that's the only stipulation; mums the word."

"Okay, doc, anything you say."

As planned, the doctor and Jack had an enjoyable afternoon. At 4:58, the doctor opened the laboratory door and switched on the light.

"Take a look at our swimmers, Jack."

Jack Albus was amazed; the three furry rodents were still vigorously stroking in that confined glass swimming pool.

"Now, Jack, I need your assistance. You'll wear tear-resistant gloves, and your only job will be to hold each of the next three rats firmly. You only have to hold them for about 30 seconds each. All you need is a firm grip. Hold them tightly, and they can't hurt you or me. Got it?"

Although a little squeamish, he replied: "I got it, doc."

After giving Jack his pair of gloves, the doctor donned a pair of reinforced rubber gloves. As Jack held each rat, with a pair of sharp scissors, the doctor clipped their whiskers. As soon as he gave each rat its shave, he deposited it into the second oblong jar. In about three minutes, all three rats were in the second jar. The time was 5:09.

"Now, watch carefully, Jack."

The albino rats began to swim, but even the first few strokes were weak. They flailed with purposeless motions.

"Doc, it's crazy, but they look like they just saw a ghost."

"Maybe they did, Jack, maybe they did."

While the three white rats in the first jar were still swimming almost five hours after they began, the second group were dead less than five minutes after their first encounter with the water.

"Isn't it amazing what a shave can do," said Jack.

"Yes," said the doctor, "for these rats, it was their whiskers; for Sampson, it was his hair."

But in actuality, the rats were stressed to death.

* * * *

Great-grandpop David took a nap while the others were snacking. It started out as a nap but wound up being a prolonged sleep. Since he appeared to be sleeping so peacefully, everyone else took off for a leisurely walk around the grounds.

The grandfather clock chimed six times — David awoke with a start. He looked around. No one was in sight. But he thought he heard a child crying. He went to his bedroom window, pulled up the shade, and looked outside. Nothing was there. Leaving the bedroom, he passed through the living room and opened the front door of the ground floor apartment. He gingerly stepped on the front walk. Looking and listening in every direction failed to reveal the source of the now-intensifying sound. Closing the door, he walked back inside. By the time he reached his bedroom, the cry became louder and more piercing. Panicking, he got into the bed and covered himself completely. Still, he couldn't block out the sound. As it intensified, it enveloped the entire room.

He tried to think, *Am I going crazy? What is it? Where is it coming from?*

He had no answers. But just then, the shrill sound changed. Instead of being pervasive, the cry localized. David was able to pin point it. It was coming from a place real close by — right near him — right next to him — from — from — from his own mouth. It was he who was crying. Why was he crying? He didn't know, but something was propelling him, something was telling him, and he had to do something.

What is it? What is it?

Waking up (this time for real), he was in a cold sweat. Then he noticed the doll on the corner shelf — the one he found by his hospital bed and was going to give to Darlene. Strange, he hadn't noticed it before.

Was that the source of the cry? No it couldn't be. I just had a bad dream.

Yet, he still felt compelled. He went over to the shelf, picked the doll up, held it in his hands, and looked at its beautiful eyes.

I wonder, he thought, *is this one of those talking dolls?*

After squeezing it gently, he carelessly dropped it. It fell with a resounding crash.

Still feeling tired, he told himself, *I'll pick it up later.*

He walked to the bed and got under the covers.

"Oh my God!," he shrieked. "Did someone stick a knife in my chest?"

He looked for the blade; he searched for his assailant. But there was nobody there. And there was no blood. Yet the blade was tearing him up inside. At least, that's how it felt. The pain was burning and boring; it was unbearably sharp and penetrating. Could the source be internal? David had never had a heart attack. In fact, aside from his asthma, he had never been sick. This pain was foreign to him, but he knew it was there and it was happening to him. Was he having a heart attack?

I've got to find Dorothy and the others. Where did they go?

He started to rise, but the pain intensified. It spread to his back and shoulders.

Be quiet; be calm; get to the phone; that's all I have to do — just get to the phone. A sledge hammer crushed through his chest tearing out his ribs. *God, get this weight off me! I can't breathe; I can't even move.*

David was a fighter; he had been an amateur wrestler in his younger days, and he never give up in business, in sports, in any endeavor. He wouldn't give up now. Regardless of the unbearable pain, he managed to get himself into the kitchen. He dialed 911 and got a response: "Please send an ambulance to 1650 North Collins Avenue, Apartment 6408. I think I'm - - - "

"What is it mister?"

"Ah, ah; I think it's my heart — a heart attack."

"Hold on, mister; we'll send someone right over."

The answer gave him a ray of hope. He would make it. Just then, the jagged-edged dagger ripped open his coronary blood vessels. He let out an unintelligible "Aaay." Dorothy heard the sound. She ran ahead of the others and leaped into the elevator. In two minutes, she was inside the apartment. David was on the kitchen floor. He wore a death mask.

2

Wednesday, February 15

The stentorian voice of President Chris Johnson boomed out: "The meeting of the Greater Miami Society of Clinical Hypnosis will now come to order."

A hush came over the packed audience in the auditorium of the Miami Medical Center in downtown Miami.

"We will postpone the business meeting until later. Our guest speaker has a tight schedule and has to catch a flight to New York in two hours. Program Chairman, Fred Hickman, will now take over."

A bearded, portly, clinical psychologist went to the podium holding his notes.

"It is with great pleasure that I give you one of the world's most renowned medical hypnotists; a man who was editor-in-chief of both major hypnosis journals; a man who has written over 250 scientific articles and ten books on the subjects of hypnosis, meditation, yoga, and zen; a man who has lectured throughout the United States and in 35 overseas countries. Without further ado, here is Dr. Vincent Simpson. Dr. Simpson will speak about control in hypnosis."

21

A subdued hand followed from the approximately 300 physicians (mainly psychiatrists, anesthesiologists, and internists), dentists, psychologists and other assorted doctors. From his aisle seat in the third row, the rat-expert doctor displayed no emotion.

"Thank you very much Dr. Hickman for the complimentary things you said about me. Since the subject today is one of control, let me first tell you a little story about lack of control.

Three elderly gentlemen were having a discussion about their relative degrees of control with respect to excretory functions. The first man — a mere lad of 65 years of age — said: 'When I get up in the morning, I go to the bathroom and stand by the toilet. I stand and stand and wait and wait. After a few minutes, a few little drops trickle out.'

'That's nothing,' said the second elderly man, who was a robust 75. 'My problem is much worse. I sit down on the toilet and squeeze and squeeze. Finally after much squeezing, a tiny little hard lump comes out.'

The third oldster — a sprightly 85-year old — countered: 'I don't know what's the matter with you guys. I have no trouble urinating, I had no trouble defecating (for this scientific meeting, the speaker used the technical terms although everyone present knew what the old man would **really** say)- - - and then, I get out of bed.' "

The audience roared, even though several of them were in their mid-eighties and knew the problems of advanced age. Once quiet was restored, Dr. Simpson resumed: "Obviously, all three men had a lack of control, but the oldest gentleman was also losing some control of his mental facilities. And that is what I shall speak to you about today. Can hypnosis cause loss of mental control? And does the individual have to be willing for this to occur?

We have all been taught that a person who is in a hypnotic trance, no matter how deep or how good a hypnotic subject he or she may be, **won't** do anything against his or her will.

In other words, a person **cannot** be forced to do something he or she doesn't want to. You may counter by saying: 'How about the person who barks like a dog in front of an audience. Does he really want to play the fool?' The answer is that maybe not consciously but subconsciously, he is willing or desirous to act in that manner. Possibly, he always wanted to be the center of attraction, and this is an easy way for him to show off. But the answer is not as simple as that.

Under hypnosis, people can do things that they would not do under ordinary circumstances. Why? Because they are tricked into believing the circumstances are different. True, according to the ethics of our professions and our hypnotic society we would never trick or deceive our patients. But the truth is that we deceive them all the time. How many doctors tell their patients the complete truth about their medical condition, especially if they are near death from cancer or heart disease? Sometimes we tell them they will get better because we have done all we could and hope for their recovery is wishful thinking on our parts.

In order to achieve a deep hypnotic trance, we lie and deceive. Just think about it. We tell them fantastic stories about being on a mountain and climbing down a cliff; we talk about a pilotless boat that will take them to a magical place of utter serenity. We stroke their hands and tell them a large balloon is attached to the wrist, and as the balloon ascends, they will get more and more relaxed. We confuse them; tell them contradictory and illogical occurrences in order to get them into a trance. Vivid descriptions are given of hands being placed into buckets of freezing cold water — resulting in pins and needles, followed by numbness. We tell them their arms or legs are rigid and immobile. We know that none of these things are happening. They are all ruses that we use in order to achieve some purpose. The purposes are noble: relief of pain; reduction of anxiety; decrease of depression; probing their minds for causes of their present psychosomatic or psychological condition. The means we use are lies and deceptions, even if they are used for noble causes."

A murmur of dissent and unrest swept the audience.
Most doctors don't like to be told that they are anything but
perfect, magnanimous, and noble. Certainly, none of them
want to hear that they are liars.

Dr. Simpson waited a few minutes for them to quiet
down. He then continued: "Now, let us consider some
hypothetical situations in which none of us would ever be
involved. But let's examine them anyway. I am going to
show the male role in this scenario, but it would work equally
as well for a woman in the opposite situation.

You are infatuated with a beautiful woman. You want to
make love to her, but it is improper and unethical. We all
know that we cannot merely have her look into our eyes and
succumb to our every desire. That wouldn't work because
she wouldn't do anything against her will. In this
hypothetical situation, the woman is happily married and has
no desire for anyone except her husband. But could you trick
her? Could you fool her? The answer is: definitely! All you
have to do is deceive her. First of all she must have trust in
you. There must be rapport between the two of you.
Second, she must be able to concentrate well. Of course,
these two factors are important for all good hypnotic subjects.
Third — and especially important for this scenario — she
must have a vivid imagination. She must be able to readily
take mental trips. You have to be able to get her into a deep
state of hypnosis; that is, into the somnambulistic stage. We
all know that about 15% of the population can achieve this
depth of hypnosis. At any rate, once she is sufficiently deep,
you then plant some major lies. You tell her she is at home,
and it is late at night. Good hypnotic subjects do not question
that they are in a doctor's office and home at the same time.
As you know, trance logic is strange and can tolerate
inconsistencies that would be considered illogical under
ordinary circumstances.

You tell her she is tired and should get ready for bed.
Then, she would have no compunctions about disrobing.
You can further suggest that her husband is coming to bed

with her and is in an amorous mood. Ladies and gentlemen, I leave the rest to your imaginations."

Now the audience was no longer murmuring. They were noisy and disrespectful. President Johnson took the microphone and roared: "This is outrageous. I am certain that Dr. Simpson has a good reason for telling us this. I will have no more interruptions. I'm sorry, doctor; please continue."

The booming, threatening voice had it effects; the shocked doctors quieted down. Interestingly, throughout all the murmuring and noise, the rat-expert doctor listened expressionlessly.

Dr. Simpson continued: "It's quite all right. Had I been listening to myself, I, too, would have become upset. But I have a reason to tell you this. I want you to be aware that what I have said is not just hypothetical. It has happened and continues to happen. As you all know, there are many unscrupulous people who call themselves hypnotists. We have to be certain that people know the complete truth. That they are aware that they should only go to accredited medical hypnotists for any kind of health-related therapy. Because, deception can be used in unsavory ways.

There is another way in which deception can be used to get a person to do something against his or her will. When an individual is in a deep hypnotic trance, it's as if a cover or cloud is placed over his or her consciousness. A person in a deep hypnotic trance is in a condition similar to being intoxicated — like being drunk or drugged. When someone has had a few drinks too many, he or she will do things that normally wouldn't be allowed. The censor has been removed, and it's then all right to flirt with someone or sing like a fool or say silly, stupid things. In this case, the person is not doing something against his or her will. He or she is doing something that would not be foreign to his or her personality. But this is the important part, it would only be done if the person was in an altered state of consciousness — like being a little drunk or stoned.

Now, let's consider that office scenario again. This time, let us say that the woman is attracted to the doctor, and the doctor knows it. However, the woman is married and realizes it is not moral or ethical for her to let her feelings be known. The hypnotist-doctor, though, is aware of how a deep hypnotic trance is similar to being drunk and uncensored. Hence, it would be relatively easy for him to seduce the woman while she is under the altered state. The point to remember here is that the woman is not doing something against her will. She is physically attracted to the doctor, but she would only consent to his advances under the special circumstance of hypnosis. Again, here my point is that we must all be aware of this possibility and therefore, pressure both the public and politicians. Let them know that only moral and ethical doctors should be allowed to practice hypnosis.

Now, let's turn away from the sexual side of hypnotic control and consider an even more sinister aspect. Have any of you read the book or seen the movie: 'The Manchurian Candidate?' "

About half the audience raised their hands. The rat-expert doctor was one of the affirmative respondents.

"Do you remember the scene in which an American soldier shoots his buddy? Brain-washing by the Chinese communists is purported to be the method by which the soldier is convinced to kill a fellow American. He ordinarily would not shoot a countryman. But he was placed into a hypnotic trance, and while he was deeply under, he was deceived. Just like I told you about deceiving a woman into believing she was at home and about to go to bed, the American soldier was deceived into believing that his buddy was a traitor. Killing a traitor would not be doing something against the soldier's will.

You might say that this was just a figment of the author's imagination, and that it can't happen in real life. Well, I tell you it can. It has occurred in the past and will happen again unless we alert the public against going to unprofessional hypnotists. Of course, no medical hypnotist would ever hypnotize a patient into believing that he or she would be doing something beneficial by killing someone. But there are unscrupulous people out there who take advantage of rapport, concentration, and especially a vivid imagination, and use deceit to commit dastardly deeds."

The audience buzzed again, but this time they soon stopped of their own accord.

Dr. Simpson then continued for twenty more minutes, giving several other examples about how deception can be used to control people's thoughts and actions. He continued to mention that doctors would never do such things because it was against their ethical and moral upbringing. Furthermore, he emphasized that doctors should use all of their means to prevent unethical lay hypnotists from harming naive and gullible patients. There was an enthusiastic question and answer session. At its conclusion, Dr. Vincent Simpson received a standing ovation. The rat-expert doctor merely smiled. He knew that he could have given this lecture himself.

* * * *

The sun was shining brightly as the rat-expert doctor left the air-conditioned medical building. Dressed in a light-blue suit, wearing dark sun glasses, and only exposing his face for a few seconds, he was able to avoid the cancer-inducing sunlight. Having worn similar garb for most of his life, at the age of 68, his skin had the unhealthy pale pink appearance of an apartment-dwelling northerner. But he was alive and well, and he meant to stay that way for many more years. After all, he had an important mission in life.

The sunlight pierced the closely cropped Bermuda grass, setting in motion the photosynthetic process that provided oxygen for the laboring ants that were busy building a home. The doctor was deep in thought. *Isn't it amazing that we, the most advanced species on earth kill each other in*

*greater numbers than all of the other species combined.
Not only that, we destroy in an incredible variety of ways.
And the most amazing method of all is by will power — the
strength of the mind.*

Just as the doctor was about to walk to his car door, his
right foot missed the pavement, and his heel came crushing
down on the newly constructed ant hill. Unlike the more
advanced humans, the lowly ants didn't have time to worry
about their impending death.

3

Friday, March, 10

It's delightful to be in south Florida at this time of the year. Warm, but not hot, low humidity, clean air, cloudless sky. When clouds and showers appear, the onset is late and the stay is short-lived. It was a typical morning. The sun's reflection off the white stone facade of the North Miami Beach General Hospital was blinding. It almost caused the ambulance driver to miss the entrance. But he screeched to a halt in front of the Emergency Room. An elderly man on the verge of death was carried inside.

Major activity was also occurring in the main operating room. The intense beam from the dazzling light was centered on the long table. The entire body was draped except for a small opening below the diaphragm. Incisions went through, skin, mucosa, muscle. Excess blood and tissue fluids were evacuated almost as soon as they appeared. Instruments were passed back and forth, and finally the gastrointestinal tract was exposed. All was hushed as the surgeon, Dr. Lawrence Humphrey, peered into the colon. Facing him were a multitude of raw, red, encrusted growths.

"The poor slob hasn't got a chance," he exclaimed.

No one amongst the remainder of the masked ensemble could offer a response.

The resident took over and sewed the thickened lining of the over-used lower gut. The last health-care worker to depart the scene was the anesthesiologist, Ralph Blackmore, M.D. Before he left, he slowly brought the patient safely back to consciousness. Seventy-two year old Henry Preston went from unconscious non-awareness to conscious awareness, a consciousness filled with pain and depression. He was on death's door, and whether he wanted it or not, he was now ready for psychological intervention.

* * * *

In a seedy corner of the Little Havana section of Miami, a small, whitewashed shop stood out from the debris-laden background. The shop was filled with dolls. They were not the typical dolls one finds in a toy store — neither Cabbage Patch nor Barbie dolls were anywhere to be found. These dark-skinned wooden dolls were clothed in native costumes. The females had bandanas on their heads and wore wide-necked, brightly colored blouses and full skirts. The male counterparts had on wide-brimmed straw hats and pantaloons. They all wore sandals. Even though well constructed, most appeared inanimate. But an isolated few were different. The difference was in their eyes — stark blue pupils that appeared to dilate and constrict as the entering light waves changed in size and intensity.

The shop owner, Ibu Mazalo, was a true African-American. Twenty-five years ago, he left the country of Dahomey (today it's called Benin) and following the relatives of his ancestors, he moved to Haiti. (In the old days, it was called Santa Domingue.) He lived in Haiti for fifteen years, but unable to tolerate any longer the Duvalier regime with its *tontons macoute* secret police and the threat of constant harassment, ten years ago, he joined about 50,000 other Haitians and moved to Miami. Once there, he opened a doll shop.   Now at the age of 73, he was a prosperous businessman. But in reality, he was much more. Ibu Mazalo was a bokor, a secret practitioner of the *ounga* — the Congo-derived form of witchcraft. Recently he began working with an American doctor.

* * * *

Henry Preston's surgeon, Dr. Lawrence Humphrey, saw him the next morning. He spoke to Henry alone for a few minutes, but his words did nothing to alleviate Henry's distress. The psychologist, Dr. Ronald Fielding, and the physical therapist, Dr. Sidney Sargent, both of whom saw Henry that afternoon,   weren't any more successful in comforting the old man. Neither was the hospital volunteer.

The doll that Henry found at his bedside made him feel good — real good — at least temporarily.

* * * *

Two days later, Henry Preston was buried. The few mourners felt that once the doctors found out he had advanced colon cancer, he hadn't a chance. His wife, Jenny, had loved him dearly, but she felt he was better off dead than alive with unbearable pain and no chance at all for recovery. There was nothing any one could have done for Henry Preston — or was there?

* * * *

At the same time, in another warm location — the town of Bizóton — in the western end of the island of Hispaniola, other mourners brought a body to a desolate grave site. Neither dancing, chanting, nor pulsating drum beating were evident. It was dark and unearthly quiet. Before the wooden box was lowered, it was opened. A hand went inside. It was holding a large black hammer. Seconds later, a long iron nail was driven deeply into the victim's forehead. All bodily functions became irrevocably interrupted. The deceased was forever protected from zombification. All was now peaceful. The only sound to be heard was the soft patter of falling dirt as each spade-full covered the wooden box.

4

Wednesday, April 12

All eyes were riveted on the podium. Dr. Harmon Rivere, a noted hypnotherapist-psychiatrist, was the featured speaker. The assembled members of the Greater Miami Society of Clinical Hypnosis listened with keen anticipation as he began:

"The results of our examinations show unequivocally that patients hear what is said when they are under general anesthesia. Not only that, what they hear can greatly affect their lives — whether they will live or die — how long they will live — the quality of their lives.

Here are the details. The first patient was a 58-year old woman who was being operated on for cancer of the right breast. She was on the operating table for one and a half hours. Recovery from anesthesia was uneventful. A few days later, I saw her for psychotherapy. The patient was extremely depressed. It is not unusual to have post-surgical depression, but this woman's state was much more severe than I would have anticipated. So, I asked her if she would agree to the exploratory use of hypnosis. Although not overly enthusiastic, she still agreed to let me try Fortunately, she was a good hypnotic subject, and without any problem, I was able to regress her to the time of the operation. According to the patient's words, this is what took place.

"*A male voice spoke first; it must have been the surgeon.*

'The tissue is deeply infiltrated; the lesions are everywhere; the axial lymph nodes are loaded. Even if we get out all the primary, we already know that she had distant metastases. This gal hasn't got long to go. I give her six weeks. What do you think, Marty?'

'Six weeks, Jack; you're optimistic. This babe will be pushing up daisies in less than 30 days.'

'Well, maybe you're right. At any rate, she's a goner!'

It was quiet for a long time. Then I heard: 'Frank, sew her up. I'm off. Now, I'll be able to make my golf date.'

Aside from the sound of instruments, that's all I heard. The next thing I remember is waking up in the recovery room, and the nurse asking me if I was cold. I sure was; I was shivering. I took the extra blankets, and they wheeled me back to the room."

While she was still in the trance, I tried to reassure her that all would be well. But it was too late; the damage had already been done. Three weeks later, they buried her."

Frequently at these hypnosis meetings, the lectures are so stimulating that the audience buzzes and sometimes even interrupts the speaker. However, following this disclosure, the audience was stunned into silence. The speaker continued.

"At first, I thought that maybe the patient was making this all up. After all, we now know that patients can lie under hypnosis, and possibly the woman was angry with the surgeon. Since I knew one of the operating room nurses quite well, I took her into my confidence and asked her what had happened that afternoon. I told her that I would keep her response in complete confidence, and would not make an incident about what had occurred. With that assurance, she went over that afternoon's events. Sure enough, she completely corroborated the patient's version. I still felt that this might have been an isolated occurrence. But I was wrong — dead wrong.

Since that first time — almost two years ago — I have found 15   other instances in which hypnotized patients remembered details of conversations taking place while they were under general anesthesia — and supposedly out of it. And the worst part is that when statements were made that the individuals had a hopeless or fatal condition, regardless of what I said afterwards, the patients died from days to weeks after the operation. I was discouraged, but I felt that I had to let the hospital staff know about my findings. We had a meeting, and I gave them the complete details of all 16 cases. The names of the surgeons were not revealed, but the involved doctors were present at that meeting. I told them that since the patients can hear while under general anesthesia, and that their bodies can negatively react to the statements made, why don't we try and do the reverse. Why don't the surgeons and all operating room personnel say positive things regardless of what they find clinically. The staff was stunned at my findings, but they agreed to follow my suggestions.

I am happy to report that the very next surgery showed a diametrically opposite result. Here are the details of that case. Almost as if it were a planned control case, this patient was also being operated on for breast cancer on the right side. She was slightly older — 58 years of age. The operation lasted a little less than two hours, and anesthetic recovery was uneventful. A few days later, when I saw the patient for psychotherapy, she appeared to be in good spirits. I knew that her condition was just as bad as the first patient. The cancer had invaded her lymph nodes and metastasized to her lungs. She readily agreed to hypnosis and was also a good subject. I regressed her back to the time of the operation. In her own words, this is what happened.

"I could hear everything perfectly. The male voice said:

'Everything came out smoothly. It looks like we got it all out.'

Somewhat later, I heard: 'The nodes were positive but, we got them out cleanly. With chemo, I bet she'll be around for a long time. What do you think, Marty?'

'I agree with you, Jack.'

'Fine, Frank, please suture the wound. Let me thank you for all your help.'

After that, there was no more talking. I still heard the sounds of instruments being passed back and forth, but that didn't last long. The next thing I remembered was hearing my nurse offering me a blanket. I was never so cold in my life, and the blanket helped me stop shivering."

As you might have guessed, the patient lived longer than the previous breast cancer patient. In fact, she lived a lot longer; she stayed in relatively good health for two years. With the use of hypnosis, her last days were painless and peaceful."

This time, the audience responded with applause. Everyone likes a relatively happy outcome. That is, everyone except the rat-expert doctor. He merely smiled.

Dr. Rivere resumed: "Well, that positive result was followed by 12 other cases in which the patients lived much longer than would be expected for patients with similar conditions. In fact, two of the patients are alive five years following the surgery, and even though their conditions were inoperable, at this time, they still show no sign of cancer.

We have all read about biofeedback experiments in which people are apparently able to control the autonomic nervous system. We are told about individuals who can block out pain, reduce muscle tension, either increase or decrease the heart rate, slow down or even temporarily stop their breathing, prevent sweating, reduce or increase salivation, and increase or decrease the flow of blood to a tissue. There is even some evidence that with the use of imagery, meditation, and hypnosis, some people can fight tumor cells and even 'cure' cancer and other serious and potentially fatal diseases. Even if all of this is true — and there are some skeptics — we don't really know how to control the autonomic nervous system. We can't give our patients a definite blueprint. But from my clinical cases, two things are apparent. First, people can hear while they are supposedly unconscious under general anesthesia. And second, what is said while they are 'under' can positively or negatively influence the remainder of their lives."

The rest of the discussion was on the hypothetical mechanisms of positive or negative control of the autonomic nervous system. At the conclusion of the question and answer session, Dr. Rivere received a standing ovation. Even the rat-expert doctor joined in the applause, but the smile never left his face. After all, he was well aware of all that had been said. In fact, he had gone much further than Dr. Rivere ever envisioned.

* * * *

The shop was closed. The bright-eyed dolls sitting in the window stared through the exterior grates to "see" the cluttered street. In a back room — off limits to everyone but himself — Ibu Mazalo was about to enter another dimension. He began by lighting two large black candles on the centrally placed wooden table. A protective lotion made from clairin, lemons, ammonia, and bayahond leaves was then rubbed into his hands. To protect his face, he covered it with a satin scarf having cut-outs for his mouth and nose. Entering the closet, he put on a black top hat, a dark frock coat, a narrow black tie, and a pair of horn-rimmed glasses. He then picked up a golden cane bearing a snake encrusted handle.

Appearing like a 19th century undertaker, he surveyed his mortuary-like surroundings: the vat was boiling; the previously prepared ingredients were ready as was the spatula and vials. Sitting on the corner shelf, the dark-skinned dolls were resting in inanimate tranquility. Their eyes were closed and lifeless.

Ibu sprinkled some water on the sawdust- and dirt-covered floor. He bent down, and using a thin, wooden stick and powdered corn meal, made a simple drawing of a dagger and a lightning bolt. It was the vévé of the *loa* , the spirit of Baron Samedi, the god of the graveyard — the guardian of the cemetery — the lord of the underworld.

"Eeh-yah; eeh-yah; oh-lah; oh-lah." The incantation began. Ibu was about to partake of *La Prise des yeux* — taking hold of the eyes. His eyes rolled; his facial muscles twitched; his body shook violently with uncontrollable vibrations. In a few minutes, the convulsions ceased, and he entered a trance-like dissociative state. As the *loa* entered his body and mind, he started to feel enormously powerful with "second sight" and other paranormal feelings.

Into the boiling water vat went tarantulas, centipedes, assorted insects, reptile bones, pulverized pieces of dried human cadavers, toad skin, and puffer fish poison extracted from female ovaries. Ibu lifted the large spatula and stirred the contents briskly.

"Mow-mo; in-go; mah-nee."

The furiously discharging bubbles bellowed out a roar as smoke and steam filled the room. The stench was unbearable, but Ibu was oblivious to everything; he was in a deep somnambulistic trance.

Several minutes later, the turbulence quieted to a steady sizzle.

"Mah-nee; mah-no; oh-rah."

A large, black, pitted ladle displaced the effervescent molecules as it was being filled to the brim. Ibu emptied the ladle's contents into several vials.

After pouring the viscous fluid from one of the vials onto the hog bristles of a well-worn toothbrush, he lifted the first doll from its perch on the shelf. Stroking the closed eyes with the coarse bristles, he emitted the final incantation: "Rah-lah; row-mah; ee-moo."

The brilliant blue pupils opened widely as light entered the doll's eyes for the very first time.

5

Thursday, May 11

Hank and Marilyn were nearing the end of their delayed two-week Hawaiian honeymoon. In addition to their joyful marriage, they were celebrating the successful outcome of the puffer fish poisoning series of murders. The killer-doctor, Mitchell Turner, was serving a life sentence, giving Marilyn some measure of revenge for the murder of her former husband, Jerry.

Lying back on the soft, contoured lounge chair, Hank said: "I can't believe it but two weeks of relaxation has driven me batty. When I was retired in Pompano Beach, before you got me involved in those bizarre killings, I was completely satisfied with fishing, walking, and just plain relaxing. But now that I had my taste of action again, I can't dream of going back to that peaceful existence."

Brushing the sand from her black, maillot bathing suit, Marilyn replied: "I'm sorry I did that to you."

"Don't be sorry, honey. When we get back to Florida, I think I'll return to the field. I'll become a private eye."

"Hey, that'll be great. Maybe I can be your partner?"

"Why not! We'll be a husband and wife team."

39

The next day, they flew back to Florida with great anticipation about their upcoming careers.

* * * *

At the time of her first husband's funeral last July, Marilyn's parents were on an extended vacation in Europe. They had now been back in their condo apartment in North Miami Beach for six months.

Marilyn's father, James Conover, was a 70-year-old retired salesman. His last position was Senior Vice-President for the New York-based Aristocratic Electronics Company. His wife, Shirley, age 67, had been a secretary for the Victor Harbis Ladies Apparel Company of New York. She, too, had retired. Petite, pretty, vivacious, and vigorous — an apt description of Shirley. She was also a caring mother, a loving wife, and a "giver" for friends and organizations. Shirley sparkled with the joy of living. In contrast, James was beginning to look and act his age. Formerly, tall, well-built, active, energetic, and enthusiastic; presently, apathetic and slovenly. Taking trips, observing new cultures, meeting different people; these activities used to stimulate James. But since he returned from their last European trip, all that had changed.

At first, Shirley thought James was depressed over the death of his son-in-law, Jerry. That bothered him for a few weeks, but his current state was caused by something else. Could it have been related to his surgery? Last September, James had noticed some dark-red material in his stool. He went to his family physician who referred him to a proctologist, Dr. Frederick Bennett. The tests revealed rectal cancer. In October, Dr. Lawrence Humphrey performed the surgery while Dr. Ralph Blackmore administered the general anesthetic. The tumor was completely removed. There was no lymph node involvement, and no evidence of metastasis was found. Recovery was uneventful. For the last seven months, there had been absolutely no sign of a recurrence.

Yet, James was acting as if he was at death's door. Why? Shirley had no idea. All she knew was that her beloved husband James — the man she had been married to for 42 years — was now just sitting in a corner of the family room staring off into space. He had been in perfect health except for that one bout of cancer; yet, at the age of 70, he appeared to be waiting to die.

Unmoving pupils, a face cast in stone, an immobile body, but an active mind. *How did it start?* James combed the depth of his consciousness. Images floated by - - - - a package of sleeping pills. Were they his? Were they Shirley's? Did he take any?- - - - his first taste of sushi, a strange taste. Did it agree with him? Or was it Shirley who got sick?- - - - a scene from a play or was it a movie? Maybe it was on TV. Loud music, chanting, dancing, colors, lights, an endless beat. *Did I like it? Did I hate it?- - - - A doctor's office. Many doctors. Talking to me; talking through me; pictures; X-rays-standing, sitting, lying on my back, lying on my chest; taking blood; drinking a powdery, chalky liquid; going to the bathroom; giving samples; taking samples of everything; talking, talking; tests, tests; all kinds of tests. What were they for? What did they mean?- - - - a lawyer; a will. Did I change it?- - - - the museum, strange objects, a doll, sticks, stones, sharp. They were all sharp.- - - - The pain, all over, all kinds: sharp, dull, deep, shallow.- - - - food — tasteless; water — bitter- - - - a dark tunnel, can't escape it; it's drawing me in, have to go in deeper, and deeper, and deeper.*

During these last six months James lost 50 pounds, and he had very little to lose. One-hundred twenty two pounds on a six foot frame didn't leave much left to ward off bacteria, viruses, and other natural human enemies. He once was virile and vigorous, but now James wasn't willing or able to fight back. Consequently, emaciation took over, and he seemed to welcome it. Shirley, though, wasn't ready to give up. She literally had to drag him into doctors' offices. And he saw them all: internists, oncologists, cardiologists,

neurologists, psychologists, psychiatrists. Batteries of tests were run; the doctors pried every inch of his body and mind, but they could find nothing wrong. They could find no reason for the weight loss, the despondency, the despair.

Within the last few days, James seemed to have lost all interest in life. Shirley had held off calling Marilyn in Hawaii. After all, she thought, her daughter had suffered so much and was finally enjoying herself on her honeymoon. But now things were desperate. *Thank God,* she said, *Marilyn will be home tomorrow.*

His body was immobile, but his mind was churning: *I know I'm dying. I can't stop it! I don't want to stop it! Do you hear my heart beat? First, so fast! Now, so hard to hear. But wait, Shirley is saying something to me. What is it? What is she saying? Why are the sounds getting so slow? Why are they getting so quiet?*

Shirley was talking, actually she was begging: "Jim, please pull yourself together. Marilyn is coming home tomorrow. She was on her honeymoon with that wonderful man, Hank. You remember him. You only met him once, but the two of you got along so well together. Oh, Jim, I love you so much. You're the only person I've ever loved. Please, Jim darling, please, get better."

What is she saying? - - - You're thah onlee perrssonn I've ehverr lovvedd - - - Why is she talking so so slowly? Why is she talking so softly? What is she saying? Oh my mind is getting so foggy; everything is stopping; it's all going; it's - - -

It stopped. Shirley was waiting for Marilyn's return, but James was only waiting to die. At 7:45 P.M. on Thursday, May 11, 1989, a little bright-eyed doll — apparently an anonymous hospital gift — fell out of his grasp, and the world was forever shut out for James Conover.

6

Saturday, May 13

Like a store front mannequin, her face was chalk-white. The news was devastating. She knew her father hadn't been up to par lately, but she had no idea that he was **that** sick. How did it happen? How could it happen?

Hank had been in the bedroom, getting dressed, when Marilyn answered the kitchen phone. They had returned from Hawaii late last night, and Marilyn was preparing a breakfast surprise when the phone rang.

Hearing a faint moan, Hank called out: "What is it hon? Is something the matter?"

Ashen, Marilyn could barely get out the words: "Oh, Hank, that was Mom; my dad died!"

Rushing to her side, he held her tightly and asked: "He died? Just like that! Had he been sick? Was it his heart?"

Sobbing as she spoke, Marilyn replied: "Mom was too choked up to say much of anything, but from what I got out of her, it seemed he just went downhill these last few days. He just plain died without any effort at all. I know he had been losing weight lately, but why, I have no idea. He had rectal cancer last year, but he had been completely cured as

far as anyone knew. Mom did tell me that none of the doctors
could figure it out, either. Oh, Hank, just when I thought my
luck had turned! When will it all stop?"

Caressing her lovingly, Hank said: "I know how
shattered you are now. But I have no doubt; things **will** get
better. With your father's death, have you any reason to
suspect foul play?"

"Why would any one want to harm a sweet old man like
him?   And it was a slow, dragged-out death.   Nobody
suspects murder. But look what happened to Jerry! Who
knows? Anything's possible."

"Do you want to see your mother now?"

"Yes, Hank, please take me to her. Maybe this is an
omen. Maybe we should forget about our private detective
venture.

"You're distraught now; let's just get you down to your
mother's home. The future will take care of itself." But
Hank was thinking that maybe Marilyn was right. They had
enough money.   Why get involved with other people's
problems? As evidenced by this latest tragedy, Marilyn and
Hank had enough of their own.

7

Tuesday, May 16

The weeping was over. Well, not really over, but now it was limited to sniffles. At Marilyn's insistence, an autopsy was performed, but the results were not convincing.

Shirley was tired, weak, and depressed. She felt fate had cheated her: "Marilyn, I still can't understand it. Your father had a good friend, Henry Preston. He was a couple of years older than my Jim. He also had cancer; his was a little higher up. I think it was in the colon. But Henry was very sick. He had been sick for a long time, and he died two months ago. I spoke to his wife, Jenny. She said that the doctors told her his cancer was so bad they couldn't even take it out. So, it was no shock when he died a few days after the surgery. Jenny's a stubborn lady. She wasn't convinced that the cancer killed him; she asked for an autopsy. When it was done, the doctor told her that the results were just as expected. Whether she believed it or not, I don't know. But your father; oh my God, your father. They said everything came out. The doctors told me he was as good as new. A horse he was. And still he died. Where's the justice? Oh, Marilyn! What am I gonna do?"

45

Marilyn hugged her mother and said: "Mom, Dad had a good life and you've got many wonderful memories. I certainly have. I know things look terrible now, but we'll be with you as much as we can. We'll get you through. Meanwhile, Hank and I want to investigate the circumstances of dad's death a little more. The autopsy findings are far from clear-cut."

Before they left, Hank went into the master bedroom. Out of curiosity, he looked around. Everything appeared to be normal: a king-sized bed with a flower-patterned bedspread; two matching walnut end tables with men's and women's dressers; a mirror and three scenic paintings on the walls; a clock radio and two lamps on the tables; a color TV opposite the bed; and books and knick-knacs on the shelves. Hank thought, *Everything looks fine — but, wait! What's that doll doing there?* On a corner shelf was an attractive, young, female doll. On second thought, Hank said to himself, *Well, old folks are no different than the rest of us. They have their quirks, too.*

Coming back into the living room, Hank kissed his mother-in-law and left the two to console each other. Later, spurred on by their interest in uncovering the cause of Marilyn's father's death, the two of them applied for their PI licenses. Several weeks later, the firm of Meltzer & Meltzer was born.

* * * *

Ernest Goodman, MD, a conscientious, dedicated, pathologist was resting comfortably in his private office at the North Miami Beach General Hospital. He was mulling over the findings from three recent autopsies.

How can anyone understand what will kill one person and allow another to survive for months or years? Bernstein had metastases all over his body. He was diagnosed ten years ago. All during that time, he lived well, played golf, flew his own plane, skied. And that was a 75-year-old man. So what happens? Two days ago, he has a stomach ache, and that night, he dies peacefully in his sleep. I open him up; cancer cells are everywhere. But they were everywhere ten years ago. CAT scans, MRI, all kinds of x-rays, every test we had; they all confirmed metastases — imminent death. Finally, with no apparent change in his condition, the disease decides to kill him. Why? What took so long? Who knows?

Then there's Conover. He was healthy all his life; that is, until eight months ago. Rectal bleeding, a biopsy, the diagnosis of Class I rectal carcinoma. If you're gonna get cancer, this is one of the best types to get. Localized, slow-growing, and skillfully removed. We check everywhere. No evidence of lymph node involvement, no metastases. All of the follow-up tests are negative. So what happens? The guy goes downhill; he loses 50 pounds; looks depressed. They tell me he just sat around staring off into space. Then just like that, he stops breathing. I open him up. What do I find? No tumors, no blockages. Yeah, there was atherosclerosis, some occlusion in his coronaries. But what do you expect in a 70-year old man? Plenty of people live for years like that with no complaints. What killed him? Who knows? Sure I found some heart muscle damage, but certainly not from a recent event. Well, I had to list something as the cause of his death. No one will question heart failure. But what really killed him? Did he will himself to death? And if he did, why?

And how about Marsch? Nowadays, most doctors leave well enough alone. Not wanting to get sued for some diagnostic or treatment error, they don't ask for autopsies, and most survivors are so distraught they don't even want to know. But for whatever the reason, Mrs. Marsch asked for an autopsy. Not that it did any good. A 79-year-old with chronic asthma. He develops severe bronchitis, but the disease is controlled. So what happens? A man with the heart of a 30-year-old dies of a massive coronary. Who can figure it out? Maybe someday we'll learn!

Just then, a forceful knock on his door jolted him back to
the present. The pathologist called out: "It's open, come in!"

Hank Meltzer, retired Philadelphia police captain,
recently-licensed private investigator, and Marilyn's new
husband and partner, entered. "Hi! I'm here for my 1:00
appointment. Meltzer's the name, Hank Meltzer."

Dr. Goodman displaced his 220 pound frame from the
leather-bound swivel chair and got up to shake Hank's hand.

Hank was no novice when it came to interviewing
pathologists. In his recent investigation of the puffer fish-
poisoning murders, he had several sessions with Dr. Peter
Simon, pathologist at Pompano Beach Memorial Hospital.
Hank was somewhat shocked at the contrast between the two
pathologists. Peter Simon was tall, thin, and gaunt-looking.
In contrast, Ernest Goodman could have been a stand-in for
Santa Claus. All he needed was the white beard. As it was,
he had a peppered, well-manicured gray beard. It wasn't that
Dr. Goodman disliked exercise; he actually was a half-way
decent doubles tennis player. His downfall was food; he was
in love with pizza and pancakes, whipped cream and waffles,
steak and swordfish. His digestive tract was a glutton for
punishment. Maybe eating was his response to all of the
death around him. He always used to say: *"You only live
once; so, you might as well enjoy life to the fullest."*

For Hank, another interesting finding was the contrast
between the two pathologists' offices. Peter Simon's office
was stark-white and reeked from formaldehyde. Ernest
Goodman's office looked like it was designed by an interior
decorator. Mauve grass cloth wall paper; hanging and upright
plants — shiffaleria, philodendrums, spider plants; colorful
pictures of outdoor scenes; comfortably soft chairs and love
seats; and the room was permeated with the odor of fresh-cut
flowers.

"Let me see now. You told me on the phone that you're a
retired Philadelphia police captain who just embarked on a
new career as a private investigator."

"That's right. A real dope am I. Can't leave well enough
alone."

"That's not necessarily true. Do what you like. That's the first key. Anyway, you want to ask me a few questions about the death of your father-in-law, James Conover. Am I correct?"

"You've hit the nail on the head, doc."

"So, what can I tell you?"

Being candid, which is not necessarily a trait of all doctors, Ernest Goodman said: "First of all, there was no obvious immediate cause of death. There were some areas of lung hemorrhage and congestion. You know, bleeding and filled with some fluid. Those findings are really non-specific. In other words, they're not related to any definite cause of death. A small area of heart damage was also found, but this, too, could have been found in a person of his age without being the direct cause of death."

"How about the cancer, doc? Was there any sign of spread?"

"No! As far as the cancer is concerned, Mr. Conover was perfectly healthy."

"So what killed him?"

"Before you came in, Mr. Meltzer, I was turning that over in my head. We really don't have all the answers. We really don't know why some people with relatively minor findings die, and others with major evidence of disease live for many more years than expected."

"Any evidence of foul play?"

"None at all; no drugs were found in his system. The body fluids were clean. No, it just looks like James Conover was ready to die; his number was up."

"So you think, there's no reason for me to carry this investigation any further."

"Sorry to disappoint you, Mr. Meltzer. But I see no reason at all. Anything else that I can do for you?"

"No thanks, Dr. Goodman. I appreciate your time. Maybe I'll see you again."

"That would be fine."

With that, they shook hands again. Leaving the room, Hank was certain that the doctor's autopsy findings were accurate, but he still had his doubts about why a man who had loved life so much should go downhill so rapidly and for no apparent reason. Remembering that Dr. Peter Simon was incorrect about the puffer fish poisoning murders, Hank resolved to pursue the matter a little further.

8

Concentric circles radiating outward, a typical bullseye except for the sharp, pointed, centrally-placed object facing the viewer.

The subject was seated semi-inclined in a comfortable contoured chair. Following directions, he removed his shoes, loosened his belt, and unbuttoned his collar.

"Get comfortable in your chair. Now look up at the diagram opposite you. See the circles. Notice the separate colors. As you concentrate, as you focus, as you stare, watch the circles move. They come in and out, out and in; they get larger and smaller, smaller and larger. Focus on the center. See the pointed stone. It is coming closer to you, moving out of the circle. Watch it move. All is getting blurry, distorted, altered, changed. Everything is moving around and around, in and out, out and in, forward and backward, backward and forward, side to side."

The old man was oblivious to everything except the monotonous tone and the bullseye picture. The only motion observable was from his quiet, even, rhythmic breathing and his fluttering eyelids.

"You're getting sleepy, tired, deeply relaxed. Everything is quiet, peaceful, calm, tranquil. As your eyes close, you feel yourself in a wonderful relaxed state."

The old man's eyes closed as his head slumped.

"Now you are at the top of a beautiful mountain. The sun is shining brightly; there's not a cloud in the sky. Birds are flying by and singing joyfully. Flowers are in bloom everywhere. You can smell the wonderful scents. Down the mountain, you start to walk. It is a very safe mountain. A few squirrels dash about in the woods. Tall graceful trees give you shade as you slowly and carefully descend. With each step you take, you feel yourself getting deeper and deeper into this wonderful relaxed state. You touch a flower. It feels so soothing. It smells so wonderful. You are approaching the bottom of the mountain. Directly in front of you is a large, beautiful, and peaceful lake. And there is a sailboat right at the end of the path. You step into the boat. The captain is there, ready to take you to your own secret destination. He asks you where you want to go. You tell him about your special place — the wonderful place that you always go to, where you go to be calm and peaceful, your own private place of happiness and joy. The captain casts off. The ship is sailing. It is a wonderful trip. As the boat sails along, you feel yourself floating along with it. You feel tingling and floating sensations, warm, pleasant, relaxed feelings. You are going to your own wonderful place. You are almost there. You feel so good — as good as you've ever felt. Now I will be quiet and let you enjoy this utter tranquility all by yourself. Then in a little while, I will guide you further."

Having completed his experiments with rats, the doctor was now experimenting with his fourth human subject. The other cases were completely successful. The hypnotist was now in complete control; the patient was drifting inexorably into a stuporous trance.

* * * *

Two days before at the North Miami Beach General Hospital, the old man, Kenneth Frankel, had been operated on for stomach cancer. The surgical and anesthesia teams led by Drs. Lawrence Humphrey and Ralph Blackmore, worked on him for three hours, but the situation was grave. A lifetime diet of rich, fat-filled and fried foods had taken its toll on his gut. As he approached his 77th year, Kenneth Frankel's future looked bleak. Considering the extent of the tumorous invasion, the operating room doctors gave him only a few months to live. The surgeon, Dr. Lawrence Humphrey, and other members of the medical and supporting medical staff saw the patient over the next few days to help him enjoy his remaining time. One of them lent a hand and gave him a bright-eyed doll, but it was not for support or friendship.

* * * *

Three days later, an obituary notice was placed in the North Miami Beach News. "Kenneth Frankel, a resident of North Miami Beach for the last 12 years, died yesterday from long-standing stomach cancer. The 77-year-old retired electrical engineer was survived by his wife, Irma, his three children, and five grandchildren. Funeral services have not yet been announced."

Although not mentioned in the newspaper notice, an inanimate human representation — a pretty little doll — also survived Kenneth Frankel. It was resting comfortably by his bed.

* * * *

The same day, a clandestine meeting was taking place at the Miami International Airport. The same two individuals had last met at this identical site exactly six months ago. At that time, they were up to no good; today was not to be any different.

The short, well-built, dark-skinned, middle-aged Cuban man was the first to speak: "I found out some more information about those two bastards; the Meltzers have opened up a private investigation agency."

Although his English was heavily accented, as a result of their last encounter, the young, dark-haired, attractive Japanese woman was able to decipher his remarks. She interjected: "Carlos, do you know where their office is located?"

Her oriental version of English was also difficult to understand, but Carlos Candiani could always get the gist of what she said.

He responded: "Yeah, Haruo, they set up shop in a small suite in an office building on Main Street in Pompano Beach."

Haruo Maruoka added: "Great! What are they doing now?"

"I don't think they're working on anything yet. But they will be pleased. We will be their first clients."

"That's interesting; tell me all about it."

"We'll give Hank and Marilyn Meltzer a case so weird and wild they'll have to get involved. And when they are in real deep, we'll destroy them once and forever. Yeah, this time we won't be fooled."

"The JRA will be pleased. No one can cause our operatives to be imprisoned and get away with it. Now, tell me all about this case. I want to know how you're going to 'nail' the Meltzers."

"Well, it involves a certain family matter - - - - "

9

Wednesday, August 16

As the front door quietly opened, a stream of sunlight entered the darkened room. The door closed; the odors of pine, menthol, and eucalyptol were intense but not unpleasant. Following a few seconds for olfactory accommodation, the visitor announced his presence.

"Good morning, Ibu. It's lovely outside," said the aging, pale-skinned, American doctor. "You should let nature's warmth and freshness invigorate you."

"Good morning, doctor. Thank you for your most considerate suggestion, but I have no need for extraneous influences. I derive my energy from the spiritual world."

The deep, mellifluous tones flowed effortlessly from the diaphragmatic depths of the tall, muscular, African-American. "Oh, by the way, did you bring my money?"

"Of course, Ibu; I would never forget you."

"I'm pleased," he said as he carefully counted out the money. "How are you feeling? Are your experiments going well?"

"Thank you for asking. I'm feeling fine, and the experimental results are splendid; the outcome couldn't have been better. The dolls are absolute charmers."

"Oh, I'm so glad. It gives me so much pleasure to find out that the results of my humble workmanship are proving so helpful. Have you need of any more of my little friends?"

"Most certainly; they are so handy. There are so many poor old folks clamoring to be put out of their misery. It's my duty to allow them to reach their heavenly rewards."

"That's good to hear. Helping mankind is a noble accomplishment. By the way, I have just made some entrancing additions to my little brood. Come inside and have a look at them."

The doctor was surprised; he had never before been permitted to venture inside. He was somewhat apprehensive but also quite curious. Since curiosity was the stronger motive, he followed the bokor.

For the bokor's part, he was enjoying his working relationship with the doctor and felt it was time to give him a glance at the deeper aspects of his artistry.

A few seconds later, they had entered the private room of the small, whitewashed, doll shop.

The air was permeated with the odor of entrails, urine, and various other bodily discharges — not a pleasant scent with which to be welcomed into a room. Swallowing deeply, the rat-expert doctor looked around. The front shop had been somewhat dark, but it was a normal-appearing room. This chamber had both surrealistic and morgue-like overtones. It could have been the "living room" of a haunted house, but then again, he might have entered the inner sanctum of a bizarre temple.

On the far wall was an altar. It was decorated with paintings of slithering snakes, fire-bellowing lizards, and ballooning fish. On its left was a wooden cross; on its right was a spear. Beneath the altar was a small red brick fireplace — the ashes were still smoldering.

Turning to his left, the doctor saw shelves holding jars filled with brilliantly colored powders and plant extracts and bottles filled with what appeared to be rum and wine.

As he faced the rear, he observed a wall decoration made up of a large sisal whip and a wooden staff of variegated wooden carvings.

Completing his turn, the doctor was now facing the right side of the room. Other shelves were present, but these were filled with diabolical-looking objects. Sitting on the spider web-encrusted shelves were assorted skulls — humans, monkeys, rats, bats, and lizards. Other bones were scattered about — scapulas, femurs, a humerus here, a tibia there; it was a frightening conglomeration. Dead bones were bad enough, but there were more than just bones. Large vats, cisterns, and barrels sat on the floor; each with its own particular emulsion, suspension, or solution made up of chemicals and components extracted from the living and the dead. They emitted the odor of formaldehyde, ammonia, hydrogen sulfide, and God knows what else.

Just when he was ready to retch, the doctor noticed the dolls. They were sitting on a corner shelf away from the assorted degradations. In some miraculous way, the noxious emanations seemed to have spared them; yet, they appeared hauntingly alive.

Observing the first group on the shelf, the doctor remarked: "Ibu, those four are perfect. A trio of oldsters are just about ready for my services, and I couldn't think of a more delightful present than the gift of one of those lovely dolls. The fourth one I'll keep as a backup."

"I'm so glad that you like them. They happen to be particular favorites of mine. They will bring you great pleasure. Oh, by the way, I have a case that demands immediate attention. The person who needs to be serviced is similar to your regular customers. I am sure it will please you. This is a case we can work on together, and in addition we will both be paid royally."

"It sounds very interesting, Ibu. I am always looking for ways to broaden my altruistic methods. Please tell me more, my good friend."

After the deal was consummated, the doctor left the shop and re-entered the world of the living, ready to continue his "humanitarian" pursuits.

10

Wednesday, August 16

After locking the door of the 1989 black Mercedes 560 SEL, they walked toward the entrance. The sun rays bouncing off the sparkling new white brick office building temporarily blinded them. Recovering their visual acuity, they went inside. Given the correct office by the guard, they crossed the tropical plant-filled lobby. Entering the elevator, they pushed the fourth floor button.

* * * *

Using a terry cloth towel, he wiped the top of the new walnut desk. His handsome visage — slightly distorted — reflected back from the polished surface. While leaning back on the brown, contoured, swivel chair, and looking out at the salmon pink grass cloth wallpaper, he said: "That does it! Marilyn, the desk is ready, and so is the rest of the office. Now all we need are clients."

Glancing above his face, she focused in on her first decorating gift — a water sketch of the Pompano Beach fishing pier. Then, her eyes lowered toward his face.

"You're right, Hank, but I really wonder if we're doing the right thing. There are really safer things we can do with our lives."

"Oh come on, hon, you know that a life without some risk is a bore."

"True, but we could take our risks on roller coasters or water-skis."

"I would never be satisfied with those peaceful kinds of adventures. Being involved with the challenges of detective work has become second nature to me. I thought you were also getting hooked."

"I guess you're right."

He got up, walked to the window, and looked out on Main Street in Pompano Beach. He noticed the black Mercedes, but he didn't think twice about it. Turning around, he patted the state-of-the-art Compaq SLT 286 SX Laptop computer on his desk and said: "Good! We've made our decision; let's stick to it."

* * * *

With his macho swagger, he led the way; with her characteristic shuffle, she was right behind. They approached the door to Room 412.

* * * *

"All we have to do now is wait. I got us listed in the upcoming Yellow Pages for both Bell and Donnelly, and I made the message tape for the answering machine. The Pompano Beach Chamber of Commerce and Police Department have been informed that we're in business. Do you think the police will be helpful?"

"Well, ever since we helped them solve the puffer fish poisoning murders, I've been on friendly terms with Captain John Macintosh and some of the other officers. I think they'll be cooperative as long as we don't interfere with their work."

"While we wait, I think I'll curl up with a good murder mystery. This one should catch your interest, being an ex-Philly cop. It's called 'Caught Dead in Philadelphia.' "

"Oh. I heard of that; it's by - - - oh, yeah, a strange first name - - - I know, Gillian; yeah, that's it, Gillian Roberts. It's supposed to be real neat. I'll read it when you're finished. Meanwhile I wanna call Dr. Ernest Goodman, the pathologist. I'm still not certain about the cause of your father's death. I also heard that a couple of other old men died rather suddenly."

Just then, a knock on the front door interrupted the discussion between the Meltzers.

"Come in," Hank called out.

* * * *

He opened the door; she followed her in. The first clients to step on the newly installed beige carpeting were a a middle-aged Cuban man and a young Japanese woman.

* * * *

The same morning, the sun was shining brightly in another warm city. The scene could have been a setting from a promotional video for an exotic Caribbean island.

The view unfolds: The copper-tinged, blue-gray mountains flanking the city serve as the backdrop. White claps of thunderous waves die peacefully as they meet the pristine white beaches of the shores of the Gulf of Gonâve. The sandy shores extend inward and blend with the tall, gracious, green palms. Then the city itself rises — the wondrous city of Port-au-Prince. It lies prostrate, stretched out in the shape of a broad half-moon across the low, Cul-de-Sac Plain. Closer to the water is the old town with its harbor, native quarters, crypt- and mausoleum-filled cemetery, two-spired cathedral, and dazzling, white government buildings. There is a stench-filled "iron" marketplace and all kinds of shops with loquacious natives hawking their wares. One can see half-finished monuments surrounded by the radiant, elegant, domed National Palace, with its spacious lawns and gardens. As the hills rise, so does the splendor of the surroundings and the beauty of the homes. The Mulatto élite and the Caucasian residents live in picturesque, pastel-colored, gingerbread villas with   weed-free lawns   and   picture-book gardens embellished with enchanting flower beds. The homes lie in relative obscurity, hidden by high, stone walls.

In the vicinity are museums — the futuristic National Pantheon and the *Musée d'art Haïtien* — parks — the *Place des Héros de l'Indépendence* and the *Place du Marron Inconnu* — and several leading hotels.

The land mass of 10,000 square miles is inhabited by over 6 million people. Port-au-Prince is a sprawling conglomeration of a city.   At first glance, it appears chaotic, but there is a sense of beauty everywhere. As they go about their arduous daily tasks, carrying goods on their heads and in makeshift wagons and carts, the people have the *joi-de-livre*, transporting themselves in a carefree, jaunty manner.

Outside the city, life is not so tranquil. In the small village of Bizóton, a few miles south of Port-au-Prince, most of the natives live in mud-plastered huts or wooden shacks. The more well-to-do have small homes made from tree bark or bamboo. But nature didn't completely cheat the inhabitants; it planted lush, tropical vegetation to provide a bountiful supply of natural food and serve as a natural barrier, giving the inhabitants privacy from their neighbors and a degree of protection from the blistering heat.

By the side of a gnarled fig tree is a voodoo prayer house — a *hounfor*. On this day, it was occupied only by Ahram Mazola, brother of Ibu and resident houngan.

In Haiti, where voodoo is the principal religion (it is said that 90% of the Haitians are Catholic, but 100% practice voodoo), there are good priests — the houngans, and bad priests — the bokors (witches, sorcerers). Both are essential for the practice of the religion and were important in the past for the survival of the African slaves. It is believed that in the slave uprising that led to the establishment of the independent republic of Haiti in 1804, part of the reason for the overwhelming success of the slaves was the result of the help they received from the houngans and the bokors. The houngans empowered the warriors with magical medicine to make them invulnerable to bullets. The bokors gave them magical poison-filled amulets, trinkets, and charms and taught them black magic to charm their enemies to death.

In Haiti, voodoo governs the lifestyle, politics, family and social relationships, and, of course, the religious affairs of most of the Haitians. Houngans are more numerous than bokors — they are all males. The smaller number of female priests (priestesses) are known as mambos. Houngans are involved in the entire management of the natives. Houngans cure the sick, but they do not participate in black magic. That is the realm of the bokor. A bokor can cast a spell on an enemy and create a zombie, but most of the time he employs his magical powers in the form of charms and amulets. These are worn for good luck, to ward off disease, and for protection against the evil eye. The symbol of voodoo is the Green Snake. The fetishes of the Green Snake are considered by believing Haitians to be infinitely more powerful than the Christian Cross.

Although they don't practice it, the houngans know all about black magic. They must be knowledgeable about evil in order to combat it. In a similar vein, the bokors know all about the work of houngans. Although the houngans are more respected, the bokors are more feared.

When the Mazalo brothers came to Haiti from Africa
25 years ago, Ibu became enthralled with the dark side of
the practice of voodoo, and he became a bokor. His
younger brother, Ahram, was appalled at Ibu's diabolical
interests, and although he still loved his brother, he turned
toward the more humanitarian profession of hounganism.
Ten years ago, Ibu left for Florida to start a new life.
During the interim, Ahram had received many letters from
his brother, and he was extremely pleased that Ibu gave
up his evil profession and became a successful doll
maker.

One of the duties of a houngan is to try and undo the
damage created by a bokor. Ahram had just returned from
consoling a family that had lost a member to a bokor's
curse. Fortunately, the deceased stayed dead (the nail in
his forehead insured that), and Ahram did not have to de-
zombify him. But he made certain that the victim's evil
soul was exorcised, and his good soul was returned to
Africa to enjoy eternal bliss. Right now, Ahram was
preparing the *hounfor* for a joyous voodoo ceremony.

* * * *

"What can we do for you?" Hank asked the singular-
looking couple.

Acting as the spokesperson, the Cuban man replied:
"We have a serious problem and hope you can help us."

"We'll try," Marilyn responded. "That is, if it's
something we can handle" *or comprehend,* thought
Marilyn. Just hearing a few words from him made her
realize that his method of speech would be difficult to
understand.

"First of all, my name is Carlos Candiani."

Not having a criminal record, he was unconcerned
about giving them his true identity. "This is my wife,
Haruo."

Since she was known in the United States as a
Mitsubishi electronics sales person, he felt that giving her
name and lying about the marriage would not be
something that would be investigated. "The problem
concerns my father. He died last week and was buried the
next day. But he has returned from the dead as a
zombie."

"Hold on!" cried out Hank. "We don't deal with any
of that spooky stuff. And anyway, how did you find out
about us?"

Haruo answered. "Please don't get upset, Mr.
Meltzer. I know it sounds bizarre, but Carlos is speaking
truthfully as far as he knows. We found out about you
from the Pompano Beach Police Department. We told one
of the officers that we needed someone to straighten out a
family matter. They gave us the name of a few private
investigators, but you were given an excellent
recommendation."

Before Hank could comment, Marilyn said: "Hank,
let's hear them out before we jump the gun; let's at least
find out why he thinks his father is a zombie."

"Okay, Marilyn, let's hear your story, Carlos. You
can call me, Hank, and as you've heard, my partner's
name is Marilyn."

"Thank you, Hank. I repeat; my father has returned
from the dead. But before I go into that, let me tell you
something about him and what has happened lately."

Peering at him with renewed interest, Hank and
Marilyn listened intently.

"My father, José, was 83 years old this past June. He
was born in the Dominican Republic. My father worked
as a tobacco farmer; he worked real hard and did well.
But he was bored with just being on the farm. He had a
lot of spunk; he was full of adventure. My father was a
very friendly man; he got along with all kinds of folks.
Like most of the Dominican people, he was raised as a
Catholic, but he wasn't too religious, and I wasn't
brought up as a strict Catholic."

Not used to talking in English for such an extended period, Carlos's throat was getting dry. "Can I please have a drink of water or something?"

"Sure, we have Cokes, Seven-ups, and beer in the back. What would you like?"

"A Coke is fine, thanks."

"Anyone else for a drink?"

Marilyn and Haruo both asked for a Seven-up and Hank got himself a "Bud."

Taking a long sip from the Coke, Carlos continued: "Anyway, my father had an open mind and liked to learn about different people and religions. You know, he wasn't educated in schools, but he had brains. Yeah, my father was smart. Living close to Haiti, he got interested in voodoo. Whenever he could get off the farm, he went to Haiti. He got to know the Haitian priests, the good ones — the houngans, and the sorcerers — the bokors. After a few years, things went bad on the farm and my father and me moved to Cuba. I had no other brothers or sisters, and my mother had died when I was young. My father chose Cuba; he was convinced that life under communism would be better than before. But he was wrong and five years ago, we escaped from Cuba and landed in Florida. Things worked out well. My father retired, and I got a job in a radio and TV store. Now it's a video and VCR store, and I own it."

Pausing for another long swig of Coke, Carlos got back to his story. "Then about a year ago, my father got lung cancer. You know, he was a tobacco farmer, and we lived in Cuba with those tasty Cuban cigars. I wasn't surprised that his lungs got messed up. I would've thought he'd have gotten it sooner. Anyway, last month they operated on him. The doctors said they got everything out."

Hank chimed in: "What hospital was he at?"

Haruo responded: "Mr. José Candiani had his operation at the North Miami Beach General Hospital."

"Good; let's hear more." Hank was putting two and two together as he considered silently, *That's the same hospital in which a few old patients were treated and died soon afterwards. There's more to this case than I thought at first.*

"The operation might have been done right, but when my father came home — he lived with us — he went downhill fast. Two days later, he was dead. I mean, we thought he was dead."

"Well, that sounds like he just died from the after-effects of the cancer," interjected Hank. "Some people just don't recover after a serious operation." But Hank was thinking about the recent death of Marilyn's father and the other old-timers.

"Please finish your story," said Marilyn.

"I'll try to be as fast as I can. Anyway, after my father retired, and before he got sick, he got interested in voodoo again. The truth is, he was always interested in it; he just forgot about it for awhile. I know that he had visited a bokor in Florida. Yeah, they have those witches here, too. I don't think they hit it off too good. When my father came back from seeing the bokor, he was real upset. Yeah, he was shook up."

"If I went to a sorcerer, I think I would be shook up, too," added Marilyn.

"Another thing, after he left Cuba, my father got a big mouth. He went around spouting about how bad things were in Cuba and what a cruel dictator Castro was. I'm sure that there were some Cuban spies planted in Florida who wanted to get rid of my father."

"But he still died from cancer, didn't he?" asked Marilyn.

"Like I said before, he's not really dead; he's one of the living dead; you know, a zombie."

"That's baloney!" Hank exclaimed.

A scornful look from Marilyn told Hank to be quiet. Marilyn nodded to Carlos, and he got back on track.

"The second night my father was home after the operation, he spoke out in his sleep. I heard him moaning and ran into his bedroom. He was mumbling some African chants — stuff like 'Ah-room; ah-reem.' Finally, he made some sense, talking about a voodoo curse, and speaking about a doll. Now that I think about it, he did have a doll with him when he got home."

Hank recalled that James Conover, Marilyn's father, had a doll at his bedside on the day he died. *I'll have to look into that*, thought Hank.

"Anyway, he looked scared to death. That night he died, and the next day we buried him."

"Where was he buried?" asked Hank.

"I can't remember the name of the place. Do you remember, Haruo?"

Without a trace of hesitation, she responded: "It was the Ginger Park Cemetery."

"Yeah, that's it. I came back to the cemetery the next day to put some more flowers on the grave, and the place was all messed up. I jumped down inside the grave and opened the wooden casket. I was shocked; my father was gone; the thing was filled with sand and stones."

"Are you sure your father was in the grave when he was buried?" asked Marilyn.

"Sure, I'm positive. We had a wake; I saw them put him into the box, and I went with them when he was driven to the grave. No, he was buried all right."

"Well then, that sounds like the work of grave robbers. Maybe they stole the body to do some experiments."

"No, Hank, the body was found. My father came back to us today."

"Yes," added Haruo: "My father-in-law is in our house right now, but he is more dead than alive."

"I couldn't understand my father; he was speaking in a weird tongue, and he looks just like a zombie."

"How can you leave him alone?" asked Marilyn.

"He's not alone. My friend, Ronaldo, is watching him until we get back."

"Let's look into this a little further," stated Hank. "First of all, who determined that your father was actually dead."

"A doctor came to the house and signed a death certificate."

"Who's the doctor? What's his name?" questioned Marilyn.

"His name is - - - - Let me think. Oh, what the heck is his name, Haruo?"

"I'm sorry but I don't know that. He signed the certificate, but like all American doctors, his handwriting was inde - -ciphe - - rable, you know, hard to understand.

"Yeah, it sure was," Carlos added, "but I know one thing, he's an old-timer, works at the North Miami Beach General Hospital. He came over to the house - - - - he might have been one of the doctors who worked on my father at the hospital. But I don't remember; it's so hard to tell you people apart." As he said that, a sheepish smile appeared on his face.

"Anyway, when we called the hospital, the doctor was sent over."

Hank chimed in: "All of this sounds very interesting and quite weird — if you ask me — but Carlos, what do you expect us to do?"

"Hank, I think my father has been cursed by a bokor. I'm sure he was paid to do it by one of Castro's agents. I would like you and Marilyn to try and find out who did it, how it was done, and whether the curse can be undone."

Hank replied: "That's a tall order, Carlos. First of all, I don't believe in voodoo curses. Secondly, I don't know any witch doctors or Cuban spies here in Florida. But I am interested in the rash of sick old people suddenly dying. Maybe your father is one of those cases. What do you think, Marilyn? Should we take it on?"

"Why not, Hank. I'm certain that there is no such
thing as a zombie, but something happened to José
Candiani. I think it will be a fascinating case."

As Marilyn finished speaking, Carlos Candiani, the
Cuban spy, gave a barely perceptible grin to his partner in
crime, Haruo Maruoka, the JRA agent.

"All right, Carlos," said Hank. "but a case like this
will involve a lot of time and effort. Our fee is $5,000
plus expenses, and we can't guarantee success."

"That's a bit high; we're not rich, but if you can solve
this mysterious puzzle, it'll be worth it."

Terminating the discussion, Marilyn said: "All we can
do is try."

With those words, the case of the Cuban zombie
victim began.

11

Friday, August 18

Hank was driving the Oldsmobile; Marilyn was at his side. With the current epidemic of car thefts, taking no chance on losing a valuable car, they left the Porsche back home in Pompano Beach.

While en route, Hank was telling Marilyn, the results of his latest meeting with the pathologist, Ernest Goodman.

"So, hon, the doc said that he was surprised about the sudden death of David Marsch. The guy was a chronic asthmatic."

Realizing that Marilyn, too, was an asthmatic, Hank momentarily winced. Seeing that the statement didn't noticeably affect her, he continued: "He was under good control. And then just like that, he got a bad chest cold, had a severe heart attack, and that was it — a goner."

"It looks like I'd better be careful."

"I'm not worried about you. Anyway, Dr. Goodman couldn't understand how the old guy died that way because his heart was in pretty good condition before he had the attack."

"Was it a coronary spasm?"

71

"Yeah, the doc thought the heart blood vessels must've closed off suddenly. I asked him if there was a chance it was a toxin. He said there was no evidence of a toxin. He wasn't certain 'cause he said he didn't use a fine tooth comb looking for one."

"What about the other old-timer who died under strange circumstances?"

"That was Kenneth Frankel. He had stomach cancer. It was bad. But they expected him to last for a few months. A few days after the operation, he was dead. It wasn't from any complications of the surgery."

"Could it have been a toxin that did him in?"

"Goodman didn't find any evidence of one, but then again he couldn't understand why the guy died so quickly."

"All four of these cases, these two, my dad, and that other old-timer, Mr. Preston, they all died strangely. Sure they were all sick, but it didn't seem as if they died just from their disease."

"Yeah, that's just what Dr. Goodman said. As soon as we finish this zombie case, I'll see if I can talk to the widows of the old-timers. Maybe there was something in common with all four deaths."

While they were talking, they entered Little Havana. Hank was paying attention to the driving, and Marilyn was surveying the sites. Passing through West Flagler Street, they next entered the principal thoroughfare of Little Havana known to the Cubans as *Calle Ocho*. (For the uninitiated, it is known as South West 8th Street.) Marilyn noted block after block filled with a hodgepodge of gas stations, fast food establishments, used furniture stores, porn shops, gun shops, drug stores, hardware stores, bakeries, and grocery shops. All the store signs were in Spanish: *Fanaciás, Pandalderías, Muebleriías, Ferreterías.* Many of the groceries had open fronts. The shopkeepers were hawking their fruits and vegetables. "*Plátanos, papaya, malanga, yucca,*" they shouted. There were dozens of cafeterias and diners. She saw people sitting outside drinking Cuban coffee and eating "*Sandwich Cubano*" — a combination of ham, cheese, and pork loaf.

The sounds were everywhere: people speaking in rapid-fire Spanish; radios blasting from a variety of sites — cars, apartment buildings, bungalows, folks sitting on steps, children walking in the streets. The radios were all turned to Spanish stations like WFAB or WQBA.

They passed people reading, *El Herald*, the daily Spanish edition of the Miami Herald, young girls dancing the samba in a side street, and in the park, old men playing dominoes.

The area had its religious shrines, too. Of course, Marilyn thought, *Not as elaborate or ornate as those in Japan or Hawaii, but they still had a unique beauty of their own with the well-constructed buildings and the small, picture book lawns.*

The omnipresent motels with their typical plaster statue pink flamingo were here as were the super markets like Winn Dixie.

"You know, Hank, this region is a cross between a foreign country and America — the way it was 20 to 30 years ago."

"That could be true, but it's also a center for drugs, gun smuggling, prostitution, and who knows what else."

Just then, they approached their destination. It was in a run-down section of Little Havana and certainly was not an ideal place for a casual visit. But this was no casual visit, and they were being paid well to solve a mysterious puzzle. Parking on the buckled street in front of the cracked and frazzled sidewalk, they locked the car and gazed up at the ramshackle structure. Actually, the red-brick, two-story house was in better condition than the adjoining dilapidated homes. Walking up the steps, while holding onto the railings, just in case the steps caved in, the visitors were being carefully scrutinized by the neighbors peering out of their windows, and the slow-paced drifters who were passing by. A surly look by Hank and a winsome smile by Marilyn were met by petulant stares from the others. Since no one advanced in their direction, and for the time being, the car was left alone, Hank rang the front door bell. After three rings, a beautiful, young, kimono-clad, Japanese woman opened the door and greeted them warmly.

"Good morning, Hank; I love your colorful Hawaiian shirt. Did you get it in Florida or had you purchased it in Hawaii?"

"Thanks, Haruo. The shirt's an original. I got it last year when me and Marilyn went to Honolulu."

"That must have been an enjoyable trip. Some day, I would love to visit Hawaii."

Turning toward her other guest, she said: "Marilyn, I didn't mean to neglect you. Your print dress is bright and beautiful."

"Thank you, Haruo; your kimono is lovely."

From the interior of the apartment, Carlos called out: "Hi Hank and Marilyn; welcome to our humble, little shack. Come inside. I've made a pitcher of sangria. Is that all right?"

"That will be fine," answered Hank and Marilyn in unison.

In stark contrast to the outside environs, the living room was cheerful and colorful without being gaudy. It exuded life — from the vigorous potted plants to the vibrant fish in the foliage-filled aquarium. Hank and Marilyn sat down, appropriately, in the love seat. Carlos and Haruo sat opposite them in inexpensive, but comfortable, lounge chairs. The noise and sunlight were effectively blocked out by the wood-shuttered windows. A small room air conditioner kept them comfortably cool.

After they were settled in for a few minutes, having had time for a sip or two of sangria, Hank posed his first question: "Carlos, is the car safe outside?"

"Don't worry, Hank. No one would dare touch a car belonging to one of **my** guests."

The emphasis convinced Hank. "That's good to know."

With the niceties concluded, Haruo got in to the purpose of the meeting. "Marilyn and Hank, I think we should now let you see my father-in-law, José Candiani."

With that, Carlos and Haruo entered the small bedroom off to their right. In a few moments, they returned with someone that Hank and Marilyn later agreed looked like no one they had ever seen before — at least, no one alive.

The first thing that hit them — literally — was the effluvium. There was a touch of ammonia and vinegar along with the stench of hydrogen sulfide and other putrescent gases, but it was none of them and oddly, all of them. It was an odor not of this life, and yet, how could they know what by-products of the nether world would smell like?

Prior to his entrance, the room had been pleasantly cool. Now, it was frigid, but not the cold of New York or even Alaska. Hell is purported to be scorching, but the room suddenly felt hellishly cold. Were the gelid conditions emanations from his body? Or was he truly a supernatural being that created his own environment?

His eyes were downcast, but once he lifted his head, they glanced at them: deep-set and blue — strange for a Latino — not the sensitive blue one might find in a young child, not the sensual blue of a seductive, beautiful woman, but the deepest, darkest, most opaque blue imaginable. They felt as if one glance into that penetrating gaze would pull them irrevocably into an unfathomable state — a condition from which they could never return. Quickly avoiding his stare, Hank and Marilyn watched as he moved into the living room.

It was not really a walk; it couldn't be called a glide; neither was it a limp, and it certainly wasn't a march. They had both seen the Frankenstein movies, but this was not of that pattern. The arms were not raised in a threatening gesture. All they could tell was that the arms hung limply on the sides, and one leg followed the other as the six-foot tall body slowly advanced in a shambling gait. Although the floor was constructed of solid oak, as each foot touch the wooden planks, a vibratory pattern was set in motion that culminated in chilling sensations traveling rapidly up the legs of the two visitors. Strangely, Carlos and Haruo seemed unaffected.

All of this was a mere prelude to the effect created by

José Candiani's nasal-type utterances. They weren't howls; they weren't cries; they certainly weren't laughs; and yet, they weren't moans. The vocal intonations were in no known language or dialect. The patterns were somewhat monotonous but not structured enough to be described in that manner. As with the other aspects of his demeanor, Hank and Marilyn could only later describe his speech as frightening, weird, and devastating.

"So, Hank, am I right? Is he a zombie?" asked Carlos.

Trying to appear unfazed, Hank answered: "I don't know about that, but he sure has been zonked. Is it all right if we examine him?"

"Certainly!"

Marilyn, with her biological background from college and teaching, had the foresight to bring along an automatic blood pressure, pulse rate, and body temperature monitor. It was a Digiprint 2000 model that they purchased yesterday from a neighborhood medical supply store.

After all, the tests might be helpful in determining whether or not José Candiani was a zombie — if indeed, there is such a thing, thought Marilyn.

"Let's go into the kitchen," Haruo spoke out. "The light is brighter there, and Mr. Candiani can sit on a straight-back chair which will allow you to examine him in a more upright position."

After Marilyn and Hank nodded their assent, the old man "walked" into the kitchen and was seated by Carlos. The room was certainly brighter, but the cold and odorous emanations followed them into that room. Avoiding his eyes, Hank looked at his other facial features. Having been a farmer most of his life, Hank sensed that the old man would have a dark complexion, but that's not what he saw. The hairless visage in front of him was sallow. The ghostly grayish-white appearance matched the color of his full head of hair. The hair color itself was not frightening, but the steel wool-like strands were erect, sort of like the fur of a cat frozen in terror.

Elephantine ears stuck out from sunken cheeks. A broad expanse of a nose took up most of the center of his face, but it was difficult to see or feel any air entering or leaving those grisly nasal passages. The thin, bluish, lips were parted enough for Hank to observe his tobacco-stained teeth. One positive finding: no vampire-like canines jutted out, but the stench from his mouth would be enough to send any dentist begging for a new profession.

Leaving his emaciated neck, Hank then cursorily examined the fragile-appearing body. Although covered by a robe, he was able to detect a literal "bag of bones" enveloped by tightly-drawn skin.

Now that the physical exam was completed, Marilyn in her medical guise, took over. She placed the cuff of the sphygmomanometer on his right arm. He offered no resistance. She then placed the thermo-tip in his mouth. Having the connections for blood pressure, pulse rate, and body temperature correctly made, Marilyn was ready to begin testing.

After a few minutes, the digital printouts were read by Hank. The findings were remarkable. The blood pressure was 80/40; the pulse rate was 30; the temperature was 96.8° Fahrenheit. Although the man was alive, he indeed seemed to be on the borderline of death.

Hank told Carlos and Haruo their findings.

"Now are you convinced that my father has been made a zombie?"

A little more shook up by now, Hank replied: "I don't know for sure, but something has put him into this death-like state. Now, we have to find out who did it, why it was done, and how we can get him back to normal — that is, if it's at all possible."

As they left, Marilyn remarked to Hank: "We have a tall order and we don't even know where to start."

"I know, but I think the first thing we have to do is try and find out if there are any of those witch doctors living in Miami."

"Right! Carlos did tell us that his father had visited a bokor, and if we find the bokor, he could have a clue to what's happened to José Candiani."

"Yeah, but considering what was done with José, I hope we're not going to be getting ourselves too involved with witchcraft, voodoo, and zombies. That puffer fish poison was bad enough."

"I know, Hank; I know."

12

Friday, August 25

Their friendship dated back fifty years, from the many years together when they endured the cold winters back up north. Each retired twenty years ago at which time they made the big move, the relocation to south Florida for a life of fun under the sun.

Jack Goldberg was an English teacher; Herman Levine was a science teacher; and Irving Moskowitz was a history teacher. They all taught at Midwood High School in Brooklyn. Now in their seventies and alone, they had separate apartments at the Sarah Beck Senior Citizen Center — a sprawling expanse in North Miami Beach.

Jack, at age 72, was the youngest. He was the only widower, having lost his beloved, Sadie, to uterine cancer six years ago. He never completely recovered from the loss. After all, to be suddenly severed from a woman you lived with through thick and thin for 45 years, is a devastating blow. The day Sarah died, Jack's gray hair turned stark-white. Two years ago, he had a massive coronary, and two months ago, he had open heart surgery — a quadruple bypass. The surgeon was Dr. Lawrence Harvey; the anesthesiologist was Dr. Ralph Blackmore.

Two-hundred and twenty-five pounds was a bit too much
for a 5'6" frame. After the surgery, Jack lost 25 pounds, but
lately he was gaining it back.

Two days ago, complaining of chest pains, he was re-
admitted to the North Miami Beach General Hospital. The
test results showed that he had angina. Jack was warned by
his doctors to lose some more weight and to begin a moderate
exercise program. Considering that he had a second chance,
with the help of psychologist, Ronald Fielding, and physical
therapist, Sidney Sargent, he was motivated to do his best to
recapture his health. *After all,* he thought, *my two life-long
friends are in similar predicaments.* He was certain they
could reinforce each other and bring back at least a semblance
of their long-lost youth.

Herman was 74 and a bachelor, although not by choice.
It's not that he couldn't have married, but as far as women
were concerned, he had a long string of bad luck. One
prolonged relationship ended by his girlfriend running off
with another guy — a butcher, of all people. It probably
wasn't that unusual, though; in those days there was a meat
shortage, and people used to crave beef. The next affair had
a tragic ending. A lovely lady, who truly cared for Herman,
was killed in a plane crash — to Florida, of all places. And
his final chance at marital bliss ended because a warm and
affectionate woman decided that her career as a physician
would not permit her to marry. Of course, that was those
days; today, many women combine marriage with a career.
But the women's movement came too late for Herman.

Herman, though, didn't feel sorry for himself. He
devoted his life to the fantastic intricacies of science. The
microscopic and macroscopic world around him was
fascinating. Every day was filled with some unique
discovery, some interesting nuance, some ethereal pleasure.
And he did have the friendship of Jack and Irving. That
friendship, as warm and caring as it was, had its drawbacks.
The three of them were more concerned with their own
esoteric worlds — English literature, science, history — than

they were about their own health. So Herman, like the others, got out-of-shape and ballooned to 225 pounds, which was much too much for a small 5'9" frame. Another sign of premature aging was the early loss of his hair; by the age of 40, his head was as a smooth and shiny as a bowling ball. Over the last twenty years, he had suffered three heart attacks, and a year ago, he had coronary bypass surgery. Since the operation, he had taken better care of himself. By watching his diet and engaging in a supervised exercise program, he had lost 45 pounds. Two days ago, he had a check-up with his surgeon, Dr. Lawrence Humphrey, and two other members of the medical staff. Fortunately, the examination and test results showed that he was doing well. Coincidentally, he met his good buddies, Jack and Irving, in the hospital.

Irving was the old man of the group, having just turned 76 two weeks ago. Of the three of them, he was known as the Don Juan, having had many romantic entanglements and three marriages. In fact, back at Midwood High he had established quite a romantic reputation for himself. Unfortunately, he didn't know how to keep his women. The first marriage to Julie lasted less than a year. She was a public school elementary education teacher who didn't appreciate Irving's extra-marital escapades. After that blow to his ego, Irving became more discreet with his dalliances. He kept his rendezvous secretive enough so that his second marriage to Phyllis, a New York bookkeeper, lasted five years. Unfortunately for Irving, he was caught in the act and was given his walking papers. The third marriage — to the lawyer, Linda — lasted the longest. They kept the marital knots tied for 15 years. Part of the reason for the longevity was that Irving lost most of his libido. He also lost a lot of his spunk. In fact, Linda became bored with him. So with the emergence of liberal divorce laws, she parted company with Irving on the grounds of incompatibility.

All of this was too much for Irving. Like his friends, Jack and Herman, he let himself go downhill physically. A man who in his youth was dashingly handsome — a Clark Gable type — wound up at the age of 70 as a thin, balding, wrinkled man with a pear-shaped pot belly and in terrible physical condition.

Unlike his buddies, Irving suffered from hypertension. Not being able to stay away from the salt shaker and rich, fatty foods, two years ago he was rewarded with a cerebral stroke, which left him paralyzed on his left side. Receiving extensive rehabilitation, he recovered most of his functions; he was left with only a minor facial tic. Having had a check-up two days ago at the North Miami Beach General Hospital, he was relieved at the doctors' reports; his condition was as good as could be expected. An extra bonus was he met his two best friends at the hospital.

This morning, Herman arose at 6:30, just about the same time he had been getting up ever since he arrived in the sunny south. Typically, it was another warm and humid day. After a healthy breakfast of prunes, All-Bran, Sanka, and an oat bran muffin, Herman felt compelled to go for a drive in his 1980 Chevy Chevette. Of the three friends, he was the only one still driving. Even with corrective lenses, Jack's vision was too poor for him to get a renewal of his driver's license, and ever since his stroke, Irving hadn't driven. So whenever there was an errand to do, a show to go to, or a restaurant to eat out in, Herman was the designated driver. Of course, nobody had to worry about drunk driving with him at the helm. He hadn't touched alcohol in 10 years. Wanting to share the joyous day with his friends, he called them on the phone.

"Hello, Jack; it's Herman. What'cha doing?"

"What could I be doing at a quarter to seven in the morning? What else? I'm making love to a beautiful woman. What did you think I was doing? Eating breakfast? Sitting on the toilet? Or maybe sleeping until I was waken up out of a sound sleep? Now that I think of it, maybe that's when I was making love — in my dreams. Anyway, enough of this fantasizing. What's so important that you had to break up my early morning romance? What's on your mind?"

"Well, Jack, I was thinking if you hadn't any previous engagements would you like to join me in an exciting cruise along Biscayne Boulevard or maybe even Collins Avenue? Who knows? We might even pick up a few chippies?"

"I do have a busy schedule, Herman, but I think I can free myself up for a little rendezvous. I could use some excitement. But you know what my doctor said; it can't be too exciting."

"No problem, Jack. By the way, I'm going to ask that lover, Irving, to join us. You don't mind, do you?"

"Well, with him around it might be a little more difficult to catch a dame, but the heck with it, the more, the merrier. And Irving has to get out of his apartment already. He's been in the doldrums. Sure, give him a call."

"Great, I'll pick you up in fifteen minutes. Wait outside the building."

"Okay, I'll be there."

"See you soon."

Having called Irving, who reluctantly agreed to an early morning drive, Herman got dressed. He was always the sportiest of the three. He put on a green Izod polo shirt, tan Bermuda shorts, a clean pair of white socks, a new pair of Reebok sneakers, and his long-time favorite, a perfectly preserved Brooklyn Dodger baseball cap. Leaving the parking lot, he pulled up in front of Building 120. Jack was ready. Dressed in a sloppy, stained, yellow, short-sleeve shirt, gray slacks, and sandals, he dragged his portly body into the back seat. Even those few short steps left him temporarily out-of-breath.

"Herman, why do they make these new cars so low to the ground? Anyway, now that I'm in, I'm rarin' to go. So, where's Irving?"

"He's coming; look, there he is now."

"Hello, boys; let's get the girls."

"Right, Irving, but first you've got to get into the car."

Irving had on a yellow straw hat, a pink short-sleeve shirt, brown socks, and gray moccasins. Shimmering his

ungainly body into the passenger side in the front, Irving got
in and moaned: "I'm ready, but I hope you've got an oxygen
tank in the car."

"Don't worry, Irving, I always keep oxygen in the car,
and I've got nitroglycerine, too. It's a real drug store, this
Chevy of mine."

"Good, boys; what are we waiting for?"

With that, the three of them buckled up for safety and
were on their way for a scintillating early morning drive.
Feeling in a decidedly upbeat mood, Herman led them in an
off-key rendition of an old-time favorite, "Mairzy Doats."

After the exuberant trio had finished their joyous
rendition, Irving had to admit: "You know, boys, I didn't
know until I was a grown man that 'mairzy doats' meant
'mares eat oats.' "

Herman chimed in: "If we were a little smarter those days,
we would have listened to those horses and maybe not have
gotten so sick?"

"What do you mean, Herman?" inquired Jack.

"Well, nowadays they tell us that eating oatmeal can lower
our cholesterol. If we had low cholesterol, we probably
wouldn't have had our heart attacks and strokes."

"How about that!" added Irving. "We should've listened
to the horses instead of our mothers."

Herman turned into Collins Avenue. The old men
couldn't help but notice the beautiful young women
displaying their natural endowments. In additional to the
physical beauty that was parading by, the natural conditions
that morning couldn't have been better: no wind, no rain, a
cloudless sky, little traffic, an air conditioned car, and an
excellent driver with a faultless safety record. Everything
was perfect except for those post-hypnotic suggestions.

* * * *

The next morning the headline in the North Miami Beach
News read: "Three Elderly Men Die in a Fiery Crash on

Collins Avenue." The story went on to say : "From eye-witnesses' reports, although conditions were perfect, the driver apparently lost control of his vehicle and drove it into an abandoned hardware store. No other cars were in the immediate vicinity, and no bystanders were injured. Although the wreckage was extensive, no immediate evidence of foul play was found. To rule out drug or alcohol use, and to determine whether or not a medical condition was responsible for the accident, autopsies will be performed on the three victims."

* * * *

In preparation for the arrival of the next of kin tomorrow morning, by 5:00 PM, the cleaning lady had finished collecting the remaining possessions of the three former residents of the Sarah Beck Senior Citizen Center. As befitted old men living alone, she found the usual assortment of worn-out clothes, well-used appliances, family pictures, and sundry small items. One thing surprised her: in each room, sitting on a shelf was a colorful native doll with the strangest looking eyes. "Well," she reckoned, "some old folks have weird tastes."

* * * *

The next afternoon, chunky pathologist, Ernest Goodman, had just returned from a detailed examination of the three car-crash victims. All were on the verge of death from their medical conditions, but they didn't die from a heart attack or stroke. Although toxicity tests weren't completed, preliminary findings showed no evidence of alcohol, illegal drugs, or toxins in their blood stream, liver, kidneys, or anywhere else. Traces of medically-indicated drugs such as nitroglycerine, verapamil, and niacinamide were found.

There's a double lesson for me to learn, he told himself. *First of all, I find it odd that so many sick old men are dying strangely. Take this case. I called the motor vehicle bureau, and they told me that the driver, Herman Levine, hadn't ever had a traffic accident. He was an excellent driver. So how come under perfect conditions, he crashes the car? Something or someone is causing these — what is it now? Six? No, it's seven! Seven sick, old men have died within the last few months. And although each was sick enough to die from the disease, I think something else killed them. The second thing I've learned from these last deaths is that most of them had heart disease or blood vessel disease. If I don't want to be joining them, I better do something about this weight of mine. The diet starts tomorrow.*

13

Saturday, September 2

The rat-expert doctor was in his private study. He had just finished re-reading the news item from last Friday's North Miami Beach News — the story about the three oldsters who died in a flaming car crash on Collins Avenue. A few minutes before, he had taken a refreshing early morning swim in his climate-controlled indoor pool. Life had been good to him — at least as far as material things are concerned. His Miami Beach home was in a perfect location, right off Biscayne Bay, and a five minute drive from the ocean. He had a gardener, a day maid, and an impeccably furnished home with the most modern decor south Florida could offer. The landscaping was flawless.

Although he had spent much of his research life with rodents, his only living companion was not of that family. He had a white Persian cat named Whiskey. She gave him the companionship he needed ever since he lost his wife, Claire, five years ago. Every day since she died he spent some time reminiscing about their wonderful life together. However at this moment, he wasn't thinking about Claire. Something else was on his mind, and he was about to make an important decision.

Having a captive audience of one, he decided to expound his philosophy to Whiskey, who was resting comfortably on his lap. Although she certainly wasn't interested, she couldn't argue with him. At any rate, in case he ever had to present his somewhat unusual views to a real audience, this would give him a chance to deliver his carefully prepared speech.

Starting quietly, he said: "You know, my little friend, euthanasia was first described 2,500 years ago by Hippocrates. Nowadays, people are a little confused by the term. What it means is: a doctor deliberately acts to terminate the life of a patient. The way it usually is performed is by an injection of a barbiturate to put the patient to sleep. This is followed by a lethal injection of curare — that causes the patient to stop breathing.

Of course, there are other ways to end a patient's life, but we don't call them euthanasia. For example, a lot of patients who are really brain dead or 'vegetables' and have absolutely no chance of resuscitation, are artificially kept alive by the use of life-sustaining methods such as cardiopulmonary resuscitation, ventilators, dialysis, or tube feeding. The way doctors end the patients lives is by cutting off the use of these methods. Anyway, Whiskey, those patients are more dead than alive.

Another way a doctor can end life is by what is called 'assisted suicide.' Here, the doctor prescribes a lethal dose of a drug, but he doesn't inject it; the patient takes it by himself. Do you understand?"

By now, the cat was quite groggy. The doctor was a good hypnotist for animals as well as humans. In this particular case, although he wasn't trying to hypnotize the cat, the monotonous speech was having that effect. Despite the cat's sleepy state, the doctor continued: "Finally, if the patient's family or friends ends his life, then it is called 'mercy killing.'

In our country, the issue of euthanasia and other methods of doctor-assisted life termination for hopelessly ill patients is being hotly debated. But did you know that in the Netherlands about 5,000 to 10,000 patients receive euthanasia each year? The Dutch have a five-part guideline. First, there has to be an explicit, undeniable decision by the patient that he or she wants to die. Second, the patient has to have extremely severe physical or mental suffering with no chance of alleviating the condition. Third, there must be no alternate treatment options. Fourth, the patient's decision must be given without duress. Finally, there must be agreement after consultation with another physician.

Whiskey, even though the Dutch think they're enlightened, I consider them backward. You see, I've gone one step beyond euthanasia and mercy killings. I've shown that the mind can control the body to the ultimate degree. I've proven that the mind can kill. Just to be sure, I used a little voodoo sorcery, along with its potent poisons. The dolls and their noxious emanations were helpful, but that was in the past. Now I'm certain that they are not necessary.

Seven old-timers who were a dredge on society with their deleterious genes and disease-ridden bodies have been taken care of for good. An eighth guy is in limbo, but he'll be gone soon. A ninth will be pushing up daisies any day now. After I get rid of him, I want to be on my own. I want to get rid of the other oldsters my own way. But I don't want interference from anyone. Nobody can be around who can in any way implicate me. After all, this society still considers what I'm doing to be a crime. That means I've got to get rid of the bokor. That would be another good deed. Black magic is evil. I must prove that my way is better. Nothing could be more rewarding than beating Ibu at his own game. Yes, I will hypnotize the old sorcerer and give him a dose of his own 'medicine.' But it won't be just a small dose. Oh yeah, the bokor will die from an overdose — a lethal concentration of voodoo poison. I can't wait."

The doctor was pleased with his uninterrupted lecture, and the cat was pleased as well; she was fast asleep.

* * * *

Back in Haiti, in the village of Bizóton, the crickets, grasshoppers, and frogs were trilling and chirping as a sonorous overture to the full-length musical presentation to follow: a presentation filled with drum rolls, spiritual singing, and frenzied dancing.

The scene was set. The tall stake in front of the hut with a horse's skull hung on the top let everyone know that the *hounfor* was inside. Today's ceremony was to take place within the *hounfor*. Inside the medium sized room, a wooden table was centrally placed. A few dingy cups and plates were the only dishes present. Empty boxes along the walls served as seats for those few who actually sat. On the walls were carved heads of animals and paintings of sacred animals and trees. To the right of the table, five giant drums — made from hollowed-out tree trunks covered with stretched out goat skin — were silently awaiting the drummers arrival.

Ahram Mazalo, the houngan of Bizóton, had a busy day helping his subjects deal with their bodies, souls, and spirits. He had to save four souls — known as the *gros bon ange* (large good angel) — that were affected by anger, resentment, lust, and suspicion. He also had to reclaim the souls of three others: one who had lost a brother, a second who had been jilted by her lover, and a third whose business collapsed. Ahram performed these good deeds by using a combination of "magical powders" and incantations. In other words, he acted like a high fashioned Park Avenue psychiatrist.

Now, he was ready to help a native communicate with a *loa*. The drummers, dancers, choir, and congregation entered the *hounfor*. A white-robed girl was the initiator — the houngis. She placed a candle on the ground and lit it. Ahram then started the ceremonial fire, placed his right hand in a bucket of water, and sprinkled the drops on the dirt floor. Using cornmeal powder, that he took out of a jar, he drew the *vévé* of the *loa* on the ground. It had the appearance of a sinewy snake. This was to call forth the spirit of the god, Wedo, the god of supreme mystery.

Ahram spun his asson, a gourd rattle filled with cemetery-derived earth, small pebbles, snake bones, and "magical powders" and encircled by a network of snake vertebrae and colored beads. Although an asson purportedly can be used to command the dead, inflame and control the *guédés* — cemetery spirits — its principal role is to regulate activities of the living. And that was what Ahram was now doing.

As the drummers beat slowly, the dancers, with their satiny torsos reflecting the crimson, orange flames, moved in a rhythmic pace. The men were naked except for a thin loincloth. The women's only wearing apparel was a narrow string of shells around their hips and a white orchid in their flowing hair.

The hounganicon — choir leader — started the singers, and soon the room reverberated with strident voices and piercing drum rolls. One native, carrying a live chicken, began to chant: "Eeh-yah! Boola-boola." Dropping the bird into the flames as a sacrifice to Wedo, he continued to chant: "Eeh-yah! Boola-boola."

The drums rolled faster and faster; it was almost as if the hands had a mind of their own, or even as if they were being directed by a supreme spirit. The dancers became whirling dervishes; the singers supplicated the spirits with their earth shattering cries; and the chanting native was spinning in a mind-altering turn. Although he appeared to be transcending this life; he was having a convulsive, orgasmic experience. He could feel the *loa* entering his body, his mind, his soul. He felt his own personality leave him as the *loa* took over. The native's facial features became distorted; his eyes were glassy; he uttered unintelligible sounds — the sounds of the *loa*. As the crescendo reached its pinnacle, he swooned. The service had concluded.

After everyone had left, Ahram relaxed in his straw bed. Having had a long and busy day, now was the time for silent reflection. Thoughts came and went; then a sudden revelation pierced his consciousness. It resulted in an important decision. *I haven't seen my brother, Ibu, in ten years. Yes, I've made up my mind; I will visit him in Florida; it's been too long.*

14

Monday, September 4

It was over two weeks since Hank and Marilyn left the Candiani's apartment in Little Havana. They still hadn't completely recovered from the shock of observing the ghoulish old man. But that didn't stop them from pursuing the investigation. After obtaining Carlos's permission, and the required financial outlay, they had José Candiani brought to the North Miami Beach General Hospital for diagnosis, observation, and possible treatment. They chose that particular hospital because it had a reputation as a premier poisoning center, and it had excellent neurology and neurosurgery departments. Hank also realized that this was the same hospital that had treated the old men who had died under rather strange circumstances within the last few months. Hank felt that the "zombie" case might be related to the others. However, so far, he hadn't any clues of what could have killed Marilyn's father, James Conover, and the others except for what the coroner had reported. Hank realized that as soon as he began to see the light with the "zombie" case, he would spend more time with the mysterious (as far as he and Marilyn were concerned) deaths of the old men.

Following several days of extensive diagnostic testing and neurological and psychiatric examinations, the doctors were just as puzzled as the Meltzers and Candianis. Although the doctors could not ascertain the cause of his limbo state, with the use of IV feeding, they were able to prevent his condition from getting any worse. There was, however, one doctor at the North Miami Beach General Hospital who knew exactly how José Candiani got into that somnambulistic state, but for the time being, he wasn't talking to anyone.

Having had just started as private investigators, Hank and Marilyn didn't have too many contacts in the south Florida area. Of course, there was Captain John Macintosh of the Pompano Beach Police Department, who was on the puffer fish poisoning case, and Captain Stu Weinstein from the Fort Lauderdale force, who had previously helped Hank with some background information, but Hank didn't think the police should be involved at this time. At any rate, he had a better contact, his old buddy, Eric Adler. Back in Philadelphia, Eric was a private eye, but now he lived in Pompano Beach. Although basically retired, he did some carpentry work. Eric had helped Hank check on circumstances surrounding the three doctors under suspicion in the puffer fish murder case. Since he knew a lot about the seamy side of life in the south Florida area, Hank believed that Eric could find some contacts in the Haitian population. That way, maybe they could find the bokor who had seen José Candiani. With that in mind, Hank contacted Eric and now, one week later he had an appointment to see him. They were to meet at the North Miami Beach Health Club.

Meanwhile, Marilyn had been following another path. An old friend of hers from Columbia University, Linda Perrin, had, as Marilyn recalled, been extremely interested in witchcraft and African religions. Following her inclination, she became an anthropologist and was now Professor of Anthropology at the University of Miami.

Marilyn felt ashamed. She had been living in Florida for 18 years, and in spite of that only saw Linda a few times; the last time was about five years ago. *Well, that's what happens when life takes you on separate paths*, she reasoned. Linda never married and was a dedicated career woman. Marilyn had kept her interest in biology and science; she was still teaching an adult education non-credit course in the high school, but she was basically a homemaker during her 22-year marriage to Jerry. His untimely death — the first victim of the puffer fish poisoner — resulted in her meeting the then retired police detective, Hank Meltzer.

Wonderful Hank, she thought. *My whole life changed after meeting him, and now Hank and I are married and run a private detective agency.*

In spite of feeling guilty, Marilyn resolved to make amends. She called Linda, renewed their acquaintance, and asked her if she could find out as much information as possible about voodooism and especially zombies. Linda was very agreeable, and told Marilyn that it was right up her alley. Her doctorate dissertation had been on voodooism.

"Had you forgotten?" she asked Marilyn.

"Of course," Marilyn replied. *"How stupid of me!"*

Today was one week since that call, and Marilyn had an appointment to see Linda at a restaurant in Boca Raton.

* * * *

Back in those days if you worked out with weights, they called you muscle bound. No respectable coach would let his athletes lift weights. Following a vigorous workout at the North Miami Beach Health Club, Eric Adler was relaxing in the sauna. His old buddy, Hank Meltzer still had a couple of minutes to go on the Lifecycle, and then he would join him for a good sweat. Aside from Eric, the only other person in the sauna at this time was a pot-bellied, bald man who appeared to be in his late 60s. Beads of sweat were trickling off his hairy chest. His eyes were closed. Eric was using the intervening time to recall Hank and his early days together at City College in New York. In those days — the early 50s —he was Captain of the Beaver Barbell Club. He could see himself now — a young man with a finely sculptured, rippling muscular, 148-pound body. Today, his 5'6," 56-year-old body was not as solid, but he had added only about 10 pounds over the last 35 years. Hank had also been well built, but he had a bulkier frame and lifted in the 165 pound class. Seeing Hank today, he was pleasantly surprised that Hank kept his 5'10" frame in remarkably good shape. Hank had told him that his only exercise, aside from fishing, during the last few years had been daily walks, but now that he saw how good Eric looked and the excellent equipment currently available, he was inclined to work out regularly and get back into condition.

While Eric was reflecting about old times, the stocky man opened his eyes, gave a couple of grunts, slowly got down from the top level, and left the room.

Before Eric could renew his thoughts, a blast of cold air came into the sauna, as muscular Hank Meltzer entered the room.

"Just like old times in Philly, isn't it, Eric?"

"Right, Hank, old buddy, but you used to run the track and lift York barbells and dumbbells — no easy stuff like Nautilus and Lifecycles in those days."

"I like it better this way; the new equipment is so much easier to use, and from the sweat pouring off me, you can see it works just as well."

"You know, I was just thinking about old times at City College. Do you remember the day I was bench pressing 250 pounds?"

"I sure do. I was the only other guy working out."

"Right, but you were so busy curling, I didn't want to ask you to spot for me in case I couldn't lift the weights. So, I bench pressed the weights by myself. The first lift was tough, but I was able to get it above my chest. The second repetition was a bit more of a struggle. The third time was too much. The weight pounded down on my chest and crushed five ribs."

"Yeah, I heard the sound."

"I know, buddy; you came to the rescue and drove me to the hospital."

Just then, the old man re-entered the sauna. Dripping wet, he obviously had taken a shower and was back for additional thermal torture.

Eric thought, *He's gonna have to sweat a long time if he wants to make a dent on that stomach.*

The old man took his previous upper level position, let out another grunt, and renewed his sweating slumber. Eric and Hank renewed their reminiscing.

"Remember, Eric, back then, there was a tremendous prejudice against weightlifting. I can still see the fury erupting from our track and field coach — What was his name?"

"Let's see, it was Jim something, now I know, Jim Blair."

"Right, didn't he explode when he found out that his star shot putter, Arty Rambler, was secretly lifting weights?

"He sure did."

"Arty was our heavyweight lifter, but he was afraid of Coach Blair's fury. Can you imagine, Eric! In those days, the coaches used to get more furious with their athletes lifting weights than today's coaches do about athletes taking steroids or cocaine."

"Hank, those were great days in City's history. The basketball team was the first and only double champion; they were the only ones that ever won both the NIT and NCAA titles."

"Can you visualize it, Eric? The year was 1951. The team brought a lot of fame to the school that year, but the next year was a year of scandal."

"Right! That was when they had the basketball point shaving scandals. Yeah, us weightlifters got nothing of the glory and nothing of the despair; we just got nothing. Remember how the college wouldn't give us money for equipment, or uniforms, or to attend meets."

"Yeah, we had to buy everything ourselves, and most of the guys, including the two of us, were poor as church mice."

"I can see it now, Hank. All the school gave us was a dark, dank basement room to work out in. It was a place that no one except rats and cockroaches could tolerate."

"True, but with it all, we brought glory to ourselves and the college. We were great, competing against all the college teams. Remember that morning in September. I think it was 1954. We drove to the McBurney YMCA in New York."

"It was great! The Beaver Barbell Club — boy, it pissed me off that we couldn't call ourselves the CCNY Weightlifting Team — came in second place; we were the second best college team in the country."

"And both of us won individual silver medals. The only team to beat the old Beaver Barbell Club was Ohio State, with its Olympic middleweight champion — What was his name? Wait I remember. It was Pete George."

A loud explosion shook the rafters. Sheepishly grinning, the portly old-timer excused himself and headed for the toilet. In a few seconds, the odor was disseminated enough so Eric and Hank could resume their conversation.

"Even back then, Eric you and I knew that working out with weights was great as long as you didn't lift too much, and that you worked both sides of each joint, you know, the flexors and extensors."

"We also knew you had to do cardiovascular conditioning. In those days, no one called it aerobics."

"Right! Aerobics was coined by that Dallas doctor, Cooper, yeah, Kenneth Cooper. We didn't need to use any fancy term. We knew that it was great to work up a good sweat — one that left you panting."

"You bet! And we did it with intercollegiate wrestling. Of course, we didn't dare tell our wrestling coach we lifted weights."

Smiling now, the stocky old guy once again interrupted their conversation as he came back into the sauna.

Eric reflected, *Well, between the sweating, walking back and forth, and relieving himself, the old-timer must have dropped some weight. I hope that's it with his interruptions.*

Again thinking about old times, Eric said to Hank: "How the world turns. Yesterday, bodybuilding was spurned; today, practically every coach in every sport has his athletes work out with weights. Even the women are using weights in their sports. Maybe I should have been a coach and- - - "

"Ah-eeh!" A loud, penetrating scream erupted. It was so piercing that it shook the wooden rafters of the sauna. Following the intense screech, a rolling crescendo was heard. It ended as a dull thump as the corpulent, bald man hit the wooden planks.

Within a fraction of a second, Hank and Eric leaped to his side. They dragged him into the tiled bathroom. Placing his ear next to the old man's nostrils, Hank determined that the old-timer was not breathing, and he could not feel any definite pulse. Hank yelled for someone to call an ambulance. A young man, dressed only in jockey shorts, ran to the telephone and called for assistance. Meanwhile, Hank began mouth-to-mouth resuscitation while Eric followed with closed chest cardiac massage.

Five minutes later, as a result of the prompt and efficient work of the good Samaritans, the rotund old man began to breathe. The ambulance arrived, gave emergency treatment, and took him to the North Miami Beach General Hospital. Although he had suffered a massive coronary occlusion, he survived because of the rapid reflexes and altruistic attitudes of two ex-CCNY weightlifters and the expeditious care by the Emergency Room personnel. Only one hospital staff member was displeased; his "humanitarian" intervention to bring portly, Aaron Bean, to his heavenly rewards had been thwarted. He had to determine who had interfered with his "magnanimous" efforts.

After recovering his breath, Hank asked: "Where did you learn that, Eric?"

"Right here in Pompano Beach."

"Me, too. I originally took a course in Philly but just last month, I took a refresher course in Pompano."

"We could've been in the same class, but anyway it was good we learned it. By the way, I remember reading about how not too long ago you were on the receiving end of resuscitation."

"Yeah, that was from puffer fish poison. I'd rather not think about that any more."

By now, they had taken a shower and were finishing getting dressed. "Anyway," said Eric, "before we were so rudely interrupted, I was about to tell you about my search for the bokor."

"So, what did you find out?"

"It was mostly negative. I couldn't find out about any bokors living here in Miami. If there is one, he isn't advertising the fact. But I did find out about a bokor who is living in New Orleans. He's an authentic witch doctor who came to the States from Haiti about ten years ago. I was informed that if there is a bokor living in Miami, this New Orleans guy would know about him."

"Well, that's a good start. What's his name?"

"Raoul LeGauche, and he lives at No. 305B Burgundy Street; it's in the heart of the French Quarter. Of course, I have no idea how cooperative he'll be. But I'm sure if the price is right, he'll tell you something."

"Thanks, Eric. We'll have to do this again. Give my regards to Susan. Oh, by the way, don't forget; you promised to cover for us when we're both out of town. Once we're in New Orleans, we'll need someone to watch the shop."

Although Eric was no longer an active private investigator, he did get licensed when he moved to Florida. He replied: "Right, Hank. Good luck! Give my best to Marilyn."

With that, Hank left the health club at his usual peppy pace.

* * * *

Dr. Linda Perrin, tall graceful, attractive, and impeccably dressed in a coral linen suit, left her office in the Department of Anthropology at the University of Miami in Coral Gables.

She was on her way to a luncheon meeting with Marilyn Meltzer. Linda was pleased that Marilyn had called her last week because she had always like Marilyn and enjoyed her company, but especially because she was excited about once again getting involved with voodoo and zombies. After completing her doctorate, circumstances forced Linda to change her interests, and she got involved with the women's movement. Her particular field of interest and expertise was religious practices of primitive women. Her new-found interest took her to strange, exotic places such as New Guinea and Thailand. Now completely ensconced as a tenured full professor she hadn't any real challenges for a couple of years. She had just about forgotten her former predilection for native religions and witchcraft. Marilyn's call stimulated Linda to re-read her doctoral dissertation. She also went to the university library several times to discover more up-to-date material. She even spoke to an associate who had visited Haiti last year and had observed a voodoo ceremony. Marilyn would be pleased with what she had uncovered; she was certain of that.

* * * *

Cruising along I-95 at a comfortable 60 mph, the Oldsmobile was purring contentedly. The romantic strands of the second movement of Tchaikovsky's Fifth Symphony filled the car's interior with ethereal bliss.

It's too bad, thought Marilyn, *Hank isn't here. This kind of romantic piece is just the type to get him into classical music. Maybe, next time.* Turning her thoughts toward the upcoming meeting with Linda, Marilyn was looking forward to seeing her former friend again. But she was really excited about the prospect of obtaining some solid information about zombies.

* * * *

They met at Davidsons, an outdoor restaurant in Boca Raton.
Seated under the spreading branches of a graceful Banyon
tree, they were cool and relaxed. Of course, the frozen
daiquiris helped maintain their present state.

After speaking to Marilyn about voodooism in general
terms, Linda concentrated on zombies. "According to Haitian
tradition, there are two souls that inhabit the living human
body. Upon a person's death, the good soul returns to Africa
to enjoy eternal happiness. The evil soul stays around the
corpse. The houngan — in return for a small payment —
will exorcise the malignant spirits. The dead person then
stays dead, and only his good soul prevails.

However, if a bokor gets to the dead person before his
evil soul is exorcised, that soul can be captured by the
bokor. Rather than dying, the person becomes a zombie.
Sometimes a houngan will be able to recapture the soul from
the bokor. But, in general, houngans don't like to confront
bokors. They fear the black magic. So, they leave the
zombie alone."

"Wow, that's chilling!"

"It sure is, but the story is not as simple as that. Bokors
and houngans are both well acquainted with hypnotic
methods, although they never call them that. They also have
a wide knowledge of medicine, especially toxins. They
know about plant poisons, like those found in toadstools and
animal poisons, you know, the kind found in toads and
frogs. A bokor can give a native an apparently harmless
drink, and from the way he presents it, and from the way he
speaks and acts, the person who drinks the brew can become
bewildered. He can act like a raving lunatic; he can become
delirious. He could walk around completely blind, deaf, or
dumb. He can go from being completely virulent to
becoming completely impotent. That's not all; he can
become cataleptic; you know, so rigid that he can't move a
muscle, and then again, he can become completely paralyzed.
A victim of the bokor's drink and actions can even become a

slave — a slave that will carry out any and all commands. Depending upon how gullible is the native, and how domineering is the bokor, determines how much real toxin is used in the brew and how many suggestions are used."

"This is wild stuff; tell me more."

"As you might have guessed, a zombie is not made merely by suggestion. There are toxins involved, and there are several formulas of zombie poisons. First, in order to defend himself from the effects of the zombie poison, the bokor rubs the exposed parts of his body with a protective lotion. The ointment is a mixture of lemons, ammonia, and clairin. The zombie poison formulas are weird: one is made from the ground leg bone of a human mixed with pulverized bits of dried human cadavers, and extracts from a sea toad and some fish. A second formula contains manchineel — an apple-like fruit — and datura — the thorn apple. Datura contains the drugs atropine and belladonna — which is known as "deadly nightshade." A real disgusting formula contains three drops of mucous which has escaped from the nose of a corpse that had been hanging upside down."

Marilyn shivered but remained quiet.

"Another formula contains pepper wood leaf powder which stimulates the mucous membrane of the victim's nose. This reaction supposedly triggers a dissociative response. That makes the individual highly suggestible.

This next formula seems to be quite authentic. First, a snake and a bonga toad are bound together in a jar until they both die from extreme rage. This is supposed to ensure that the poison from the toad is at maximum strength. Sometimes, they substitute a worm and a white tree frog, but the frog also becomes quite poisonous. Then, ground millipedes or centipedes and tarantulas are mixed with - - - -"

"Eeech," cried out Marilyn, "I'm getting sick just listening to you."

"Wait, the best part is yet to come. Anyway, the ground-up bugs are mixed with some native seeds and plants; there are seeds of tch-tcha; seeds from a mahogany-like tree, and leaves of a relative of poison ivy plants. All of this stuff is ground up into a powder, placed into a jar, and buried below ground for two days."

How revolting, thought Marilyn, but for the time being, she said nothing.

"Next, the jar is dug up, and the native plants, tremblador, desmembre, and another one called, zombie's cucumber, are added. Four plants that contain formic acid, which gives the pain of ant bites, are mixed in. Pine cones, which are real sharp are added along with a plant that contains calcium oxalate needles. And this is the most potent part, four species of puffer fish are - - - "

"What did you say?" screamed Marilyn.

"Calm down, Marilyn, I only said that they use puffer fish preparations. The most poisonous kind of puffer fish in the Atlantic Ocean is found in the waters of Haiti."

"I can't believe it. Hank and I were involved last year in solving a series of murders committed by a crazy dentist. He used puffer fish poison he got from Japan. The first victim was my late husband, Jerry."

Saying that, Marilyn became teary-eyed. Linda came over to console her. "I'm sorry, Marilyn. I should have remembered. Now I recall reading all about it in the papers."

After a few minutes, Marilyn recovered and said: "That's all right. I couldn't expect you to remember. Please continue."

"There's not much more. I don't have to tell you how toxic puffer fish poison is, but I was informed that the variety they use is 160,000 times more potent than cocaine. Anyway, it seems that by varying the amounts of the puffer fish poison — along with the other ingredients, and the amount and types of suggestions, the bokor can come up with a zombie that can live for days, weeks, months, or even years."

"Wow! Wait till I tell Hank."

After finishing their vegetarian lunch, the women embraced and promised that they would not wait so long to see each other again.

15

Thursday, September 7

Lighting up the full-flavored Cuban cigar, he said: "As long as the JRA supplies the money, we'll let Hank Meltzer dig his own grave. Not only dig it, we'll throw him in and never let him out."

"Yes, Carlos, my brothers back home in Japan are pleased that you have devised a plan to get rid of him and his wife, Marilyn. They said that money is no object. But you've only told me the bare outline of the plan. Now that we have some time, fill me in with the details."

They were sitting in Carlos's living room. It was mid-afternoon of a drab, rainy day. Carlos was a secret agent for Castro's Cuba; Haruo was a secret agent for the Japanese terrorist group, the JRA. They were working together to gain revenge for the jailing of two of the JRA "freedom-fighters" as the result of Hank Meltzer's interventions. Working in close proximity over the last two and a half months had resulted in their relationship going well beyond that of mere business. In fact, they were now not at all anxious to have the "zombie" case end quickly.

"Well, as you now know, it had been carefully thought out. Most of the information I supplied the Meltzers was true. What I didn't tell them was that I am a Castro agent, and I hate my father — that turncoat. So, I devised a plan to destroy the old traitor and trap the Meltzers as well. Looking through my father's papers, I found out about Ibu Mazalo, the bokor that my old man had a run-in with. His shop is not too far from here. Although he tells the world he's a doll maker, I knew better. He has a brother who is a houngan in Haiti. I also found out that Ibu is working with an old American doctor. It seems the doc wanted to get rid of some sick old people, and Mazalo was helping him with some of his poison-loaded dolls. Meeting Mazalo and enticing him with a little money, I was able to convince him to use his magic on my old man. Since the doc was such a good hypnotist, Mazalo got him to help in the creation of the zombie. The old doctor is also a big phony. He makes out that his is such a noble cause, but when Mazalo offered him money, he quickly agreed. Of course, the old doctor and the Meltzers didn't know about my part in the plan.

So, the doc and the bokor did a real number on old José and turned him into a number one zombie. After he was buried, I had three of my comrades dig up the body and fill the casket with sand and stones."

"That was great. How long do you think your father will remain in that state?"

"He can stay that way for months, but we'll see to it that he goes to Hell sooner."

"Aren't you concerned that Hank Meltzer is now going to New Orleans to meet another bokor. Maybe, he'll find out about Mazalo."

"No sweat. Both Mazalo and the Creole witch doctor, LeGauche, are working with me and have been paid off. I saw to it that Hank Meltzer's buddy, Eric Adler, was fed information about the Creole bokor. When the Meltzers get to New Orleans, LeGauche will tell them that he doesn't know where Ibu Mazalo can be found. But LeGauche will send

them to Haiti to see Mazalo's brother, Ahram. He's a
houngan there. Ahram Mazalo can't be bought, and I don't
know if he's gonna lead the Meltzers to his brother in Miami.
But I have two of my men in Haiti. If the old houngan
doesn't tell them where his brother is living, then my men in
Haiti will kill the Meltzers there. If the Meltzers do get to see
Ibu Mazalo, with the use of his voodoo magic, we'll get rid
of them here. No matter what, they're goners."

"You're a genius, Carlos; that's a great plan."

Saying that, displaying the mannerisms of a geisha, she
slithered over to him and meticulously unbuttoned his
shirt. Her kimono gracefully fell off her shoulders. She
may have been a hard-boiled terrorist, but there was at least
one soft spot in her heart.

* * * *

Their last flight together was in May, the return trip from their
Hawaiian honeymoon. Today's trip was much shorter, but
they also were anticipating a pleasant encounter with the
"Crescent City." It was 6:00 P.M. when the Delta jet began
its descent into New Orleans International Airport. Marilyn,
as was her wont, was reading the tour guide.

"Hank, listen to this: 'Between the years of 1712 and
1803, the province of New Orleans had changed hands six
times. As a result of continual battles among France, Spain,
England, and the United States, the region was in constant
turmoil. In addition, there were Indian rebellions and slave
uprisings. The main influences on the present day culture
were the French, the Africans — primarily from Guinea, the
West Indians natives — with many from Haiti, the Spaniards,
the French Canadian Acadians, German farmers, and some
other Europeans. Native-born Louisianians, who were
descendants of the original French settlers are known as
Creoles. The Acadians formed their only separate group, and
today they are known as *Cajuns.* The descendants of the
slaves from Africa and the Caribbean islands have retained
many of their native customs, including the practice of
voodoo.' "

"That's interesting, Marilyn. Maybe if we're lucky, we'll meet up with one of the practitioners, this bokor, LeGauche."

"Even if we don't, as long as we're here, let's live it up a little. New Orleans sounds fabulous. You know, I don't only love classical music; jazz has always been one of my favorites."

"Me, too. Back in Philadelphia, at the Academy of Music, I once heard the Preservation Hall Jazz Band. They were just super. Of course, that was the only time I went to the Academy."

"I hope I can change that. For now, I think the Preservation group will be performing while we're here. And New Orleans has Bourbon Street and the intriguing architecture of the rest of the French Quarter. The Garden District is supposed to be fabulous, and that 'Cajun' cookin;' it's supposed to be out of this world."

"Yeah, and I love the praline chocolates. But don't forget; we've still got a job to do. Speaking of that, I still can't believe that tetrodotoxin — the same puffer fish poison that the crazy dentist used — is a major ingredient of zombie poison."

"You know, Hank, I just thought of a wild thing. If the dentist-killer had known that the puffer fish in Haiti had tetrodotoxin that was just as potent as the type found in Japan, he never would have had to go all the way to the Far East to get his supply."

"That's right, and then he wouldn't have furnished his waiting room with Japanese decor, and we might never have found him out."

"It's a good thing that Dr. Turner wasn't interested in zombies."

Just then, the wheels hit the turf with a slight jolt, the engines raced mightily, and the plane taxied in effortlessly. The first leg of their voodoo venture had begun.

* * * *

At that very moment, a few hundred miles away, another plane was landing. For Ahram Mazalo, the only familiar aspects of his encounter with Miami International Airport was the weather. Upon first leaving the plane, the air that greeted him was just as hot as it had been back in Haiti. Of course, once he was inside the terminal, the air conditioned environment was vastly superior to that of his native country. Ahram had no trouble finding a taxi and talking to the driver in Spanish. Ahram was fluent in French and English as well. The driver had no difficulty finding Number 2405 La Venetia Street, the home and shop of Ibu Mazalo.

* * * *

After picking up a white 1989, Chrysler LeBaron convertible from Alamo Rent A-Car, they headed for their hotel in the French Quarter, The Royal Orleans. The early evening traffic was heavy, and they were unfamiliar with the city. But with the help of a city map, they finally reached the French Quarter. As they approached the entrance, Marilyn remarked: "Oh, Hank, look at the lovely balconies; the wrought iron work is exquisite. I know we're going to love it here."

"I'm sure we will."

They left the car and the bags for the car attendant and bellhop to attend to and took a brief tour of the hotel and its grounds. Stopping off at the front desk to register, upon Marilyn's request, the clerk filled them in about the hotel's history.

"The hotel was first built in 1836 and was called The St. Louis Exchange Hotel. It was considered to be one of the most elegant hotels of the era. The St. Louis was a focal point of the social life of New Orleans right up until the latter part of the Civil War. At that time, it became a hospital for wounded soldiers — both Northerners and Southerners. Later, it served for a short time as the state capitol building. The wondrous reign of the St. Louis came to a devastating end when it was toppled by a 1915 hurricane. For 45 years, the site was unused. Finally, the Royal Orleans was built and opened its elegant French doors for the first time in 1960."

Thanking the clerk, the couple looked around at the splendid surroundings. Marilyn spoke first: "Have you ever seen such a fantastic lobby? Can you believe the elegance of the marble and brass? And those crystal chandeliers, aren't they incredible?"

"Well, you know I don't know too much about those kind of things, but I do know that to build a place like this today, would cost a small fortune."

"You're right. But enough of this dilly-dallying, I'm starved, and I bet you are, too. Let's take a quick shower, change into something clean, and come down for dinner. Why don't we eat over there. It's called the *Café Royale*. It has a lovely garden setting. Look at it, Hank!"

Hank didn't have to be asked twice. The place looked great, and he was famished. Showering and changing quickly, they had a great meal in the garden and an after-dinner drink in the *Esplanade* lounge. Upon returning to their impeccably furnished room, two mints greeted them from the soft pillows. New Orleans was basking in a steamy night, and the passionate lovers were just as steamy. It was a fabulous introduction to New Orleans for Meltzer & Meltzer, Private Investigators.

* * * *

For Ahram Mazalo, the Haitian houngan, the introduction to Miami did not proceed as smoothly. At 6:45, he rang the front door bell to the upstairs apartment. A few minutes later, his brother, Ibu, appeared. The two brothers, with their similar-sized, muscular bodies, hugged each other affectionately. After finishing a fine Haitian-style dinner enhanced by a few rum swizzles, Ibu, at his brother's behest, opened the door of the downstairs doll shop. Ahram was pleased that his brother had given up his nefarious role as a bokor, and wanted to see evidence of his new occupation.

Feasting his eyes on the inanimate splendor, while speaking in cultured French, Ahram said: "I must say, Ibu, you certainly haven't lost your touch. The craftsmanship in these dolls is superb."

"Thank you, brother dear," responded Ibu. "it gives me so much enjoyment to improve the quality of life for all those poor suffering children."

Two rapid flashes of lightning momentarily brightened the darkened room. A few seconds later, the rumbling thunder sent shivering waves through the wooden internal structures.

As the voluminous drops pelted the building, Ahram remarked: "As often as I've been caught in these tropical storms, I still can't get used to them."

"My brother, you should know; it's only a sign from the gods, telling us to mend our ways."

"If that's true, it warms my heart to know that you've mended your ways."

"As you can see, I am now only a humble craftsman trying to eke out a mere living."

"I am pleased; the gods will bless you."

Another lightning flash illuminated the far corner of the room. Ahram saw something moving. Ten hairy legs attached to an oval head and bulbous trunk were moving synchronously under a door. The thunder-induced vibratory pattern had shaken a shelf; a bottle fell off; its lid dislodged; the living inhabitants gained their freedom. A few seconds later, another member of the Therasphosidea family joined its brother as it crept through the door. And then it became a veritable stampede as a dozen more tarantulas followed their leaders through destiny's door.

"Open that door!" demanded Ahram. Although, it was too far to see them clearly, he thought he had recognized the spiders; they appeared to be a type of tarantula indigenous to Haiti.

"What are you shouting about? It's only a closet. There are so many stinkin' bugs around here. I just can't get rid of them."

His brother's remarks only served to anger him further. "I said open that damn door."

"But - - - -"

Ibu's pleading was in vain. Finally, he had to relent and open the door. Gazing inside at the diabolical surroundings while inhaling the putrescent odors brought forth an immediate recognition. He knew that the room was a bokor's sanctuary. The revelation triggered an intense reaction from the cultured, normally mild-mannered houngan. The preceding thunder and lightning was mild compared to the auditory explosion that then ensued. Civilized as he was, Ahram did not resort to violence, but following his verbal tirade, he stormed out of the building vowing never again to set eyes on his brother.

16

Friday, September 8

They arose bright and early; it was destined to be an event-packed day. Today they had planned to seek out the bokor, but to make sure the day was at least partly entertaining, the morning was to be devoted to enjoying the sites of the French Quarter.

The car was parked in the garage. Armed with a guide book to New Orleans and a walking tour map of the French Quarter, Marilyn was ready to lead the expedition through that historical 90 square blocks. To work up an appetite, they took a brisk walk toward the fabled Mississippi River. Having reached Chartres Street, they turned left and walked several more blocks until they arrived at Antoine Alley. They followed the Alley to the French Market. By then, it was 8:30, and they were famished. Since it was relatively early, the Market was not yet hectic. They thought it would be enjoyable to do some "people-watching" while having a unique New Orleans breakfast.

Seated at an outdoor table of the illustrious *Café du Monde*, they glanced at the abbreviated menu.

"Not much to choose from, Hank, but the beignets are considered to be a must."

"Yeah, but with all that sugar and who knows what else, these doughnuts or crullers or whatever they are, are no good for my cholesterol."

"One order is not going to kill you. They're supposed to be real delicious."

"You win; I'll have *café au lait* along with them. Is that all right?"

"That's fine! Now, let's relax and look around."

Sitting under the large awning, they were invigorated by a delightful river breeze. It almost made them forget the mounting heat and humidity.

Sipping her coffee, Marilyn was looking across the way at Jackson Square; she fixated on the imposing bronze statue of General Andrew Jackson. Munching on a beignet, Hank was viewing the neatly lined up horse drawn carriages.

"Wasn't life peaceful and relaxed when people drove around in horse drawn carriages?"

"For the passengers, it was, but think of the poor horses, especially in this kind of sweltering heat."

"I guess you're right, Marilyn, but life has become so hectic lately. It would be - - - -"

* * * *

Fate and fatality — two similarly sounding words that are often inexorably intertwined. Yet, is it fate that leads to premature death or is it the foibles of individuals? Why do some people drive when they're drunk? Why do some individuals drink early in the day? Why don't more of us use seat belts? Why do unlicensed drivers get behind a wheel? Maybe part of the answer to all of these questions is the uncontrollable desire for excitement — a drive that irrationally refuses to accept the nature of risks and the potential damage to oneself and others. On this particular morning, Steve Farrington was living that kind of distorted reality. Young, reckless, and fearless, he thought that the best way to overcome a morning hangover was to start off the day with a drink.   Following his impulse with a stiff jigger of scotch, he got   into   his black 1973 Volkswagen coupe. Having nothing better to do (having recently been fired from his gas attendant job), he decided to head for the Mississippi docks. As he drove down St. Phillip Street, the car swayed in harmony with the beat of the rock tune blasting away on the car radio.   The right turn he made on Decatur Street was exceedingly wide. Even though he had lost his license, it wasn't because of deficiencies in the ability to handle a motor vehicle. So, when a blue Plymouth Valiant headed straight for him (after all, he was on the wrong side of the road), he quickly straightened the wheel and avoided the oncoming car. He missed a head-on collision. But his compensatory turn was markedly accentuated, and he was going too fast. With the seat belt neatly tucked into its compartment, he put his right foot on the brakes.   His foot strength was too weak, and his timing was too slow. Seeing the tables coming to meet him, he cried out; and then someone turned out the bright sunlight.

* * * *

Since Hank and Marilyn were both looking to their left in the direction of Jackson Square, it would have been difficult for them to observe an oncoming vehicle from their right — difficult but not impossible. Before Hank could finish his sentence, he heard the roaring engine and the squeaking brakes. Without a second's delay, he grabbed Marilyn and leaped out into the street. Falling hard onto the pavement, he cushioned Marilyn's fall by taking the brunt of the punishment himself.

"What happened, Hank? Are you all right?"

"Just a little bruised. The guy must have been drunk or stoned or both. The hell with him! How are you?"

"A little jittery, but I think I'm okay."

However, the driver was not so fortunate. He was flung out of the car into a metallic pole, one of the four that had held up the awning of the restaurant's outdoor pavilion. The pole cracked, and Steve Farrington was impaled on its jagged edge. Miraculously, no one else had been in the vicinity, and only inanimate destruction occurred.

Getting up and verifying that she had no broken bones or any other serious problem, Marilyn said: "Can you believe it? Even when we're not driving or flying, we still can't get away from these near-misses."

"As I said, honey, life used to be so peaceful. Let's get out of here before fate delivers us another blow."

By that time, the police had arrived. Hank and Marilyn gave their statements. The other patrons, the owner, and the employees, who were all within the protective confines of the inner dining room, had little, if anything, to add.

Shaken up but undaunted, Marilyn and Hank resumed their walking tour, but their pace slowed down considerably. They stopped off at many of the major highlights, having abbreviated views of the St. Louis Cathedral, Pirate's Alley, Royal Street — home of the "Streetcar Named Desire" — and the *La Branch* House, with its fancy iron grillwork. Marilyn captured many of the sights with her Minolta. They also passed by the infamous haunted house, the *La Laurie* Home, but no ghosts came out to greet them. In a similar vein, they observed the site where Marie Laveau, the New Orleans voodoo queen, had reigned. No pin-filled dolls were visible, but thinking about it, Hank remembered the strange doll by James Conover's death bed. *I have to look into that when we get back*, he told himself.

Having finished a delicious Creole luncheon at the picturesque Court of Two Sisters, they were now ready to meet the bokor.

* * * *

It was 1:45: fifteen minutes to go before he had to re-open the shop. Raoul LeGauche was smiling. He was a bokor and looked the part: tall, swarthy, and roguishly handsome. He could have passed for a movie star. Even now in his late 60s, he gave the appearance of someone decades younger. America had been good to him. The sale of amulets, charms, and trinkets proved to be a financial windfall. Gullible tourists paid inflated prices for his wares believing that they would be protected against demons, enemies, jealous spouses, and even so-called friends. He learned a lesson early in life: you get much further by appealing to people's fears and worries than by considering their aspirations and good nature. Knowing the power of hatred, he used his knowledge of sorcery, mind control, and toxins, to extricate large sums of money to help individuals avenge wrongdoings. Among his clients was the Cuban, Carlos Candiani. Carlos's case was going to be one of his easiest paychecks. One thousand dollars and all he had to do was steer the Meltzers to Haiti. And the Meltzers would have to offer him some more money. His smile broadened. *God bless America!*

* * * *

Pulling back the lacy iron grill gate, he placed his right hand on the emblazoned brass knocker. He rapped it a few times. This generated a low octave sound that traveled in the form of waves through the thick wooden door, the inner room, and the auditory apparatus of the two ears of the reflecting African American. The noise startled him and interrupted his reverie. His cerebral cortex interpreted the generated nerve impulses. Realizing the implications, he walked to the front door. Looking through the tiny peep hole, he saw the middle-aged couple. Recalling the description he recently received, he assumed that this must be the American private investigators.

"Please come in," he said in a powerful, resonant voice, spoken with just a touch of a French accent.

As they entered the Haitian voodoo objects shop, they were impressed with the light, uncluttered appearance of the surroundings. Ivory colored walls, spotless pine wooden floors, colorful lamp shades, paper mache macaws and parrots on decorated stands, small palms and tropical plants, and several glass enclosed display stands with all kinds of trinkets.

Hardly a place where voodoo would be practiced, thought Marilyn.

"What can I do for you?"

"Hi, my name is Hank Meltzer, and this is my wife and partner, Marilyn. We are private investigators and were told that you might be able to help us find the location of a certain person living in Miami."

Taking their hands and bowing gracefully, he said: "I am pleased to meet you; have a seat. I would like to help you, but I don't have too much free time; the shop re-opens in ten minutes."

"We'll get right to the point," Marilyn stated.

As she was about to start, Raoul interjected: "Before you begin, I must let you know that if I can be of service, there is a fee."

"We understand," Marilyn responded. "This cashier's check is for $500 and it's yours if you can give us a lead to the location of a particular person who is practicing as a bokor."

"I do have good contacts among the Haitian immigrants, but I, myself, only sell amulets and various charms, as you can see in the display cases. I do not engage in any evil or despicable practices."

"Oh, we didn't imply that- - - "

Interrupting Marilyn, Raoul stated: "Regardless, the $500 is sufficient. Tell me who you want to find."

Hank replied: "The man's name is Ibu Mazalo. I've been told that he practices his profession in the Little Havana section of Miami."

"The name sounds familiar. I may be able to help you. Stay here a minute. I will go inside where I keep my reference materials."

With forceful steps, Raoul LeGauche went to his private back room — the secret chamber where he delved into his devilish pursuits. Meanwhile Hank and Marilyn looked at each other with a mixture of anticipation and anxiety.

A few minutes later, displaying an impish smile, he was back in the room. "To quote an American adage, I have good news and bad news. The good news is I do know about Ibu Mazalo, and I'm aware he's in Miami. The bad news is I don't know his location. But there is a definite possibility that you can find him. Ten years ago, I left Haiti for New Orleans. When I left, I remembered that another Haitian who was versed in voodoo lore took off for Miami at the same time. That person is Ibu Mazalo. Now Ibu has a brother back in Haiti who is a houngan; that's a voodoo priest. I am certain he can tell you where his brother is located. If you kindly give me the check, I will give you his address. However, if you would rather not go to Haiti, I'll forget about the whole thing, and there will be no charge."

Hank looked at Marilyn. She shook her head affirmatively. They got the address and directions, and would soon be off to the heart and soul of voodooism. But for the rest of the weekend, the sights and sounds of "the Crescent City" would be keeping them busy while temporarily taking their minds off of any future calamities.

* * * *

Meanwhile, another conversation was taking place at the North Miami Beach General Hospital. It was in the private office of psychologist, Ronald Fielding. A large clutter-free walnut desk separated him from his friend and colleague, internist, Arnold Banks.

Both men were in their late 60s and had been practicing their specialties for over 35 years. Ronald had thinning gray hair, an aquiline nose, tobacco-stained teeth, and tiny gray eyes. His outstanding feature was his Amish type salt and pepper beard. He was small-boned, but tall, and had a cone-shaped pot belly.

Arnold was quite the opposite: thick, horn-rimmed glasses, a large button-shaped nose, protruding teeth, and a pock-marked complexion. He was large-boned, also tall, and his belly started at the middle of his chest, overlapped his thighs, and joined with his oversized backside. Neither of the doctors was the picture of health.

Leaning back on his reclining chair, the psychologist, Fielding, spoke first: "I'll tell you, Arnie; I've had it with working with these sick old fogies. When I was younger it wasn't so bad, but now that I'm getting a little older myself, I've just got no patience for them. Especially when I know that my counseling isn't really doing much good. Most of these oldsters either don't understand what I'm saying, or they kick off before my advice and suggestions can do them any good. I know it's blasphemous to say it, but considering their condition, I wonder why the heck we try to keep them around. What do you think?"

Leaning forward in his chair and looking directly at his friend, the internist, Banks, replied: "You won't believe it, but lately I've been thinking along the same lines myself. For most of these sick old codgers, my medications just keep them going for a short time. And a lot of them don't even thank me. They're more concerned with the cost and whether their insurance will cover it. And God forbid if something should go wrong, the malpractice summons is there almost before you finish talking to them."

"How about that! We think alike. Maybe it's time for a change."

"Yeah, Ron, maybe we should retire before working on these oldsters drives us crazy."

"Or drives us into deciding to help them end their misery and keep ourselves sane."

"You don't really mean that; do you?"

Before he could answer, there was a knock on the door.

Dr. Fielding said: "Come in."

A tall, slightly stooped, handsome older man entered.

"How are you, Dave? We were just having an interesting little talk."

"About what, Ron?" asked David Lavier, a hospital volunteer.

"We were discussing how difficult it's getting to be working with these sick old people," said Arnold. "You're one step ahead of us, Dave since you've retired from surgical practice. But how can you take working with them even as a volunteer?"

"Well, I guess I'm just a little more tolerant than you guys."

They continued the conversation for a few more minutes.

While they were talking, a couple of doors down two other doctors on the verge of retirement were concluding their own conversation. They were in the private office of physical therapist, Sidney Sargent. Sidney, a well built, balding, fair-skinned, native Floridian, was emphasizing a point to his colleague, anesthesiologist, Ralph Blackmore.

"You might think that after all these years of working with sick and injured senior citizens, I would be burned out. Sure, at times I get stressed from the patient load. But in general, I really like working with my patients. The vast majority of them are very appreciative. I know, by necessity, your experience is a little different."

"Not that much, Sid," said the Cary Grant look-a-like. No doubt, most of my patients are under general and can't communicate with me, but I do converse with those under local. And I talk to everyone before and after their surgery. I also do get bombed out at times from the workload. But overall, I would say that my experiences with older patients are quite favorable. As long as I do my job well, they appreciate it and we get along fine. In fact, I really think that most old-timers are more appreciative than their younger counterparts."

Walking out of the office, they met the other three doctors who were heading in their direction.

After a few seconds for an exchange of greetings, the five doctors rekindled their previous discussion. Leaving the building, one of the five — the rat-expert doctor — smiled broadly to himself. After all, he knew much more than the others; he was the only one who had taken things into his own hands.

17

Tuesday, September 12

Elliot Palmer felt frightened, defenseless, and dependent. Having lost all control of his life to the medical staff, he was afraid of everything and everyone. Almost all of his life, he had been in charge of stressful situations. Whenever there was a problem, the first one to be called upon was Elliott. Everyone could depend upon him, and he was secure in his knowledge and ability. When his wife's sister had been brutally raped, he was the one who came to her aid, got her to the hospital, and eventually nailed the criminal. When his father died, he made all the arrangements for the funeral, comforted his mother, and managed the estate. His brother and sister were too grief-laden to do anything productive. Even when he was personally involved in catastrophic occurrences, he managed them well. In one month, he lost $20,000 in the stock market, $15,000 in a land deal, and $10,000 in a company that became defunct. Undoubtedly, he was a poor businessman, but the triple blow didn't cause him to become depressed and suicidal. He didn't even seek revenge on those who had suckered him into those shady deals. He took control of his life and since that time 30 years ago, he had never lost a penny in business or investment scams.

That was then, and this is now. *Why, he wondered, does the body have to fall apart as one ages?   I was fine until I got diabetes. For 45 years, I had nothing worse than a cold and a sore throat — the picture of health. And then I got the sugar disease, and the next 25 years everything changed. But I really didn't have too much to complain about until recently. Then my eyes went bad, I got arteriosclerosis, and last year, of all things, I came down with tuberculosis. A few days ago, I got a nasty foot infection. Then my diabetes got worse, and here I am back in the hospital for all these tests. I hate this gown. Me who always was dressed so well, I have to walk around with this ugly frock. And then all the waiting: sitting around on hard chairs waiting to be called for tests, and then waiting around for hours or days worrying about the results. Taking those tests was no fun, either. Sticking needles and probes into every orifice in my body, that was pure hell. Going to the dentist was a pleasure compared to some of these ancient forms of torture. Gee, I'm feeling so scared and nervous. I feel so weak; I'm so tired. Oh, I just want to go to sleep and let it all end.*

Elliott Palmer had a right to be frightened. He had been admitted to the North Miami Beach General Hospital in the stage of diabetic acidosis. Before admittance, he had been feeling extremely weak and tired. Having developed a severe headache and feeling just plain "blah," he called his son, Charles. One glance at his father's sunken eyes, bright red lips, and flushed cheeks convinced Charles to have him admitted. That move saved his life — at least temporarily.

Quick work by the Emergency Room physician, the anesthesiologist, and other members of the staff stopped the disease before a fatal coma occurred. The rapid, feeble pulse and falling blood pressure were restored to near normal, and for a while the patient was resting comfortably. Later, he had a reassuring chat with the psychologist, Ronald Fielding. Nurses, aides, and a hospital volunteer stopped by to attend to his needs. Much later, the patient's mood changed. He became extremely apprehensive. Changes occurred in his body as well. A marked increase took place in blood glucose which then spilled over into his urine. Ketone bodies began accumulating in the blood. Soon disturbances took place in acid-base equilibrium, and acidosis re-occurred. While Elliott was feeling so tired and wanting to go to sleep, he was approaching the stage of diabetic coma.

* * * *

The clinical-pathological conference that was held two days later concerned itself with the sudden death of Elliott Palmer. In attendance were: six residents; the hospital administrator, Joel Glick; the Chief of Staff, Richard Adler; the Emergency Room physician, Carl Alvarez; the anesthesiologist, Ralph Blackmore, the psychologist, Ronald Fielding, the pathologist, Ernest Goodman; and the internist, Arnold Banks.

Carl Alvarez was addressing the group: "I can't understand it. When he came in, all of the signs pointed to diabetic acidosis. He had marked dehydration of the mucous membranes; his skin had abnormal turgor. His tongue was red and parched; his eyes were sunken. Hyperpnea was present, and he had acetone breath. His pulse was 100 and quite feeble, and his blood pressure was 90/50. After fluid and metabolite restoration and oxygenation, his pulse went down to 80, and his blood pressure went up to 135/85. He looked better, and was able to talk. I left him resting comfortably. I just can't understand it."

Richard Adler, commented: "Carl, who saw the patient after you left him?"

"I think Ronald had a brief chat with him."

"I did," responded the psychologist. "When I left him about 10:15, he appeared to be fine."

Dr. Alvarez then commented: "The nurses on duty that night were Maria Gonzales and Joy Reiss, and they reported that he was doing well while they were in attendance. The night nurse, Caroline Abrams, saw him at 11:30 and didn't find anything unusual."

"But he still died during the night. Ernie, what did you find to be the apparent cause of death?"

Ernest Goodman, replied: "The islets of Langerhans showed hyaline degeneration and sclerosis. His kidney showed pyelonephritis; there was marked arteriosclerosis, and retinitis was also present. But he could have lived for years with those complication. Richard, there is no doubt in my mind; he died from diabetic coma. There was glycosuria, marked ketosis, and acidosis. How it happened so quickly after apparent restitution is difficult to understand."

Internist, Arnold Banks, interjected: "I know it sounds way out, but I remember reading that extreme stress can trigger rapid diabetic changes."

Dr. Adler added: "It is true that stress can precipitate a diabetic flare-up, but to have caused such marked changes, that's difficult to fathom."

Dr. Goodman, who had seen several other strange deaths of old-timers lately, commented: "It may be difficult to understand, but with all we've been reading and hearing about the psychological control of the autonomic nervous system, it could be possible. We've all heard of anecdotal reports of people suddenly dying after a stressful event — whether it's good or bad. You know, things as disparate as winning a lottery or being mugged in a park.

"Yes," replied Carl Alvarez, "something could have frightened him to death. But what?"

The conference continued for several minutes more, but no decision could be made. It was apparent that no one knew that a doctor had visited the patient at 11:30, and before the next nurse's call in the middle of the night, Elliott Palmer was in a terminal coma.

The entire hospital staff was upset about this occurrence. Pathologist, Ernest Goodman was even more troubled about this latest unexplained sudden death of a sick old person. However, one doctor was smiling — a doctor who liked to experiment with rats and humans.

18

Friday, September 15

The weekend in New Orleans was therapeutic. The jazz, the superb cuisine, the trolley car rides, the riverboat cruise — excitement, pleasure, and relaxation all rolled up into one satisfying package. Today, it was back to business. Eric Adler had taken care of a couple of new accounts: gathering evidence for a divorce, and tracing the whereabouts of a lost child. Hank and Marilyn were so pleased with the work of Hank's old buddy, Eric, that they convinced him to come out of retirement and stay on as a permanent addition to the team.

Having booked a flight to Haiti for Monday, the Meltzers decided to spend today at Marilyn's mother's house. Marilyn hadn't seen her mother for awhile, and Hank wanted to see if that doll was still around. Considering that the "zombie," José Candiani had muttered something about a doll, Hank thought that there might be something "fishy" about James Conover's doll.

It was over four months since James had died, and although she was still grieving, the acute stage was over. Shirley Conover, wearing a bright yellow print dress, greeted her daughter and son-in-law.

"Hello, children."

"Hi, Mom; you're looking great."

"Oh you don't have to fool me. I'm looking as plain as ever. But you, Marilyn, you've never looked better. Hank must agree with you."

"Thanks, Mom. He sure does agree with me, but doesn't he look good, too?"

"Of course, Hank. You look wonderful. Lost a little weight, haven't you?"

"I'm glad you noticed, Mom; I've been working out lately — ever since I met up with my old buddy, Eric."

"Mom, Hank wants to look around a little. Actually, he's looking for something in particular. A doll, you know, that doll that dad got at the hospital."

"Yes, the cute little West Indian doll. It's on the shelf in our bedroom. When your father died, he had dropped it and - - - -"

Thinking about James brought tears to her eyes. Marilyn and Hank came over and comforted her.

"Thank you, I'm all right. Anyway, I don't know why Jim brought that doll back with him from the hospital. It seemed to comfort him, so I just kept it. Why did you ask? Is there some problem?"

"We don't know. It's probably nothing, but Hank had a hunch. So, he'd like to take a look at it."

"Fine, be my guest."

"Thanks."

Shirley Conover and Marilyn went into the kitchen for some tea and conversation. Hank headed for the master bedroom.

It looked just as he had seen it several months ago. Picking up the doll, he gazed into the luminescent eyes. *What strange eyes*, he thought. *They almost look alive.* He felt the doll without squeezing it and looked for any openings. None were apparent. No unusual odor was present, and there was no sign of anything coated on its "skin" or clothing. Aside from its eerie eyes, it appeared to be just a child's doll.

Hank wasn't convinced; he would first go to see the pathologist, Ernest Goodman, and find out if there were any new, hard-to-explain deaths of older folks. Then he would pay a visit to the toxicologist, Jonathan Milton — the doctor who helped him solve the puffer fish poison murders.

* * * *

Marilyn decided to keep her mother company while Hank made his calls. Having reached Dr. Goodman at the hospital, he was able to get an appointment at 1:30. Dr. Milton was pleased to hear from him and would be able to see Hank that same afternoon at 5:30 in his office at the University of Miami School of Medicine.

Arriving at Dr. Ernest Goodman's cheerful office right on time, Hank knocked on the door.

"It's open, come in, Hank; what's on your mind?"

"You know me, Dr. Goodman, suspicion, that's what's on my mind."

"There's nothing wrong with an inquisitive mind. By the way, please call me Ernie. I've got the feeling we'll be seeing each other a lot more. I know that once you've got your mind made up, you don't give up. Peter Simon, the pathologist at Pompano Beach Memorial Hospital, told me how your persistence paid off with the tetrodotoxin cases. I've never seen any cases of puffer fish poisoning. Anyway, that's not what you're here for today; is it?"

"No, Ernie, I wanted to know if there were any more unusual deaths of old-timers."

"Now that you've asked, I must tell you that there have been a few more. Since I last saw you four months ago, there have been five more sudden deaths of very sick old men. Again, it would be reasonable to expect that they died from their diseases, and aside from the three that died in a car crash, the disease process could have killed them."

"So why are you hesitant?"

"Because I think something else killed them — even

those killed in the car crash. The only thing is I don't know what."

Dr. Goodman went on to give the details of the deaths and his pathological findings.

Hank then asked: "Ernie, I found something a little bizarre associated with the death of my father-in-law, James Conover. There was a West Indian type doll in his room; he got it at the hospital. It has the strangest looking eyes. Here, take a look at it."

Dr. Goodman scrutinized it carefully and had to admit that the eyes appeared weird.

"Another case I'm working on involves a strange coma that an old man has been put into; he's supposed to be a zombie."

"A what?"

"Not that I believe the guy's a zombie, but he was also involved with one of these strange kind of dolls. I wonder if any of the other old folks that died recently brought home a West Indian type doll."

"I don't know, but I'll ask around."

"Thanks for your time. Later, I'll be seeing the toxicologist, Jonathan Milton. I want him to examine the doll. Maybe there's a toxin hidden somewhere inside that's related to Mr. Conover's death."

"Another thing, there's the possibility that some psychological methods could've been used to precipitate those deaths. I have no evidence, but it remains a possibility. Anyway, Hank, good luck."

"Thanks."

Dashing out of the building, Hank, said to himself, *Psychological, hmm; that's interesting."* One thing he was certain; he was on to something.

* * * *

The palm tree-lined path to the entrance of the pharmacology building looked just as it had last December. Like he was reliving a dream, Hank got into the elevator, and pushed the fourth floor button. Rapping gently on the door to room 477, he awaited a response. The Chairman of the Department of Toxicology, Jonathan Milton, opened the door.

Putting his arms around Hank, he said: "I'm so glad to see you, especially since you're so robust looking." He had remembered that the last time he saw him, Hank was near death.

Hank was thrilled with the warm response, and the office was still as colorful and comfortable as it had been previously.

Lighting up his favorite pipe and looking at the doll in Hank's right hand, Jonathan asked: "So, Hank, what have you got for me? You didn't really have to bring me a present. I've got to tell you I'm a little too old for dolls."

"I should've brought you a present, Jonathan for all you did for me. But this is no present."

Hank then explained to Jonathan the details of the eight deaths and his suspicion about the doll.

"I would appreciate it if you would look into this doll and see if there is any evidence of a toxin."

"I'll do the best I can, but considering it's been over four months since Mr. Conover died, even if there had been something there originally, I doubt that I'd detect anything now. Nevertheless, I'll see what I can find."

Hank then told him about the upcoming trip to Haiti and the "zombie."

"I know that zombification is related to toxins. I wasn't aware that puffer fish poison is a component, but if that's what Linda Perrin told Marilyn, I'm sure it's true. She's one of our best anthropologists. Have a good and safe trip. Give my best to Marilyn."

"Thanks, Jonathan."

* * * *

Arriving back at his mother-in-law's home at 7:30, the three of them had a leisurely dinner. By 10:00, Hank and Marilyn were back in their Pompano Beach home. The strains of Howard Hanson's Second Symphony — the Romantic — put them in an appropriate mood. A wonderful night of love followed, and when they fell asleep, Hank dreamed of killer dolls, and Marilyn dreamed of fighting fish. Undoubtedly, something was preying on their minds.

* * * *

Arnold Banks was doing a different kind of praying. He was praying to the assorted gods in his expensive religious collection. Dr. Banks, a respected internist, was a man with multiple interests and many hobbies. Included among these was a fascination with the occult, the strange, and the bizarre. One of his hobbies was to collect objects of worship from the world-wide religions. An entire room was devoted to his accumulation of relics representing mankind's hopes for placating the deities. Present were statues, icons, idols, and paintings. Arnold was standing face-to-face with these representations from most of the -isms: Judaism, Catholicism, Protestantism, Hinduism, Mohammedism, Buddhism, Confucianism, and Pantheism. Not taking any chances, in turn, he was praying to them all. The aging internist was praying for strength — the strength to implement his decision.

* * * *

A retired surgeon, presently a hospital volunteer, he was a man with widespread interests including a belief in ESP. The truth was that David Lavier didn't really believe in ESP, but the subject fascinated him greatly. Mind reading, telekinesis, prescience, clairvoyance — he found the entire field intriguing. Considering the important event about to happen in his life, he couldn't afford to pass up an opportunity to gain foreknowledge. Opening the front door of Madame LaForce's suite, he was somewhat apprehensive about what the reader's crystal ball would tell him about his future. Still, he didn't really believe in this pseudoscience — or did he?

* * * *

"Keep your head in the stars but your feet on the ground." That was one of his favorite sayings. He interpreted the saying to mean: have dreams, aspirations, goals, and ambitions. "Reach for the moon" but, at the same time, know where you are starting from. Take small steps and don't get upset if you trip now or then. Always reach for those stars. Never be completely content because things always change. When you're reaching, while you're climbing, make sure you look where you're going. If you come to obstacles in your path, don't step on them. Instead, bypass them or change your route. He wasn't just a philosopher; he followed that saying to a "t."

But he also had another interpretation for the saying: when you have to make a decision, don't only look at the solid evidence of science, but consider heavenly or spiritual influences.

To outsiders, Sidney Sargent was a pragmatist, invariably making decisions based on logical analyses paired with practical compromises. But deep inside him, he wasn't certain that science was always correct. Sometimes he felt that life was somewhat of a gamble. He considered that luck and fate had as much to do with outcomes as logic and reason. Tonight, he was looking to the stars for advice. He really needed it; the aging physical therapist was about to make an important move.

* * * *

A psychologist with tarot cards, a psychologist who sits in at
séances, a psychologist who reads palms, a psychologist
who constantly knocks on wood and crosses his fingers, a
psychologist who avoids black cats and refrains from
walking under ladders — such a psychologist was Ronald
Fielding. His scientific training taught him that only
controlled experiments could be believed. Yet, he didn't
think it strange that he delved into these pseudo-scientific
fields. After all, he wasn't convinced that psychology was as
scientifically versed as its proponents believed. He also felt
that by learning parapsychological practices, it might make
him an even better psychologist. At any rate, it was fun, and
with all the stress he built up from working with sick and
dying old patients he felt entitled to some enjoyment. Right
now, he was reading the cards. He was interested in what
they would say about his future. For the aging psychologist,
an important event was about to take place.

* * * *

Ralph Blackmore was an anesthesiologist with extensive
training. Like all members of his specialty, he was well
versed in the various techniques of local analgesia and
anesthesia, general anesthesia, and intravenous (IV) sedation.
But he also had expertise in the psychological methods of
inducing anesthesia and analgesia. Having had taken
extensive courses in meditation and hypnosis, he was
currently the only anesthesiologist in the hospital who used
those methods in the operating room. In most cases, he was
quite selective in the use of psychological modalities;
hypnosis and meditation were primarily used to supplement
IV and general anesthesia. Right now, Ralph was in a self-
induced hypnotic trance. The deep state of relaxation would
help unchain his conscious constraints and give him the
courage to make a major move.

* * * *

Belief is a major determinant of motivation. It doesn't matter whether the belief is logical or erroneous, whether it is true or false, whether it is triggered by internal or external forces, whether it is instilled by force, reason, or emotion. It only matters that it is held firmly. Once that happens, it can act on the person's autonomic and central nervous systems to such an extent that the involved individual has increased strength, augmented abilities to fight infections and tumors, and as with certain doctors from the North Miami Beach General Hospital, renewed motivation to carry forth a plan of action.

* * * *

The religious relics "told" Arnold Banks that the timing was correct for him to follow up on his decision. He felt, however, that something was missing. What it was, he wasn't sure. There was still a little time.

* * * *

Madame LaForce's crystal ball showed that danger lay ahead. David Lavier wasn't convinced. His interest in the occult didn't extend to the point that he believed in parapsychological prognostications. He believed more in his own convictions.

* * * *

The stars were bright; the glow of the reflected light portended good happenings. Sidney Sargent's belief in the wisdom of the heavens convinced him that the forthcoming move would be successful.

* * * *

Could the cards be wrong? Ronald Fielding was in the midst
of a quandary. He wanted to believe in the readings, but the
evil bodings shown by the tarot cards did not please him.
His scientific training took over — at least for this time. He
told himself, *The cards must be mistaken. Too much is at
stake.*

* * * *

From the depths of his unconscious mind came the answer.
It wasn't in the form of an explicit thought. Rather, it was
more like a series of positive vibes. Whatever it was, Ralph
Blackmore was certain; the time had come.

19

Monday, September 18

It was sixteen days since he made his decision, and in a few minutes it would be implemented. He had an appointment with Ibu Mazalo, ostensibly to purchase two more dolls, but in reality it was to be a more sinister meeting. He conveniently arranged it for 9:45 — after business hours and before the area's evening activities would begin. Parking the distinctive 1979 brown and gold patterned Honda Civic in an alley three blocks away, he glanced at his watch. It was 9:30. With arthritic knees, his usual walking pace would get him to the shop at just about the appointed time. The doctor was keyed up but ready.

* * * *

Today was a hectic day. Although many businesses are slow after the weekend, Ibu's was different. In this tempestuous region, among drugs, alcohol, and hot-blooded temperaments, the weekends were anything but a time of rest and prayer — at least for many of the occupants. On Monday, repentance and revenge were foremost in the minds of these individuals. Some of them felt the need to placate the gods by giving the gift of an enchanting doll. Others had a more nefarious purpose; they purchased one of the activated dolls to avenge an enemy. In addition, this past weekend a full moon added to the devilish desires. Whatever the reason, today, Ibu's shop was a beehive of activity.

He was only able to grab a snack for lunch, and he had just finished a late dinner. Tired and full, he was in no mood to conduct business; he hoped he would be able to get rid of the old doctor quickly.

* * * *

No fancy platitudes filled the air when the two older professionals met. For Ibu, it was to be all business; for the doctor, it was to be all mind control. The stage was set, but there were two different scripts. The next few minutes would determine which one the "actors" would follow.

The doctor was well prepared for his part. As he entered the shop, he removed his thin, light, tan jacket. For the occasion, he was wearing a special tie. It was a paisley, made of soft silk and woven with colorful curved abstract figures. But this was not an ordinary paisley. After many years of experimenting with hypnotic induction devices (the doctor didn't just work with rodents), he designed a tie with an admixture of iridescent colors and snail-like shapes. Orange, red, pink, blue, violet, green, and black blended together into a mixture of hues and shapes that enticed one to look and entranced anyone who did look. Although it might appear to be an arbitrary configuration of sizes, shapes, and colors, every aspect of this tie had been carefully designed and tested. Today, the doctor would give the tie its most important test.

"Good evening, Ibu; I hope this is not an inconvenient time."

"I am tired, doctor, but as long as the transaction does not take long, everything will be fine."

"No, it should only take a few minutes. Is it all right if I sit down? My knees are aching me."

"No problem," he said as he sat opposite the doctor in a darkened area of the room. "Now, what's on your mind?"

But even as he asked the question, he was being irrevocably drawn to the tie.

Answering in carefully measured words and speaking in a low monotonous voice, the doctor responded: "I am now about to engage in a more pragmatic humanitarian enterprise. The individuals concerned are in the throes of despair, but they are infatuated with their inconclusive lifestyles. As a result, they are seeking redress, but do not know where to turn. I have offered them a solution, but it requires your careful and considerable help. First of all, I will need to avoid lassitude and indifference. Ibu, you can help in this endeavor, and all mankind will ultimately benefit."

Ibu Mazalo was hearing the words. He knew English was being spoken, and yet he was finding it difficult to associate the phrases with anything that had meaning. He was tired and wanted to get to sleep more than anything else; yet he was fascinated by that tie. The snails were moving in and out; they were spinning and jumping. They were reaching for him. There was much that he wanted to ask, but he could only say: "What can I do for you?"

"Please do not become pedantic with me. I know you can be abstruse at times, but the clarity of my expression is unambiguous, and you, of all people should know that - - - - - Heavy eyes, the lids are closing, let them close; beautiful, wonderful, sleep. - - - This is the plan. I supply the archaic demeanor; you supply the preternatural predilections. I am willing to pay you with a huge sum of gilders and marks."

What is he saying? Am I going crazy? My eyelids are so heavy. Sleep would be so wonderful. He is a good man. I should listen to him; I am so tired, so very tired.

"There are three hermaphrodites involved. They have a predilection for fig newtons and cigars. - - - - The cave is open; it is unlike any cave you have ever seen before. It is not dark and damp but light and dry; you walk inside. It is perfectly safe and clean. The air is pure and has a flowery odor; it is very pleasant."

The doctor continued to speak in slow, monotonous tones; he walked over to Ibu and stroked his shoulders and arms; the touch was ever so gentle.

"You've had a hard day, so many distractions, so much work. Isn't it wonderful to feel so relaxed now, to allow the worries to melt, to let yourself go? There are steps inside the cave and a wrought iron railing. You hold on to the railing and slowly descend the steps. As you go down, you feel yourself sinking deeper and deeper into this wonderful pleasant state. At the bottom of the steps, you see it. It beckons you. 'Come relax with me,' it says. You walk over and see it. There's a mist over it, but you can barely begin to make it out. The mist lifts; now you can see it clearly; it's a hammock, and it awaits you. You let yourself fall into it; it begins to rock — back and forth, back and forth. As you sway, you feel yourself getting deeper and deeper; you are so very tired, and now you are in a perfect peaceful abyss.

Now listen carefully to every word I say. I want you to be able to stay in this wonderful relaxed state forever, this state of pure bliss. But while you are in this heavenly state, the earthly part of you can respond to my directions. First, I want you to open your eyes. Fine, now I want you to - - - - - ."

Ibu Mazalo was in a state of perfect serenity and tranquility; he had no pain, no worries, no anxieties; he was listening to one of his gods, a god who was leading him to eternal peace.

Hearing the directions, Ibu carefully got out of the chair, and effortlessly walked to the back of the room. The doctor continued to speak as he slowly followed the bokor. "Take out your key, unlock the door."

Ibu unhesitatingly complied. Somewhere in the back of his mind, he knew he was being led. Even though he was a powerful man who could easily outmuscle the doctor, he was powerless to resist. Now he had entered his private domain, that nether world, that chamber of pestilence and poisons, but he was oblivious to his surroundings. The only world he knew was represented by the gentle, guiding voice. For him, nothing else existed.

"Go to the shelf, the shelf where you have the beautiful dolls, the dolls that you had prepared so carefully. Take the first one, that's right — the pretty little girl with the green print dress and pink bow in her hair. Isn't she adorable? Hold her to yourself. Embrace her. Let her cheeks touch yours. Look into her eyes — deep, deep into her eyes. Be eye to eye with her. Now squeeze the doll; feel her life; let it enter; let it come into your eyes; You will feel a slight tingle; that is her essence. It is combining with yours to give you eternal bliss. Your breathing is getting slower and slower; your heart is beating slower and slower; every nerve, every organ, every fiber, every cell is getting quieter and quieter. Your good soul is leaving for its heavenly place; your bad soul has been set free. You now will reach your ultimate reward; now and forever. You are there!"

The doctor's voice became silent. He watched as Ibu reacted; it happened just as he planned. Falling backwards, Ibu's head landed on the dirt-covered, hard, wooden floor. The doll fell out of his grasp; its eyes remained open. For the next few minutes, there was complete silence. Then sounds of life returned. The principal one was from the old doctor's gimpy gait as he began to walk out of the room. He had achieved his goal. Using a combination of a confusion technique, his unique paisley tie, and a toxin-laced doll, he had hypnotized the bokor into eternal sleep. Now, in case any of the previous dolls were found and in some way linked to the death of the sick old men, it would be assumed that it was the work of a psychotic old bokor who accidentally died from a dose of his own "medicine."

But there was another sound in the room. It was so quiet that the old doctor couldn't hear a thing. He placed his hand on the door between the inner sanctum of witchcraft and death and the outer chamber filled with colorful dolls. The rat-expert doctor thought to himself, *Now I am free to continue my "humanitarian" experiments without any fear of reprisal.*

"Ouch!" he screamed out loudly, "What the hell was that?"

Reacting quickly to the painful bite, he smashed the culprit on his neck, killing it instantly.

"Damn spiders! Let me get out of this God-forsaken place."

With that, he closed the door, walked to the front of the store, locked the outside door behind him, and headed for his car. He expected that shortly he would be home resting comfortably on his lounge.

What he didn't know was that he had been bitten by a unique tarantula, the most toxic member of its species — one that is capable of killing small animals with one bite. After the storm a few days ago in which the tarantulas had escaped, Ibu Mazalo had retrieved them all and replaced them in another jar, to be used for future experimentation. But one of the spiders hid under a cabinet, and only now came out into the open. Ibu Mazalo would never know it, but a potential member of his deadly formula had exacted a measure of revenge for him. Once the old doctor reached his car, he would have an unexpected surprise.

20

Monday, September 18

While a death rattle was quietly reverberating in the back room of the doll shop in Little Havana, the rumble of jet engines was loudly reverberating in the ears of Hank and Marilyn Meltzer as the Pan American Boeing 727 was about to take off — destination: Port-au-Prince, Haiti.

Armed as usual with tour and guide books — this time to Haiti — Marilyn was looking forward to the trip, but knowing about the dangers of voodoo and the zombie toxin, she was also somewhat apprehensive. Hank was all business; he wanted to get to the bottom of this bizarre episode — to find out, by whom, and in what manner, José Candiani was being placed into a zombie state.

To help pass the time, Marilyn was telling Hank some of the facts she uncovered about the mystical region of Hispaniola, now known as Haiti.

Using the guide book as reference, she said: "Hank, I know we didn't treat the American Indians well when we colonized our country, but according to what I just read, we were more humane than the invading Spaniards. When the Spanish settlers first came over to this Caribbean island in the

1500s, it was occupied by a gentle people called Arawak Indians.   Their   main   occupations   were   fishing   and agriculture. From the Arawaks, the Spaniards learned how to smoke tobacco, how to make bread out of the poisonous cassava root, and how to live in the countryside without getting destroyed by the natural events and eaten alive by the numerous insects and small animals. Just think, all these natural dangers are still present today.   They have treacherous rapids, dangerous whirlpools, and destructive floods. Many people come down with the potentially fatal nutritional disease, beriberi. There are also mosquitoes that cause malaria and yellow fever as well as blood-sucking leeches. A tiny green lizard is prevalent; its bite causes immediate death, and they have some of the most poisonous toads found anywhere in the world."

"Why the hell are we going there? There are enough ways to get killed back home."

"That's just the point; the Arawaks taught the Spaniards how to avoid jungle death. Anyway to go on, the place is loaded with poisonous scorpions and snakes, and we already know the sea water around Haiti has a thriving population of poisonous puffer fish."

"It seems we can never get away from those deadly creatures."

"One thing is sure; we won't go fishing here."

"That's certain; I'll wait 'till we get back to Pompano Beach before I lift another fishing pole."

"Right! Just to complete the list of dangers, they have one of the only poisonous tarantulas in the world. You know, honey, people all over the world are afraid of spiders, especially the tarantulas, but incredibly, over 99% of them are harmless. Yet, Haiti is blessed with one variety that is deadly."

"Just the thought of those crawling bugs gives me the creeps."

"To get back to the point of all this, the Arawaks were very helpful to the Spaniards; in addition to helping them survive, they also gave them golden trinkets. So what did the Spaniards give them in return? From what it says here, they gave them death from overwork, smallpox, and warfare. In fact, the Arawaks were decimated so quickly that the Spaniards needed help and in a hurry. So they imported Africans by the shipload to be slave laborers in the fields and in the mines."

"Not a pretty picture. And to think, honey that today, Haiti is a center of another disaster."

"What's that?"

"You know; the Haitians are loaded with AIDS."

"Of course! Maybe you're right; let's get on a return flight before we get involved with any of this."

"Don't worry. We're going to a nice hotel in Port-au-Prince. We're not going fishing; we won't go out in the jungle unprotected; and we certainly aren't going to shoot ourselves up with drugs or have sex with any natives; are we?"

"No way, Hank, no way!"

* * * *

While the Meltzers were talking about tarantulas and AIDS, the old doctor was about to start his car. He was feeling more than the effects of an insect bite. Actually, he was dying. Although the toxin released by the Haitian type tarantula is dangerous, it usually is not lethal. Unfortunately, the doctor was highly allergic to the protein portion of the toxin, and as a result, he was now in the midst of an anaphylactic response — a severe allergic reaction — that could in a matter of minutes kill him; that is, unless someone could give him a shot of epinephrine. Since the doctor had parked the car in a remote alley, there was little likelihood that a physician would be in the vicinity; in fact, there was hardly a chance that any human would soon pass by.

It started off innocently enough:

Boy that bite is itching me, he said to himself. Ignoring the severe irritation for the moment, he started the car. As he pulled away from the curb, he suddenly let out a violent sneeze. *Am I getting a cold, too?*

As if to answer him, his body shook from the prolonged coughing fit that followed. Although he never had previously been asthmatic, he started to wheeze. Now, the irritation spread. He had to scratch; the craving was impossible to avoid.

"God, almighty, I can't stand this," he shouted and pulled the car onto the side of the road. No one was around. Drastic internal bodily reactions were taking place. Simultaneously, his blood pressure spiraled downward and his pulse weakened. Just before he fell unconscious, his past flashed in front of him — how and why it had all started.

21

He was born in Hollywood, not the tinsel-town, movie screen landmark but the Florida version. No malevolent influences lurked in his family background. Just the opposite: as an only child with both parents as physicians, he was given every possible advantage. He had a nanny who catered to his every whim. He went to top-notch preparatory schools, starting with the structured environment of a Montesorri school right through a top-rated private high school. His premed and medical school training was at the University of Miami, and a residency in surgery was completed at the Fort Lauderdale General Hospital. Lessons by the truckload were given: piano, painting, tennis, golf, horseback riding, swimming. Possibly the only deleterious influence on his make-up was the family ideal of perfection: study hard, work hard, exercise hard, eat well, and don't accept substandard performances from yourself or others. Sometimes this worked against him. Two particular events stood out in his memory. One was the time his test average was 89 in a college genetics course. Going strictly by the book, the instructor gave him a B as the final grade. Even though he was a "real" man, he cried like a baby, berating himself for only getting a B. After all, both of his parents graduated summa cum laude from college, and he was from the same genetic stock. Although it was a disturbing blow to his ego, he recovered, but the incident left an indelible scar on his psyche.

Then there was the time he was playing third base for the Hollywood Hawks, a semi-pro baseball team. It was the bottom of the ninth; the score was 5 to 4 in favor of the Hawks. Two men were out; the bases were loaded. The count went to 3 and 2. A low sinker was delivered by the Hawk's star southpaw. He saw the pitch leaving the mound and knew it was a winner. The right handed batter was fooled. Meeting the ball on its top surface, the bat imparted a downward swing and a sharp grounder went in the direction of third base. Since he was playing close to the bag, he was in perfect position to retrieve it. Bending down low, he placed his glove and bare hand between his legs. All he had to do was scoop up the ball and step on third. The game would be over, and the Hawks would be champions. But he failed to observe a basic tenet of fielding: keep your feet together. His feet were separated. The ball went through his legs and down the left field line. Two runs scored; the game and championship were lost. He was devastated. As before, he recovered, but another psychological scar was added.

Although he enjoyed sports, his other hobbies, and school, his perfectionistic drive got in the way of lasting friendships. As a result, his principal companions were non-human. Starting in high school, and continuing through college and medical school, he involved himself with animal research. As an undergraduate, he became known as a pithing expert, often helping out squeamish classmates in their frog and toad assignments. In comparative anatomy, he excelled in dissections: the spiny dogfish was one of his favorites. But he really got a charge from working with white rats and mice. Dogs and cats were difficult to anesthetize and even if he got by that, he really felt bad if they were harmed.

Deathly afraid of getting sick or seriously injured, he avoided working on monkeys and other non-human primates. Even before the AIDS epidemic, he knew that they were frequently contaminated with dangerous viruses. Rodents were different. They could be controlled, and as long as care was taken, biting could be prevented. As a researcher interested in improving the human condition, he felt that white rats were the species that could give him substantial help in that endeavor. And with all the anti-vivisectionists starting to crop up, almost none of them stood up for the lowly rats. Rats fascinated him. He loved to watch them scurry for food or freeze from fear. But best of all, he was thrilled at his ability to control them.

Not only did he want to control rats, he wanted to be in complete charge of his own destiny: to avoid getting 89s and baseballs skipping through his legs. To be able to effectively manage his mind and his body, to eliminate apprehension — no matter what the situation — that was his goal. And he was remarkably successful in achieving it. While he was in medical school, he enrolled in an elective course in hypnosis. Enthralled by his ability to concentrate, block out distractions, become relaxed, and even feel euphoric, he soon became an expert hypnotist. Not only was he able to control himself, but he learned subtle ways to control others.

In the beginning, he only used his hypnotic expertise to help people. He was able to facilitate anesthesia, overcome needle anxiety, block out surgical apprehension, and in selected cases, do surgical procedures with hypnosis as the only anesthetic. Both within and outside the hospital, his uncanny ability was recognized. He soon achieved an excellent reputation in hypnotic circles and was elected President of the Greater Miami Society of Clinical Hypnosis. It was only after his wife's illness and subsequent death that he decided to use hypnotic techniques for a more malevolent purpose.

* * * *

The wind kicked up. The front page of *El Herald* — dated Monday, September 18, 1989 — landed on the Honda's windshield. The Spanish language headline described another drug-related death in Little Havana. Inside the car, the old doctor's body began to convulse and as it did, he regained consciousness. A short-lived episode, he soon lapsed back into an unconscious state. But before that occurred, he thought of the one love of his life, his beautiful Claire.

* * * *

They met when he was a college sophomore, and she was a freshman. Like him, she was an only child, but their interests were markedly divergent. Her parents had wanted a son and were blessed with a beautiful daughter. Undaunted, her business executive father (Vice President of the Kargen Kitchen Appliance Corporation), groomed her to be an athlete and a scholar. As an obvious choice, she majored in health and physical education.

He never forgot the morning when they first met. His memory had been reinforced by her retelling the scene innumerable times. She was sitting at the eastern end of the indoor, Olympic size swimming pool. At the other end, she saw a tall, darkly tanned, muscular young man execute a perfect swan dive and then swim the entire length of the pool underwater. Using his two arms as levers, he elevated himself out of the pool, and turned around to face her. He smiled broadly.

His recollection of the morning was of a beautiful young woman with an exquisite figure lying inclined on a lounge chair. For some strange reason, she was looking in his direction. Preparing to dive, he told himself, *"It has to be perfect,"* and it was. While underwater, he drove himself to swim the entire length although he had never previously performed that feat. Although out of breath, he reached inside of himself for an extra measure of strength to gain, what appeared to be, an effortless exit from the water. Seeing her beautiful almond-shaped green eyes, he was captured by their luminescent intensity, and he smiled at her. She smiled in return.

"Hi," he said shyly.

"Hi," she responded coyly.

Even though they liked different things and had disparate interests, that one brief encounter led to a deep romantic entanglement that culminated in a simple marriage ceremony in his senior year.

No marriage is ever ideal, but their 41 years together were as close to perfection as could be attainable. Not being able to have children and deciding against adoption, they devoted their lives to each other. He worshipped the ground she walked on, and she supported him in all his aspirations and endeavors.

Seven years ago, the calamities began. It started with the sudden rapid deterioration of both sets of parents. Slow insidious deaths from a variety of cancers — cervical, pancreatic, liver, colon — and then they were completely alone. Claire was now all he had. But before he could get over his grief from the horrendous losses, fate struck again.

It started so innocently. That first episode: he remembered it clearly.

"Claire, what was the name of the movie we saw last week? You know, the one with Marlon Brando."

"Marlon who?"

Claire had always been a stickler for details, and her memory for names was uncanny.

"Oh," she responded. Putting her head between her hands, she tried to concentrate. Observing her, he watched the furrowing of her forehead. As the ridges deepened, she said: *"I'm sorry, I don't remember the movie."*

"That's all right, sweetie."

About one hour later, she spoke to him as if nothing had happened. *"Oh, honey, the movie was 'The Godfather;' you know, the movie with Marlon Brando."*

But then the memory lapses became more frequent and intense. It was a slow, insidious, downhill process. Each day, she became a little more distant, and the pain inside him became more and more unbearable.

A few months later, another event occurred. The painful memory came back.

"You are a very handsome man," she said. *"I'd like to go out with you."*

Shattered, but smiling broadly, he said: *"Oh thank you, young lady, I would consider it an honor and a privilege to go out with you on a date."*

"That would be nice. Are you free tonight?"

"For you, I am always free."

From that day on, she rapidly went downhill. He couldn't stand it. He loved her more than anyone or anything, but she was gone, irrevocably gone. Not only didn't she recognize him, she didn't know who she was or where she was.

He tried to get the anesthesiologists at the hospital to give her a lethal injection — to end it all. They flatly refused. He knew he could do it himself, but as much as he wanted to, he couldn't face it. Finally after two years of seeing her deteriorate before his eyes, fate relented. Claire suffered a fatal stroke. Her living death and final demise left one final scar on his battered psyche. He was never the same. Seeing what happened to sick old people like their parents, and especially observing the mind-destroying death of his beloved wife, his own distorted mind came to a conclusion: he would help sick old people get out of their misery. No one would have to suffer as long as he could intervene.

How to do it? That was the challenge. The hypnotic training taught him that the mind can control the body in a variety of ways. Personally, he had used hypnosis to block pain, stop bleeding, reduce salivation, and decrease fear and anxiety. Incredibly, he was even able to get rid of warts — just with the power of the mind. He knew that with the combination of an effective hypnotist, a suggestible patient, and good rapport between the two, hypnosis could control the patient's autonomic nervous system and immune responses. But could hypnosis be used to end life? That was an unknown factor. If it could, it would be the perfect way to kill — no weapon, no toxin, no evidence. Certainly, stress could kill! Many sudden deaths had occurred after stressful incidents such as sudden death of a loved one, being involved in a robbery, or getting "caught in the act."

From his readings, he was aware that there was a will to die, just as there was a will to live. However, how does one induce the will to die? How does one induce stress in a predictable manner so that it could be used to end a person's life? The answer came from an unlikely source. He read an article by W.B. Cannon — the originator of the "fight or flight" stress response. The article appeared in a 1942 issue of *American Anthropology*. It was simply titled: "Voodoo death." In the article, from his research on the subject, Cannon hypothesized that it was the mind of the victim that reacted to the bokor's curse and led to the deadly reaction. The Haitian and Congo societies believed in the ultimate power of the voodoo curse. The bokor believed in it; the victim believed in it. If a bokor cursed you, you were expected to die. Bokors were also accomplished hypnotists, and invariably there was rapport between the bokor and his intended victim. The results affected the victim's autonomic nervous system to the point that he just gave up. Death could come suddenly from a massive release of catecholamines — adrenaline like compounds — that would cause the coronary blood vessels either to go into spasm and cut off the blood supply to the heart or cause a ventricular arrhythmia — wild, uncontrolled heart rhythms leading to sudden death. The doctor also had read that the opposite response — vagus nerve hyper-reactivity — could slow down the heart rate and that could produce death-inducing arrhythmias. Or death could occur more gradually. In the latter scenario, the victim, believing that he was doomed to die, would either stop eating or drinking completely or would gradually reduce his intake of food and beverages. He would then die from either malnutrition, dehydration, or some intercurrent infection that overwhelmed his weakened body.

It is now well known that the immune system of a stressed person — related to the release of cortisone and related compounds— impairs the immune system. The microbes and viruses are unimpeded by the body's defenses. They then go on a rampage, and ultimately, the person dies from some kind of an infection.

Social relations also contribute towards the victim's death. Once he has been cursed, family and friends alike do not expect him to live.   Recent studies have shown that sick people without social support die much sooner than sick people with supporting family and friends. So, everything works against the victim. For a while, he may be alive physically, but psychologically and socially, he is dead.

With this background knowledge, the doctor had to figure out a way to utilize "voodoo magic." From his interests in hypnosis over the years, he had many contacts in strange and exotic places in the greater Miami area. A fortuitous meeting with one of those contacts put him in touch with a bokor. Offering the bokor both a challenge and financial incentives, he was able to get the bokor to work with him to develop an effective means of mind control that turned out to be a perfect way to put ailing people out of their misery. But the old doctor, who had been enamored with his ability to control, soon went beyond his original premise and decided to end the life of sick old people — whether they wanted it or not. Armed with his new knowledge, he had acquired another mission in life: a mission to end life.

* * * *

On this fateful September morning, the doctor's mission appeared to be ending. Once more, he awakened momentarily. Gasping for breath as his body temperature rapidly rose, he called out: "Claire, I'm coming; please be there; I love you so much."

His respirations became more shallow with each passing moment. Within a fifteen minute time span, the bokor and the doctor had met their destinies, but the doctor's was not yet final.

22

Monday, September 18

No one can account for the movement of people. Scientifically, there is a ready explanation for the action of nerves and muscles. However, aside from reflex activities, all other forms of human motion are dictated by either cognitions, emotions, or environmental pressures. Even with these, responses are either immediate or delayed, depending upon the situation. With this in mind, at first glance it would appear incongruous that a prosperous physician from an elite neighborhood would decide to take a drive in mid-afternoon through an isolated section of a "foreign" enclave? What at first glance appears to be purposeless, under deep scrutiny manifests a certain degree of logic. That was the case this balmy Monday afternoon.

Dr. Arnold Banks, an icon collector, early this morning had realized that he had searched the world to amass his impressive collection of religious relics, but neglected one religion that had about 60,000 members right in the very midst of south Florida. Considering the importance of his forthcoming decision — the determination that this week, he would retire forever as an internist — his superstitious mind

155

wanted the support of another religion. Therefore, he went to his telephone table, picked up the heavy book, and let his "fingers do the walking" through the Yellow Pages. The first stop was the category, "Voodooism." As might be expected, there was no such direct listing. Trying other categories, he next examined, "Churches." He found listings for many esoteric religions including Armenian, Charismatic, Byzantine, Jewish Messianic, Swedenborgian, Bahai, and even, Miscellaneous, but no voodoo temple could be found.

As he was closing the book, serendipitously, the book caught on the page with listings from DOG through DOOR. Opening it, his eyes gravitated to the heading, DOLLS — RETAIL. One listing caught his fancy. It simply said: "Dolls — for Fun and Prayer." Thinking about the popular notion of pins and voodoo dolls, he dialed the number and reached the shopkeeper, Ibu Mazalo. When he told Mr. Mazalo his interest in voodoo religious objects, he was told to come over about 3:00 P.M., and his desires would be accommodated.

After having finished a fat-laden cheeseburger and a large order of fries — portly Arnold did not subscribe to the hypothesis of cardiovascular disease-inducing aspect of ingesting saturated fats and cholesterol — he left the restaurant and entered his 1989 metallic blue Lincoln Continental. The directions he received from Ibu Mazalo were perfect, and he now had only about two blocks to go until he reached the shop at No. 2405 La Venetia Street. Arnold was driving slowly to make sure he didn't miss the building. He also was careful not to injure his car on the buckled roads. At first, he was somewhat hesitant about taking the Lincoln into this neighborhood, but considering he had an elaborate alarm system including motion detectors and a direct signal into the police department, he felt it was relatively safe. Nevertheless, he was still driving at about only 10 mph.

As he was driving, out of the corner of his eye, something on the left caught his attention. Slowing the car down even more, he now looked directly at the site. Something quite distinctive was there. In fact, he couldn't believe his eyes. A car with it's engine racing had smoke coming out from under the hood, but it wasn't moving. Normally, he would have just driven on by. He was a member of the school of thought that said: *"Why look for trouble?"* But this was different. No one else could have had a 1979 brown and gold patterned Honda Civic. *Why that car belongs to - - - ,* but before he could finish the thought, he heard a faint moan. Now he was certain. Someone was in peril. He pulled his car directly behind the Honda. Fortunately as a practicing physician, he kept an emergency kit in his car.

Staring inside the open window on the passenger side, he saw a man slumped over the wheel. Pulling his head up, he immediately recognized his hospital colleague. Shutting off the engine, he thought to himself, *The old guy was lucky in one respect: the window was open or else he could have died from carbon monoxide poisoning. But if I don't act soon, he'll be dead from another cause — but what had happened. Was it a heart attack? Could it have been a stroke?*

Looking at the victim, hearing his labored breathing, and being somewhat knowledgeable of his past medical history, he was fairly certain that it was not a heart attack. He had to make an instantaneous decision. His judgment was that it must be an anaphylactic reaction. Ripping off the old man's coat, he pulled up his sleeve, but the veins were collapsed. If he had been in his office or at the operating room, he could have attempted a direct intracardiac injection. Here, he didn't have that option. Taking out the glass syringe with its attached thin bore needle, he placed in a cartridge of 1:1,000 epinephrine. Lifting up the old doctor's tongue, he directed the needle into the sublingual mucous membrane in the floor of the mouth. He hoped that the stimulant would get into the blood stream fast enough to save his colleague's life. He even prayed to the voodoo gods — the ones he had yet to meet.

23

Monday, September 18

The multi-dented, chocolate brown, 1982, four-wheel drive Jeep was parked in a depression about 30 feet away from the airport entrance. Wiping the strands of jet black hair off of his sweaty forehead, the thickly muscled, middle-aged man called out in rapid-fire Spanish to his companion: "There they are, Jorgé; it's the Americans."

"Are you sure, Roberto?" answered his thin and wiry young companion. "I mean, how can you tell?"

"Oh, I can tell; the descriptions I got fit them perfectly. Now, listen carefully: Our instructions are to tail them, but we've gotta make sure we're not seen. We gotta find out what hotel they're staying at."

"What then?"

"Well, they're scheduled to meet the houngan, Ahram Mazalo, sometime tomorrow. I've got compatriots at all the major hotels. As soon as the Meltzers leave their hotel room tomorrow, one of my comrades will bug their room. That way, when they return from their meeting with the houngan and talk about what happened, we'll know whether or not they'll be returning to Florida to meet the bokor, Ibu Mazalo. You know he's Ahram Mazalo's brother."

"Roberto, I'm not as smart as you; all of this is very confusing and complicated."

"It's not that hard to understand. Listen. If the houngan, Ahram Mazalo, gives the Meltzers the location in Florida of his brother, the bokor, Ibu, then our instructions are to leave the Meltzers alone and let them go back to the States."

"What will happen then?"

"Carlos and Haruo will help the bokor terminate the Meltzers."

"And if this houngan guy doesn't give the Meltzers his brother's address?"

"Then we are to arrange for the Meltzers to be destroyed right here in Haiti."

"I like that arrangement better."

"That's fine but before we do anything, tomorrow I have to check in with Carlos."

"Okay, but I'm itching to finish them off as soon as we can."

* * * *

Unlike the situation with their previous trips to Tokyo and Honolulu, here in Port-au-Prince, Hank and Marilyn didn't have a variety in their choice of a means of transportation. After leaving the airport, from the one car rental agency, they got into the available black 1979 Buick Regal and headed for their hotel, the Haitian Vodun.

Hank concentrated on the broken-pavement, dust-filled roads. Marilyn looked at the picturesque countryside. In the distance, the copper-red mountains stood out like the scene from a picture post card. Passing open fields, luxurious forests, bamboo plantations, pellucid blue lagoons, and a variety of simple, primitive homes, Marilyn was impressed with the earthy elegance of the surroundings. After taking in the natural beauty for several minutes, she picked up the Haiti tour book. Reading to herself for a while, she came across an interesting finding that she wished to share with Hank.

"Tomorrow when we get to see the houngan, Ahram Mazalo, let's ask him to to give us some magical medicine."

"Are you talking hokus-pokus now?"

"No! I really mean it. It says here in the war that the Haitian African slaves fought against the Spanish, which ultimately led to their independence, the houngans empowered the warriors with magical medicine that made the soldiers invulnerable to bullets. If that works, we'll have no need for bullet-proof shields."

"Right! And when we get the magical formula from Mazalo, we can get it packaged and mass produced. Then, we can sell it worldwide to the armies and police forces and make a fortune."

"Good thinking," Marilyn said as she burst out laughing. "Seriously, not only did the houngans work in the war effort, but the bokors joined forces with them. Pooling their spiritual and psychic powers, they supposedly used curses — called obeah — along with toxins on the enemy. Poisoned darts and verbal incantations helped destroy the Spaniards. Cleverly, by the use of oaths, they also sealed the mouths of the slaves. That way the enemy couldn't extract any information from the slaves."

"You know, if only one-tenth of the info' you've given me is true, we'd really be onto something great."

At that moment, they entered the principal city, Port-au-Prince.

"It's certainly no Tokyo or Honolulu. It looks more like a waterfront shanty town."

"You're right, Hank, but there have been many interesting things that have taken place within its boundaries. Listen to this: 'Haiti has had more political uprisings than any other country in the world, and most of them were involved with this city. The country's coat of arms exemplifies that. It is extremely martial. In the center is a palm tree having a *sans-culotte* cap perched on its top. On the sides are flags and cannons and between them a drum and cannon balls placed in a triangular shape.' "

"A flag that's armed to the teeth; that's something else."

Driving through the crowded streets, they observed the masses of humanity, the gaudily-painted, cheerful-looking, colorful buses, the ramshackle huts, the unfinished monuments, and the dazzling white government buildings.

"Hank, look at those buses. Aren't they really something to see? I never saw buses that were painted with such bright colors. Look! Each one has its own name. That one is called: 'Jerusalem, Cité de Dieu.' That means, 'city of god.' These buses certainly cheer up the dismal streets. I wonder if the people's homes are as cheerfully decorated as these buses."

"Well, maybe we'll find out. Speaking of bright, look at that building; it's so bright, it's almost blinding."

"I think that's the presidential palace."

"What a city: on one side they're as poor as church mice, on the other side, they've got more money than they know what to do with."

"I don't think that this situation is unique to Haiti. Many Third World countries have a blend just like that. In fact, even some American cities, with their slums, are almost as bad."

"You're right; that's why we're damn lucky to be living where we are in the States. Look ahead of us; I think that's our hotel."

"It says: 'The Haitian Vodun.' By the way, I know you're not thrilled with my tidbits of information, but at any rate, vodun is another name for voodoo. Vodun has several meanings. The main ones are 'spirit' or 'sacred object.' Vodun represents the various gods. There are a lot of them. A vodun can 'live' in the spiritual realm — just like the Hebrew and Christian God. But voduns can live in actual places, too. They can be found almost anywhere — even in a jar."

"Man-made gods, huh?"

"Something like that. Each god has his own specific music, type of dance, offerings, taboos, and functions. For every problem or need that a person has, there's a particular god to be called upon."

"Sounds good; remember Jizo, the Japanese god of travelers? He helped me out, didn't he?"

"He sure did! That's why I don't downplay any of these beliefs."

"I'm with you completely, but for now I'll be happy at the Haitian Vodun if we'll be able to get a good meal and a decent night's sleep."

"I'm positive they only used the name, vodun to stimulate curiosity and interest. They wouldn't dare employ any witchcraft, would they?"

Hank shrugged his shoulders and smiled as he pulled into the circular driveway in front of the imposing facade.

* * * *

Jonathan Milton was doubly amazed. First of all, he was shocked to have found anything still present in the doll's eyes. True, it was only a trace, but there was definitely a toxic substance present. Using the most up-to-date methods of gas chromatography, mass spectrophotometry, and radioactively-labeled antibodies, he was able to detect the identity of the chemical substance. When he obtained the results, he felt as if he could have been knocked over with a feather. It was — of all things — tetrodotoxin, the same neurotoxin that was involved in the series of murders committed last year by the crazed dentist, Mitchell Turner.

Yet, he said to himself, *maybe I shouldn't be surprised after all. Linda Perrin told Marilyn Meltzer that zombie poison contains tetrodotoxin. This usage may just be a variant on that formulation. But what a strange coincidence. For my entire professional career, I've never come across a case of puffer fish poisoning — that is until last year. Now, in less than a year, I'm involved in another series of murders related to that fatal neurotoxin. Of course, I'm jumping the gun a little. I'm not certain tetrodotoxin is implicated in more than this one case, and even in this James Conover case, I don't know for sure that the poison killed him. But it sure sounds suspicious. I'll have to call Ernest Goodman. A more thorough examination of the body is now needed. And if he finds something, then I'll ask him to get a court order to exhume the bodies of the other recent old timers who died in suspicious fashion. A more thorough check of their tissues might just come up with something. Wow! This is getting stranger by the minute.*

24

Tuesday, September 19

Not only did they have a good dinner and a wonderful night's sleep, but the breakfast was superb. Everything seemed to indicate that today would be exciting and fruitful for the Meltzers.

All her adult life, Marilyn was used to planning vacations, and this Haitian trip, although it entailed business aspects, was no different. Therefore, at breakfast, Marilyn outlined for Hank the details of the planned adventures for the next two days.

Glancing at her note-pad, she said: "How's this for an itinerary? After breakfast, we go into town, visit the National Palace and the major museums, drive up the mountains to Pétionville, see the National Park, and go to Jacmel, where we have lunch overlooking the Caribbean. Then we head back to Bizóton and see the houngan. If all goes well, tomorrow we'll go north to Cap-Haitien and see Citadelle National Park and Fort Liberté. Along the way, we can also stop by some beautiful waterfalls. And as planned, we'll leave for Miami Thursday morning."

"As usual, you've done a great job. That is unless this Mazalo guy decides to cast a spell on us."

"He wouldn't do that; he's a good priest."

"Oh, I almost forgot. Have you finished your coffee?"

"I sure have!"

"Great! I can't wait to get started. Judging from past experiences, our trips together have always been a ton of fun."

"You're not being facetious, are you?"

"Me facetious?   I don't even know what the word means."

* * * *

Nothing funny was happening to Carlos Candiani this morning. Wanting to confirm with Ibu Mazalo the previously made arrangements about dealing with the Meltzers, Carlos picked up the phone. Dialing the bokor's number — the time was 10:30 — he waited for several minutes, but there was no response. He was taken aback. *Where could the old bokor have gone? His shop always opens at 9:00.*

Informing Haruo that he was going to check out the inconsistency, he left for the doll shop.

* * * *

Fifteen minutes later, he got out of his car and knocked on the front door. No one answered. Turning the knob, he found it to be unlocked. As he entered, he looked into the brightly lit shop. He saw that the door to the inner sanctum was open.

What the hell is going on?

Locking the front door, Carlos walked by the collection of dolls and entered the bokor's private domain.

The familiar odors were present, but another emanation — a putrescent smell — alerted him to the presence of death.

"Eee-yah!" His shriek shook the room like the after-effects of a mini-earthquake.

A few seconds later, he was recovered sufficiently to approach the body on the floor. It was Ibu. His eyes were open; they appeared to have been frozen in terror. Carlos knew that the old bokor was now in the voodoo version of Hell.

Did the old witch doctor have a bad heart? I never questioned him about his health. Was it something more sinister?

Looking at the body from a distance — he wasn't going to touch him — he could see no immediate evidence of foul play. The only thing unusual was the one doll lying on the floor. It was a few feet to the right of the bokor's head.

A female doll with a green print dress and a pink bow in her hair. Gee, her eyes are open. I wonder if that's one of the - - - but that makes no sense. Why would Ibu fool around with one of his own poisoned dolls? Unless - - - unless it was an accident. The heck with this; I'm not gonna let myself get involved. I'm out of here and quick.

Taking out a handkerchief, he wiped the knobs of the inside and outside doors. Before departing, he locked the front door.

Getting into his car, he thought to himself, *Later, I'll have to call Roberto and Jorgé and have them set plan B into motion.*

A broad grin crossed his face as he thought about it, *The Meltzers are doomed; they will die in Haiti.*

* * * *

For now, the Meltzers were alive and well. They had just begun the first phase of Marilyn's itinerary.

"Hank, did you know that Haiti was named by the original inhabitants, the Arawak Indians?"

"No kidding! What does Haiti mean?"

"It means, high mountains. Eighty percent of Haiti is mountainous."

Looking up toward the north, she pointed in that

direction and said: "You see that ridge. It's called, *Massif de la Selle*; those are the highest mountains in Haiti."

"I've gotta hand it to you. When you go to a new city or country, you really pick up a gold mine of information."

"I think I'm a frustrated anthropologist. I'm a little envious of my friend, Linda. But then again, I'm really enjoying our private investigation agency. So far, it's been quite exciting."

"Wait 'till the bullets start flying."

"I don't think we'll be getting involved in those sort of things; will we?"

"You never know; you never know."

Hank parked the car, and they spent a few minutes examining the *Place du Marron Inconnu*. Marilyn was particularly impressed with the statue symbolizing the Black struggle for freedom.

Next, they visited the *Place des Héros de l'Independence*. It was situated in a beautiful park shaded by royal palms and flowering trees.

"Marilyn, these palm trees remind me of the majestic ones in Royal Palm Boulevard in Palm Beach. These here are graceful, but I've never seen anything like those in Palm Beach."

"I know what you mean. There is something uncannily statuesque about these tall and stately royal palms."

After spending a few minutes with the heroes of the war of independence, they headed for the futuristic National Pantheon Museum. Marilyn's anthropological interests were brought to the forefront by the museum's contents. The exhibits depicting the life style of the Arawaks enthralled her. Then she noticed something else.

"Can you believe it? This is the actual anchor from Columbus's flagship, the Santa María. Did you know that Columbus stopped at Haiti before he landed in America?"

"Yeah, that's one thing I did know. But if I remember correctly, he abandoned Haiti quickly."

"That's right. The Spaniards didn't find any gold there. They moved toward the east and cultivated what is today the Dominican Republic. Then, they went on to America, leaving Haiti to the French."

"It's a good thing. If Columbus stayed in Haiti, who knows, we might be Haitians now."

Getting back into the car, they headed south. Passing streets lined with flowering trees and gingerbread houses set back from the road, they arrived at the *Musé d'Art Haitien* and the *Centr' d'Art.*

"You know, Hank, Haiti has some excellent artists, and the art movement began and is centered right here."

"That's great for them, but for me, I never got past finger painting. How about you, hon, did you ever paint?"

"I took an art course in college; after that I did a little dabbling, but I wasn't too good."

Following this museum visit, they drove east of the city along *Avenue Panamericanine.* It was a pleasant route that climbed the mountains. As the car ascended, impressive views of Port-au-Prince came to the fore. To the sides of the road could be seen beautiful homes and gardens. Off in the distance was the *Trou d'Eau* Mountains. Reaching Pétionville, they got out of the car to look at the vistas and saturate their lungs with the unpolluted air.

Returning to the car, they drove for a few minutes until they reached the *Morne La Visite* National Park. It was on the crest of *Massif de la Selle.* Although life in the city was turbulent and chaotic, this region was like a glimpse into paradise. Tropical trees and shrubs were abundant: trembling panax, Picard's bayberry, lyconia, tree ferns, podocarpus. Birds chirped and trilled. It was like a forest scene from Bambi. Parakeets, hummingbirds, parrots, warblers, swallows — they were all in fine tune.

After enjoying this brief glimpse into Paradise, they returned to the car and headed for Jacmel. Arriving a few minutes later — it was now 12:15 — they were even more impressed with the natural and man-made beauty.

"Hank, look at the beautiful wrought iron balconies. Don't they remind you of those we saw in New Orleans?"

"They sure do, but that's not unusual. Both are French-derived."

"I'm really impressed. You **do** know more than police work and fishing; you're becoming quite observant."

"Thanks, that's a real compliment — coming from you — Now, let's eat something; I'm starved."

Finding a delightful small hotel overlooking the sea and the pristine sandy beach, they had a light, tasty lunch.

"It's such an unspoiled setting, Hank. I wish life could always be so pure and pleasant."

* * * *

But there were two men close by who would ensure that the Meltzers' life would not remain pleasant. Roberto Gonzalez and Jorgé Rodriguez were again sitting in the beat-up Jeep and observing. Having followed the Meltzers all morning, they were getting a little impatient.

"I hate these damn tourists, Jorgé."

"Me, too. When the hell are they gonna stop this touring crap and go see the houngan?"

"I don't know, but I hope it's soon. I can't take much more of this garbage."

But they would have to endure their impatience for a little while longer.

25

Tuesday, September 19

Arnold Banks never did get to see the doll shop owner, Ibu Mazalo. Dealing with his colleague's anaphylactic shock occupied him for the rest of the day. For the time being, he forgot about his desire to obtain a voodoo object of worship. This morning, however, he was feeling better, and so was his colleague. After administering the sublingual injection of epinephrine, Arnold drove the old doctor's distinctive Honda to the North Miami Beach General Hospital. The Emergency Room personnel were exemplary and by that evening, the old doctor was well on his way to a complete recovery.

Last evening, another one of Arnold's colleagues — the surgeon, Lawrence Humphrey — drove him back into Little Havana to retrieve the Lincoln. Fortunately, it had been left untouched. The logos on the window indicating that it was armed with a sophisticated alarm system must have done the trick.

Now that Arnold had performed his good deed for the day (actually, it was more like a year since he had gone out of his way to help anyone), he decided to call the doll shop owner again. So, at 10:45, he dialed Ibu Mazalo's number.

After eight rings, there was no response. Arnold deduced, *Something's strange. I don't have my first patient 'till 1:00. I've got some time; I think I'll take another drive down to Little Havana.*

* * * *

Slowing down the Buick, they observed the rusty, crooked street lamp. Just below it, the weather-beaten sign said, Bizóton. Passing mud-plastered, tree bark, and bamboo shacks overgrown with tropical vegetation, they approached a clearing in the woods. A tall stake in front of a shack told them this place was different. Stopping the car, they got out. Examining the stake, Hank pointed out to Marilyn the horse's skull hung on top at an acute angle. Yes, this was it; the *hounfor* — Ahram Mazalo's prayer home. They entered gingerly.

* * * *

It was less than two weeks since Ahram had left his brother, Ibu, vowing never to see him again. His need to forget his brother and his devilish pursuits stimulated Ahram to re-dedicate his life as a houngan. Like a physician redoing his office, Ahram decided to refurbish his *hounfor*. Just this morning, the work had been completed. Looking around, he admired his accomplishments.

Clean straw matting covered the floor. On the walls were paintings with representations of serpents, goats, crocodiles, iguanas, flamingos, crosses, and cottonwood and fig trees. Around the periphery of the room were narrow wooden benches.

In the center of the room was the altar. It held an iron bell, thunder stones — magical rocks — the asson, head pots set on China plates, and large, clay, water jugs. Surrounding these articles were handmade candles jutting out of a large, decorative, black, forged-iron, six-branched candelabra.

A elegantly carved, wide, wooden table was in front of the far wall. Neatly placed on it were jars containing incense, herbs, scented soaps and perfumes, flour, eggs, sugar, and coffee. Adjoining the jars were bottles filled with clairin, rum, and liqueurs. Decorative trays were filled with bananas, oranges, mangoes, coconuts, and yams. Fetishes made from small dried animals — moles, mice, rats, and bats — were in open display, as were abundant amulets. Colorful feathers were everywhere.

Inside a drawer, Ahram kept his medications and antidotes for voodoo curses and zombie toxins. There were canisters containing camomite flower, which is believed to be useful in reducing swelling and tumors; hogwood bark, which purportedly enhances urination; wild plum leaf, which is supposed to reduce chills; and soaked cedar bark, which is apparently useful in the treatment of diarrhea. Ahram had set aside a freshly made zombie protective lotion containing a mixture of clairin, ammonia, lemons, aloe, guaiac, basil leaves, sulphur powder, and some other secret ingredients. Various other powders were in labeled packets. Two new decks of playing cards were in a corner by themselves.

In the far left corner of the room was a free-standing ten foot replica of a wooden sailing ship outfitted in full regalia. On the room's far right corner wall displayed was a strange looking carved animal head. Its long pointed ears and narrow snout gave it the appearance of a pig-like rabbit. Beneath it were five giant drums; they were the only leftovers from the previous furnishings.

In the near right corner of the room was a bizarre wooden life-sized statue of a man. The football-shaped head had a long, pointed nose, slit-sized eyes, and a partially opened mouth with a huge, protruding tongue. Plastic molds of saliva could be seen descending onto his chin. The thin shoulders sloped downward to a narrow, sunken chest. From the undersurface of the chest a round protuberance overlapped the rest of the body. This gigantic stomach covered the thin legs and tiny feet and acted as the base of the statue.

The near left corner of the room was the dining area with a small wooden table, six wooden chairs, and about a dozen assorted cups, plates, and silverware. Ahram had discarded all his former serving dishes and utensils.

Descending from the peristyle — the roofed ceiling — were various necklaces made of snake-vertebrae, colorful beads, and variegated shells. Brightly colored flags and emblems alternated with the necklaces. In deference to modern times, a large wooden electric fan was the most centrally located hanging object.

In contrast to his brother's choice of dolls, he assembled an assortment of stylized Haitian native dolls. Set on shelves hanging from all four walls, the dolls were clothed in brightly colored satin costumes. Some had large, round heads; others had tiny, feathered heads. The bodies were either chunky or thin. Some had pitcher-handle shaped arms; others had arms that resembled string beans. One thing the dolls had in common; they were all smiling. Congo figurines, with happy faces, were sitting on shelves of their own.

* * * *

Walking into the renovated voodoo temple, Hank and Marilyn caught sight of the tall, muscular, distinguished looking, dark-skinned man. They were certain they were eye to eye with Ahram Mazalo.

Although startled to see the Caucasian couple, he maintained his composure as he said in French accented, cultured English: "To what do I owe this unexpected pleasure?"

Speaking for the two of them, Marilyn responded: "Please excuse our unannounced intrusion, Mr. Mazalo. It is Ahram Mazalo, is it not?"

"It certainly is, but how did you know my name?"

"That's what I was about to tell you."

"Before you do, please come in; make yourselves comfortable. Sit down. How about a piece of fruit or some coffee?"

Agreeing, they sat around the dining table. Hank took a banana; Marilyn chose a mango.

"Before you begin, since you already know my name, how about introducing yourselves?"

"I'm sorry that we've displayed such poor manners. My name is Marilyn Meltzer. This is my husband, Hank."

Saying, "Pleased to meet you, folks," he extended his right hand first to Marilyn and then to Hank. Both were impressed with his firm handshake.

"Now that the formalities are over, Marilyn, will you please continue."

"Thank you, Mr. Mazalo."

"Ahram, if you please."

"Anyway, Ahram, Hank and I are private investigators. We were hired by a Miami couple, the Candianis, to help solve a strange occurrence. You see, the older Candiani man was made into what appears to be a zombie."

"A zombie? And this happened in the United States?"

"Well, we're no experts on zombies," Hank added, "but from what the Candianis said and from what we observed, the old man sure is in a sorry state."

Hank then went on to describe in minute detail Carlos Candiani's story and the events Marilyn and he personally observed.

"It sounds to me," Ahram said, "that you really have a zombie on your hands. But how did you get to see me?"

Marilyn then resumed the story, telling the houngan about Eric Adler's findings and their encounter with the New Orleans bokor, Raoul LeGauche.

"Raoul LeGauche! That name sounds familiar. But go on."

"Yes, it should sound familiar. LeGauche told us he knew you and your brother, Ibu from Haiti."

"Don't mention his name to me. Of course, now I know LeGauche is also a bokor, and he went to Louisiana about the same time that my former brother went to Florida."

"Former brother?" questioned Hank. "Is he dead?"

"No, he's not dead, but he might as well be. For ten years, I thought he was just a doll maker. Then two weeks ago, I paid him a visit in Florida. It was then that I found out that the dolls were just a cover up; he was a bokor and practicing in Florida. Now, I've disowned him."

"Gee, I'm sorry," added Marilyn. "Raoul LeGauche didn't admit to being a bokor either."

"I'm sure he's one."

"Anyway," interjected Hank, "he told us that your ex-brother, Ibu, was probably the bokor who made a zombie out of José Candiani."

Marilyn added: "LeGauche said that you might be able to give us Ibu's address in Miami. That way we might be able to coerce him to de-zombify José Candiani."

Their story both angered and fascinated Ahram Mazalo. Believing their account and considering that they appeared to be an honest and forthright couple, he made a decision.

"This sounds like it could have been done by Ibu. Since I am so furious with him, I am going to help you. I will give you his address and telephone number. However, I do not want you to let him know that I had anything to do with it. Is that clear?"

"Certainly," said Hank.

After receiving the slip of paper with Ibu Mazalo's address and telephone number written on it, Marilyn said: "Thank you for your help and hospitality."

"Now that this matter has been settled, let's all relax a little. Let me show you around my newly decorated *hounfor*."

Ahram then took them on a narrated guided tour of his facilities. Marilyn and Hank were greatly impressed with the man and his sanctuary. Before they left, Marilyn asked Ahram a favor.

"I know that you're an excellent priest. I can tell that by talking with you and looking at your temple. Hank and I know that there is more to the world than what can be scientifically explained. Considering that, we wonder if we could purchase an amulet or fetish that might help protect us?"

"Don't say another word. I wouldn't think of taking any money from you. I have something for each of you."

For Marilyn, he had two gifts. First, he gave her a beautiful carved combination sea shell and snake vertebrae necklace.

"This is especially potent against bokor's curses."

"Thanks a lot, Ahram."

"Wait! I have something else for you." Taking out a violet charm bearing the face of a beautiful dark-skinned girl with large mysterious green eyes, Ahram said: "This charm is for good luck, and it will protect you from the evil eye."

"That's great, Ahram; thanks again."

For Hank, he had three gifts. Taking out a small amulet bearing a snake wrapped around a cross, he said: "Hank, this will help you ward off disease."

"Don't worry, Ahram, I'm not gonna mess around with that AIDS virus."

"Even I haven't anything potent enough to deal with that, but this should help you with other infections."

"Great!"

"I have two other things for you, Hank, because my instincts tell me you will need them more than Marilyn."

"Thanks **a lot**, Ahram."

"First, take this bat fetish. Don't worry about how it looks. It will help you when you get confronted by the bokor. But just in case you run into any serious trouble, here is a special mixture for you to take with you. There are instructions inside the packet. It is an antidote for zombie poison."

"Thanks, Ahram; I like the little old bat, but I hope to hell, I won't need the antidote."

Giving it to Marilyn, Hank said: "Here honey, you keep it. I want to be sure it's safe."

"How long are you folks going to stay in Haiti?"

Marilyn then gave him the details of the rest of their planned itinerary.

"That sounds fine. In case you need me for anything, I will be here most of the time. I'm not going anywhere for the next few days. Keep me informed about your progress with the zombie case."

"We sure will," responded Hank.

Shaking hands, they left the *hounfor* just in time to gaze upon a wondrous Caribbean sunset. They weren't aware that the next day's sunrise would usher in a day unlike any other they had ever experienced.

Having a premonition, Marilyn slipped the packet containing the zombie antidote into Hank's right back pocket.

* * * *

Just like Carlos Candiani before him, Arnold Banks was going to have a shock to his system. Arriving at No. 2405 La Venetia Street, he parked his Lincoln, activated the alarm, and rang the front door bell to the doll shop. After a few minutes of silence, he rapped the knocker. Again, his efforts were met with an eerie calmness. Trying the door knob, he found it locked. *Something's fishy; I know it. I'm gonna call the police.*

Getting back into his car, using his recently purchased car phone, Arnold dialed the Miami Police Department Headquarters. He told them about his unsuccessful attempts to get into the shop and about his suspicions. There was no great enthusiasm on the part of the respondent to hurry on over. However, since Arnold reminded the officer that he was a respected physician at North Miami Beach General Hospital, the officer reluctantly agreed to send a squad car over.

"It should be there in about ten minutes, Dr. Banks."

"Thank you, officer."

Arnold Banks remained in his car. He would not have long to wait.

* * * *

That evening, Jorgé Rodriguez received a call from Carlos
Candiani. Carlos's concluding remarks were: "Since Ibu
Mazalo is dead, it doesn't matter what his brother, Ahram,
tells the Meltzers. They are to die in Haiti. Contact the
bokor, Pierre Mancion. He'll know what to do. But just in
case, he fails, put a slug in both of them. Remember, they
are not to get out of Haiti alive."

"Taking care of them will be our pleasure, Carlos."

When Roberto Gonzales was informed about the
conversation, a big, broad grin flashed across his face. *Haiti
will soon be minus two tourists*, he told himself.

* * * *

Lieutenant Archie Braverman of the Miami Police Department
Headquarters was the first one inside. Sergeant Chubby
Corcoran was right behind. Holding up the rear was Dr.
Arnold Banks. Walking through the decorative doll shop, the
lieutenant spotted an open door in the rear. As he approached
it, he was overwhelmed by the complex odors.

"Hold your nose, guys," he shouted, "and Chubby, keep
your gun ready."

Heeding his advice, the other two advanced slowly.

When he heard about the gun, Arnold Banks increased his
distance from the sergeant. He was certainly not going to
chance getting hit by a stray bullet.

Once they were inside the inner sanctum, Chubby was the
first to spot the body.

"Now I know why he didn't answer the telephone or the
front door bell."

"Good deduction, doctor," responded the tall, thin
lieutenant.

His chubby companion merely smirked.

"It doesn't look like homicide or suicide. Probably the
old guy had a heart attack."

"That might be, lieutenant, but I'm sure the old codger was up to no good. Look at all these weird things."

"You may be right, sergeant. By the way, Dr. Banks, why did you want to see this guy, anyway?"

"Oh, lieutenant, I'm a collector of religious icons and paraphernalia. I was going to purchase some voodoo religious items from him."

"Voodoo!" they both exclaimed.

"There's more here than meets the eye. Call headquarters, sergeant. Tell them to send over an investigative team. Dr. Banks, after you give me your home and business addresses and telephone numbers, you're free to leave. Thank you for calling us so promptly."

Shaking their hands, Arnold Banks left the shop and entered his Lincoln. *This is really strange. I wonder why what's his name was parked so close to this shop. Could he have had something to do with this? That's stupid; he's a peaceful guy. Why have I blocked out his name? It's a good thing I'm retiring; I'm getting so forgetful. No matter, his name 'll come to me. Anyway, I'll see him in the hospital tomorrow and ask him to tell me what he was doing in this neck of the woods.*

* * * *

Meanwhile, back in North Miami Beach General Hospital, the rat-expert doctor was not doing much of anything. He certainly was in no mood to conduct any experiments: rat, human, or otherwise. Mainly, he was just thankful to be alive. With his exceptional retentive memory, he had no problem remembering names. Silently reflecting, he said, *I know Arnold saved my life. But what was he doing in Little Havana? I'm sure he's asking the same question about me. What can I tell him? What the hell happened to me anyway? All I can remember is having been bitten by a spider, scratching the bite violently, and then out I went. Oh my God, I must have had an anaphylactic reaction to the bite.*

But anyway, what can I tell Arnold? I've gotta come up with some good answers. Why was I in Little Havana? Where did I get bitten by a spider? Let me close my eyes and meditate. The answers will come. I'm certain.

* * * *

Dr. Jonathan Milton was also involved with unanswered questions. Having called pathologist, Ernest Goodman, and reporting his findings, he was keenly awaiting Dr. Goodman's response.

Just then, the phone rang: "Listen Jon, I really examined Conover thoroughly. Although I didn't do extensive toxicological testing, from what I did, I found no evidence of a toxin in any part of his body. You know we would require a court order to exhume the body, and I don't think Conover's wife would want to do it on such flimsy evidence. His daughter, Marilyn and her husband, Hank were somewhat suspicious about the old man's death. But as you know, the two of them are out of the country. Even if there was a toxin present, I'm certain it would have been broken down by now — especially if it was tetrodotoxin. If he did have tetrodotoxin poisoning, it would have been in such a minute amount. That would have made it undetectable. He had to have been given a trace amount. You know why? Before he died, he showed no sign of tetrodotoxin poisoning. There was absolutely no evidence of respiratory paralysis."

Ernest Goodman paused for a moment to let Jonathan Milton fully digest what he told him.

Jonathan was disappointed in what he heard, but for the moment he said nothing.

Ernest continued: "You know what I think killed him?"

"What, Ernie?"

"I know it sounds crazy, but I think he was scared to death."

"Scared to death! Have you any proof?"

"No, but lately there have been several suspicious deaths of old people. And there is a possibility that each one of them could have been severely stressed before death."

"That's an interesting hypothesis. When the Meltzers return, let's all get together and brainstorm a little about it."

They were planning, when the Meltzers got back, on having a discussion on the possible relationships among stress, toxins, and death. But as evening descended on the Haitian Vodun in Port-au-Prince, Haiti, the odds on that discussion taking place didn't look too promising.

26

Wednesday, September 20

They awoke as the searing tropical sun illuminated their small bedroom. The fan was set on high, but all that did was evenly distribute the hot air.

"We've got an exciting day ahead; rise and shine."

"I just wanna sleep."

Marilyn gave him a petulant look.

"Only foolin.' I'm rarin' to go."

* * * *

The back seat of the battered jeep had another occupant this morning. For the occasion, the short, wiry, middle-aged African was dressed in native garb.

Speaking in broken English, Roberto said: "Pierre, from the tape, we know they're gonna drive to Cap-Haitien and then on to Citadelle National Park. Where do you plan on meeting them?"

Answering in cultured French-accented English, Pierre Mancion said: "I will conveniently be close to them when

183

they arrive at the park. Saying that I'm a friend of Ahram Mazalo, I'll ask them if they would like to observe an authentic native ceremony. Once I've got them inside my sanctuary, I'll apply my magic."

"Yeah," interjected Jorgé Rodriguez, "they're tourist nuts; they'll jump at the chance."

* * * *

Forgetting about fat and cholesterol for the moment, Hank and Marilyn had croissants and coffee for breakfast.

"That was delicious. But we better do a lot of walking today. Gotta watch those coronaries."

"Don't worry, Hank; today's tour will be great on that score. There's a picturesque waterfall we can go to; there'll be plenty of climbing and hiking along the way."

Getting into the Buick at 9:15, they anticipated a relaxing but exciting day. They would be correct about the exciting part.

* * * *

As the Buick pulled out of the parking lot, Jorgé started the Jeep. Following the Buick, it remained about 300 yards behind.

* * * *

From Port-au-Prince, they took Route 100, the only paved highway going north. With map in hand, Marilyn took charge of directions. Although she learned how to drive a shift car, all her life she drove in cars with automatic transmission. Letting Hank drive the gear shift Buick, Marilyn was pleased to be the navigator.

It was a picturesque drive with scenic views of the blue-green waters of the Gulf of Gonâve. As the road took hairpin and snake-like turns, they passed through the towns of Cabaret, L'Arcahale, Montrous, and St. Marc.

Looking out at the rapid descent to the sea, while firmly holding onto the wheel, Hank reassured Marilyn: "Don't worry; I only like that water for fishing. If I have anything to say about it, we're not going fishing today."

The road then left the scenic sea route and veered in a northeasterly direction; it stayed that way for about twenty miles. Like a neurotic person not knowing which way to go, the road suddenly did an about-face and headed in a northwesterly direction. Reaching the coast again at the town of Gonaives, the road once again turned in a northeasterly direction. Driving a few miles further, they came to the approach of a large mountain. The Buick sputtered as they began the ascent. For the car, it was a torturous task, but with a sudden gasp it reached the summit.

Getting out of the car for a breath of fresh air, they came upon a breathtaking view.

"How can a country as beautiful as this be plagued with so many problems? You know: AIDS, voodoo death, zombies, dictators, deadly secret police, and who knows, what else."

"It's not just here, Marilyn. Many picturesue countries are war-torn or disease-ridden. Look at South Africa, Northern Ireland, Lebanon, Israel, Iran, Iraq. It's just a crazy world."

"When I look at the wondrous panorama in front of us, I can't but hope that things will get better."

"I hope so; I really do."

* * * *

Peering at them from around a curve in the road were the Cubans and the bokor. Speaking in Spanish so Pierre wouldn't understand them, Jorgé said: "Roberto, why don't we forget about the voodoo crap and just push them off the cliff? It's hundreds of feet down. That would finish them off once and for all."

"I'm tempted, but what will we do with the bokor? Carlos told him to take care of the Meltzers. If we do the job instead, Carlos'll find out about it, and we'll be in big trouble."

"All right; it was just a thought. But watching them fall and crash would've been a beautiful sight."

* * * *

Getting back into the car, they felt invigorated. The overused Buick was also relieved as it coasted down the mountain. As they approached the base, a large, clear, sparkling body of water was visible on the right. It appeared to be a mountain lake. Driving slowly, they could observe the vibrant life in and around the beautiful blue water.

"Hank, let's get out; this is better than a zoo."

"It looks to me to be more like a bird sanctuary. What the hell, let's take a look."

As if they were aware of the appreciative audience, the grebs, spoonbills, and herons swooped, splashed, and swam. The pastel pink colored flamingos were content with strutting. Teals and terns joined in with their own inimitable styles. The surrounding vegetation of sedges, palms, and cattails encompassed the playful residents with an esthetic border. Taking out her Minolta, Marilyn permanently captured the scene. As she was kneeling over the water's edge for a better view of a pirouetting flamingo, the shell-snake necklace got in her way. Pushing it aside, she was about to click the shutter.

* * * *

At that moment, Hank Meltzer's endodontist, Dr. Jacob Epstein — the man who saved his life in the puffer fish murder case — was in the midst of giving a lecture. He was addressing the Pompano Beach Rotary Club. The subject of his lecture was: "The Structure and Function of Teeth of Humans and Other Species."

"Teeth and mouths come in all sizes and shapes. Consider our own. In the front are the single-edged incisors — used for cutting and biting. Next to them are the single- cusped canines — used for tearing and grasping. Behind these are the multi-cusped premolars and molars — used for grinding and chewing. Incisors come in all colors: white, pink, yellow, gray, and various combinations. They can be flat-edged, peg-shaped, smooth, or jagged. Molars are generally darker in color and also have various shapes. They can be short and stocky — bull-like — or long and narrow — trunk-like.

Mouths vary as well. Some are small with thin, pursed lips. Others are huge with massive lips. When one person opens his mouth, the passageway is so slight that only a portion of the tongue is visible. With another, the opening is so cavernous that the larynx is in full view. But that's the way it is with people. Now, let's look at some other species - - - "

* * * *

It appeared to be a reel from a motion picture running in slow motion. The right index finger was closing down. It had exerted about half the amount of pressure required to complete the click.

"Aaay!"

The shriek was so loud that it reverberated across the mountain.

Staring Marilyn in the face was the largest jaws she had ever seen. Row after row of small, sharp, pointed, identically-appearing teeth were moving en masse. Firmly embedded in a huge snout, they were carrying out their intended purpose. Moving from opposite directions, they were going to meet in the middle to cut and slice a particular object. The jaws were about to close with a powerful snap, and Marilyn's head was about to be severed.

* * * *

Humans are not supposed to have instincts, but Hank Meltzer
reacted instinctively. Seeing the attacking crocodile begin to
close its jaw, he immediately leaped to Marilyn's side.
Knowing that if he went for her legs, the force would most
likely propel her into the crocodile's snout. So, he jumped at
her upper body. Pushing her back firmly but gently, he
twisted his body in mid-air and landed first. She fell upon
him. The crocodile's jaws clamped shut, but its only prey
was the captured air.

Marilyn and Hank were unscathed. Hank even managed to
"fish" out the camera from a watery ditch close to the bank.
A few minutes later, after they had both calmed down, Hank
said: "You were right; it's more like a zoo. But enough of
this nature worship. Let's get back into the car and stay in it
until we get to Cap-Haitien."

"I'm with you. Thank God, I was wearing the necklace
and had that native girl charm in my pocket."

"Forget about necklaces and charms; let's just get out of
here and not tempt fate any longer."

This time as the car ascended and descended another
mountain ridge, Hank's eyes were glued on the road.
Marilyn's eyes were glued shut. She was simultaneously
meditating and praying.

* * * *

From his vantage point behind a huge rock formation, using
his powerful Zeiss binoculars, Roberto witnessed the close
encounter.

"Jorgé, you nearly had your wish. A big, mean crocodile
almost finished Marilyn Meltzer for good."

For the time being, although still somewhat frightened,
Marilyn was alive and well.

* * * *

Dr. Epstein was continuing his lecture: "Humans and other mammals have a heterodont dentition with teeth modified by size and shape to carry on different functions. These we have already discussed. Fish and reptiles, such as crocodiles and lizards, have a homodont dentition in which the teeth are identical in appearance and function. People have a good reason to fear the jaws of sharks and crocodiles because their teeth are extremely sharp and effective in cutting and shredding. However, as dangerous as these species are, they usually do not attack unless they are provoked. Nevertheless - - - - "

* * * *

Driving due west, they came to the town of Ennery. Passing through fields of prickly pear cacti and assorted palms, the road changed directions again. It headed straight north for about seven miles until it reached the town of Limbe. At that point, it altered its course into a more westerly direction. They could smell the salty breeze from the Atlantic Ocean as the car approached Cap-Haitien — Haiti's second largest city. Spread out in front of them was an admixture of pastel-shaded colonial buildings and Victorian-style gingerbread homes. Rising from these structures, the land gradually sloped upward until it peaked as an imposing mountain — Hait du Cap.

As they pulled into the city, Marilyn looked around. She spotted fields of mango, coffee, sugar, and sisal. Hank wasn't interested in the view. He was more concerned with his growling stomach.

"With all the excitement, we forgot about eating."

"I didn't forget, Hank, but I didn't want to eat in any of those small towns. Here in Cap-Haitien, I'm certain we'll be able to find a decent place to eat."

At 1:30, they pulled into the parking lot of a small, clean-looking, seaside hotel. While viewing the incoming waves, they had a delicious, relaxing lunch.

* * * *

Not far behind were the pursuers. The Cubans and the bokor had to be content with eating in the parked car. Not wanting to take a chance on losing the Meltzers's trail, when they had started out this morning, each of them had packed a lunch.

Again speaking in Spanish, Jorgé said: "You know, Roberto, it looks like it's gonna take all day until they get to the park. Now that the Meltzer woman almost got eaten up alive, I hope they don't change their mind."

"Don't worry; they're not getting out of Haiti alive. By the end of today, one way or another, we'll get rid of them."

Sitting in the back seat, Pierre Mancion was calmly eating a yam. But inside he was churning. He didn't like it when people talked in another language to exclude him from the conversation.

* * * *

"Marilyn, I don't know about you, but I'm bloated. If you're feeling up to it, I wouldn't mind going for a hike around that waterfall."

"Why not! I feel all right. Nothing wrong with a little exercise. If we can trust what it says in this guidebook, it won't take us long to get to the waterfall. Would you care if we don't stick to the itinerary?

"Fine with me. What do you have in mind?"

"Well, to reach Fort Liberté, we would have to drive about 30 miles east on Route 121, and Citadelle National Park is just a few miles to our west. It's already after two, and we do want to get back to our hotel by a reasonable hour. So I think we should forget about the fort."

"No problem. First to the waterfall and then to the park. Let's just hope this struggling Buick cooperates."

The car chugged along. Fifteen minutes later, they parked in a small clearing in the woods. They could hear the bubbling water close by.

* * * *

It wasn't Niagara or Iguazu, but it still had a drop of about 100 feet.

"It reminds me of Bushkill Falls. Did you ever go there, Marilyn? It's in the Poconos."

"I've been there a couple of times. This waterfall is majestic — just like the big one in Bushkill. But one thing I like better about the falls back in Pennsylvania is the surrounding foliage. In the Northeast, there's such a great variety. Down her, you've got a lot of trees and shrubs, but not the kinds we've got back home."

"You're right, but the difference is that they have green stuff all year round. In the winter, we've only got those scrubby evergreens; you know pines and stuff like that."

"Anyway, let's try to enjoy what we've got here. The guidebook says that if we keep to the left side and tread carefully, we can walk down around the edge of the falls. From the base, there's a dirt path about a hundred yards further on the left that gradually goes up to the top of the ridge. It meets the stream that empties into the falls."

"Sounds all right to me. Let's just make sure we hold on to each other. Don't worry; there's no crocodiles here."

Descending the escarpment, they were becoming hypnotized by the swirling waters. It was just a light trance so they remained firmly bound to each other while keeping a watchful eye on the slippery rocks.

* * * *

By the time Hank and Marilyn were about 50 feet down, the Jeep had been parked in another secluded clearing about 75 feet behind the Buick. Roberto and Jorgé slowly advanced toward the edge of the waterfall. They wanted to see how far the Meltzers had gone. A few feet behind the Cubans, Pierre began to chant in a monotonous voice. It was quiet but penetrating.

Speaking in Spanish, Jorgé said: "What's that gibberish?"

"Aw, that's just some voodoo mumbo-jumbo. Leave the witch doctor alone. He's just amusing himself."

"Do you think they'll hear it down there?"

"No way; the sounds of the falls block out everything."

* * * *

It was as if a detergent factory exploded. The force of the cascading water upon the jagged rocks beneath created expanding eddies which, in turn, gave rise to massive soap-like spumes of frothy water. Hank and Marilyn were enjoying the aquatic show.

* * * *

The repetitive drone could have sounded to the Cubans like gibberish, but it was creating its intended effect. The combination sounds of the cascading water and the monotonous chants were putting Roberto and Jorgé into a hypnotic trance, and it was getting deeper and deeper.

* * * *

It was only about three feet long and six inches wide. Having fallen a few months ago off of a beautiful red mountain palm, it was now lying unobtrusively on the

ground. Pierre stealthily advanced and picked up the branch.
While still chanting, he advanced toward the waterfall's edge.

* * * *

For the Meltzers, who were about fifteen feet from the base
of the falls, the sound was completely blocked by the water's
onslaught. At the top of the falls, the force created by the
meeting of the palm branch utensil with the backsides of the
stooping Cubans was loud and intense. Even the sound of
their screeches was masked by the cascading falls.

* * * *

The foamy water at the base was violently disrupted as the
two hurtling men bounded off the rocks and crashed at the
bottom.
    "Oh my God, Hank; did you see that?"
    Stunned by the rapid-fire event, he was still dimly aware of
what transpired.
    "I'm not sure; I think that was two people. They're goners
by now; there's no way anyone could have survived an
impact as forceful as that."
    Hank was right. Their bones and brains were crushed
amongst the rocks and foam; the remains were carried down
river to a watery grave.

* * * *

*Now, I will follow those two myself to Citadelle. I'll do the
job the way Carlos wanted me to.* Reassuring himself, Pierre
Mancion had gotten revenge against two Spaniards who were
foolish enough to have cut him out of their plans.
Unfortunately, they did not realize that the bokor was also
fluent in Spanish and multi-talented as a killer.

* * * *

As they slowly began the upward trek, Marilyn said: "It seems no matter how peaceful the scene starts out, some kind of violence has to creep in."

"You're right. I hate to see these things happening. I saw enough violent deaths in my detective days in Philly, but as long as we're not caught in the middle of it, I'm thankful."

"This day of planned relaxation so far has been anything but that. You don't think we'll run into anything crazy at the park; do you?"

"I don't think so; at least, I hope not."

But Hank Meltzer didn't know that there would soon be another bokor in his life.

27

Wednesday, September 20

It was 2:30 when they arrived at the base of the path leading to the Citadelle. Looking up, they gazed upon an awesome site. Sitting, like a majestic crown, on the summit of Pic Laferriére was a mighty fortress.

"Quite a sight, isn't it?" said the stranger.

"It sure is," replied Marilyn.

"It was built by Henri Christophe with the help of 200,000 laborers. It took ten years to complete, and 20,000 men died during the construction."

"Wow," said Hank. "Are you a guide?"

"No, I'm not. I'm sorry for being so rude. My name is Pierre Mancion. I am a houngan — that is, a priest. I had the afternoon off, and I never can get enough of this impressive sight. I thought from your appearance that you might be Americans and would be interested in some background information about this fortress."

"That's very nice of you. By the way, my name is Marilyn Meltzer. This is my husband, Hank. Yes, we are Americans, and we would be pleased to learn more about this place. Wouldn't we, Hank?"

"Sure."

Resuming, Marilyn said: "We know about houngans; we just met Ahram Mazalo from Bizóton."

"That's very interesting. Ahram is a good friend of mine. Maybe if you have time later, I can show you my *hounfor*. It's not far from here."

"Sounds great; doesn't it, Hank?"

"Okay, just as long as we don't have to spend too much time. You know it's about five hours to get back to Port-au-Prince, and we don't know what's gonna happen with this neurotic Buick."

"No problems; you can stay as long as you want. Meanwhile, let me tell you some more about the Citadelle. Henri Christophe was a young Haitian who fought for the Americans in their revolution. He was a top notch warrior. Later, he fought for the Haitians against the French, and when they were expelled in 1803, he proclaimed himself as King of Haiti. As a monument to himself and the victory, he had this colonial fortress built. Not content with that, he had a beautiful castle constructed. It was located in the village of Milot — just south of here."

"Can we see it?" asked Marilyn.

"I would love to take you there, but unfortunately, now it is only a pile of ruins. The castle was named *Sans Souci*. It was really a magnificent structure. The building and grounds were laid out in the style of Versailles."

"It's a pity that it's gone," Marilyn interjected.

"Yes, it is too bad, but the Citadelle is in good condition. It is Haiti's preeminent historical feature, and it is one of the most significant and magnificent fortresses in the entire Western Hemisphere."

"He must have been quite a powerful and influential person to have been able to become the king and have had the fortress and castle built."

"Yes, Mr. Meltzer, he was a unique ruler. He also had clever advisers. For example in the construction of *Sans Souci*, in order to cool the castle, the water from two streams was diverted to run down a slope and under the castle's marble floors. The run off was then used to water the gardens."

"Interesting," said Hank, "a combination natural air conditioner and sprinkler system."

"That's an intelligent way of putting it. Anyway, enough history for now. It is time to explore the fortress. That is, if you would like to."

"Of course," they said simultaneously.

"Well, folks, you have a choice for transportation. You can either walk to the top; it's about a 45-minute climb. Or you can take a mule. The mule ride takes about the same time, but it is a lot easier on you."

"Hank, when I went to the south rim of the Grand Canyon many years ago, I walked down to the Columbia River. But I was pooped out when I got down to the bottom. There was no way I was going to go back up on foot. So, I took a mule. The ride was a bit bumpy, but it was a lot of fun. I think I'd like to try the mule. What do you think?"

"Look, we got enough exercise and excitement from trekking around the waterfall. I'm all for the mule."

"Good! I'll arrange for the ride."

With that, the three of them took the mule ride to the Citadelle. They spent an enjoyable and interesting hour exploring its intricacies.

At 3:45, having completed the tour, they were back in the parking area.

Pierre said: "My *hounfor* is only about a fifteen minute drive from here. Its in the town of Limbe, which is on your way back to Port-au-Prince. You can stay with me for a few minutes and be on your way back by 4:30. I suggest that you stop off for dinner at Gonaives. It's on the coast."

Taking out a sheet of paper, he wrote down the name, address, and location of the restaurant. Handing the slip to Marilyn he said: "This restaurant is located in a small hotel. The food is good, and the view of the gulf is impressive. The hotel is inexpensive, and the rooms are clean. If you feel

tired, you might want to spend the night there and leave for
Port-au-Prince in the morning."

"Thanks, Mr. Mancion. I'm not sure if we'll stay over.
We have a plane to catch at 11:00 tomorrow morning, but the
dinner thing sounds great."

Hank nodded in assent.

"Fine, just follow me. I'm riding in that Jeep."

"So, they were off, ostensibly to visit a *hounfor*, but they
would soon become firsthand participants in the art of
voodoo.

* * * *

His previous night's meditation didn't give him any
monumental solutions. He realized that Ibu Mazalo's death
would have been reported, and Arnold Banks would be
suspicious of his presence in Little Havana, close to the doll
shop. Reflecting silently, the rat-expert doctor thought, *I've
got to check out now — before Banks comes to see me. As
soon as I get home, I'm gonna leave this area. I've got no
ties except for the house. It's paid for, and if I get caught, I
wouldn't be living in it, anyway. Sure, my mission is noble
and important, but the hell with it now. I almost lost my life
once. I'm not going to let it happen again. I've got plenty
of money. The way I figure it, I've got two choices. If I
stay in the States then I get plastic surgery. I've got a friend
who'll do it for me. If I leave the country, then I don't have
to touch my face. I can live out my remaining time in a quiet
villa. But where should I go? One of the islands? Mexico?
When I get home, I'll make some calls. Whatever, I'm out
of here and fast. Soon, I'll have a new, peaceful life.*

* * * *

Pierre Mancion was planning a peaceful life for the Meltzers,
but it wasn't the kind of tranquility they would enjoy.
Opening the door to his temple, he said: "In a way, we are like

the Japanese; we prefer our guests to remove their shoes and socks before they enter the sanctuary."

Although considering it somewhat odd, Hank and Marilyn agreed to the request.

The bokor also removed his shoes and socks. Entering first, he said: "Welcome to my humble little temple. I hope you will not be disappointed."

Passing through the threshold, their eyes were drawn to the crossbar across the opening. A horse's skull was held in place with a large rusted nail.

Hank became suspicious. *I don't think a priest would have a weird object like that in front of his temple. I better be ready for anything.*

Marilyn felt uneasy. *This doesn't look right to me. I better be careful.*

They didn't notice the cross-like pattern at the entrance way of the sand-covered floor. Walking in, their soles contacted the roughened surface.

* * * *

Anesthesiologist, Ralph Blackmore, was thrilled. As soon as he got home, he made the calls. Completing them successfully, he packed the two suitcases and the one carry-on bag. That was an hour ago. Now that everything had been done expeditiously, he was about to begin a new life. Glancing up, he saw the time. It was 6:15. The plane to St. Maarten was scheduled to depart Miami International from Gate 11 at 6:45. He still had a little time left for silent reflection. *God, it's good to get away. I'll have a brand new start. I know I'll miss the hypnotic society meetings and the other guys at the hospital, but there's no turning back now.*

* * * *

Hank recognized the odor of garlic, but it was an abnormal smell — sort of like garlic that had become rotten. Marilyn recognized the acrid odor as being part ammonia and part formaldehyde. They both realized that something was wrong. As she walked into the darkened, foul-smelling chamber, Marilyn remembered a phrase that her anthropologist friend, Linda Perrin, had told her at their last meeting: *"A bokor is knowledgeable about all that is good in life, but he serves the darkness. A houngan is knowledgeable about all that is evil in life, but he serves the light."*

"Please come in; have a seat on the bench. It's right there, in the middle of the room."

They heard the mellifluous tones. They were already feeling light-headed, and in that state, his voice was even more compelling.

In the center of the room was a thick, cast-iron post. It held up the covering peristyle. At the base of the post was a cement altar. The altar contained structures found in other *hounfors*, but this sanctuary had` unique characteristics as well — and they portended evil. In front of the altar was a wooden bench.

As they walked toward the bench, Marilyn and Hank's eyes fastened on the altar. The life-like structures facing them were evil incarnate — a large, spotted snake, two crosses which looked like diabolical caricatures of the Christian cross, a pair of jet-black, horned goats, and grossly distorted phallic symbols.

"It gives me great pleasure to show you around. As a way of introducing you to the ceremonies that take place in my *hounfor*, let me give you an example of a Congo chant."

They realized that they had been drugged, but when, how, and why, they couldn't fathom. Wanting to turn around and run, all their weakened bodies could do was to inch forward.

The chant began: "Ha-reem; ha-rah; ha-reh."

It made no sense to them, but it was enticing, enchanting, entrancing, and unavoidable.

Marilyn succumbed first. The room had been dark, and then even that little bit of light disappeared. The transition was from soft sounds to deadly calm to absolute nothingness.

Hank tried fighting it, but it was something for which he had no weapons, no plan, no concept (except maybe for the three gifts in his pocket). After a while, he didn't even want to fight. *Why don't I just give up?* he thought. *It feels so good.* And then he felt nothing, nothing at all.

* * * *

Pierre Mancion was feeling smug and secure. Now all he had to do was carry out the plan. Placing them in a supine position on the floor, he walked to the entrance way and retrieved his shoes and socks.

That was a good ploy to tell them it was like a Japanese custom, he thought. Before he put on his socks, he removed the plastic inserts that had been attached to the soles of his feet — the devices that protected him from the voodoo poison that had been dispersed on the floor within the sandy cross.

Hah, he laughed to himself, *clever of me, wasn't it? I poisoned them through the soles of their feet.*

The diabolical plan was to make Hank Meltzer a zombie. Getting out the mixture containing sea toad extract, Zombie's cucumber, puffer fish poison, extracts of snakes, tarantulas, and toads, and pulverized bits of human skulls and leg bones, he injected 0.5 cc of the solution into Hank's right deltoid muscle. The intramuscular injection of the toxic substances would not be enough to kill him, but when he would awaken in about five hours, he would be an entombed zombie — at least that was the plan.

The plan did not include a similar fate for Marilyn. Pierre Mancion was a ladies man; he appreciated Marilyn's beauty and intelligence. Hence, she would not receive any further toxic substances. The initial dose that she and Hank had received was just sufficient to cause them a temporary loss of consciousness. In about two hours, the bokor expected that Marilyn would recover completely. She would probably be groggy, but judging from prior use of the dose for a person of her size, he considered that she would be physically undamaged.

When she finds out about her husband, her mental state won't be too good. But I'll take good care of her mind, and then she will be mine. It'll be great. I can't wait.

* * * *

Psychologist, Ronald Fielding, was pleased with himself. He had made a major decision. Although he was no youngster, his altered appearance would give him a new start in life: hair transplants to replace the thinning gray hair, plastic surgery to correct the aquiline nose, and crowns for the tobacco-stained teeth. Ronald was proud of himself. He quit smoking, so the teeth would stay white. He'd soon shave off the beard. No longer would anyone think he was Amish. A rejuvenated face, a new start, a new life. He couldn't wait.

* * * *

Hospital volunteer, David Lavier, completed all of the last-minute arrangements. Soon he would be airborne, and tomorrow, he would be sunning himself in Cancun.

* * * *

Physical therapist, Sidney Sargent's head was no longer in the clouds. His mind was made up. The call confirmed it; he was off to Chicago in a few hours. His friend had agreed, and major changes were going to be made.

* * * *

When internist, Arnold Banks, arrived at the hospital at about 4:30 to see his colleague, he was shocked when he found out about the sudden departure. Now, he definitely suspected foul play.

Dialing the Miami Police Department Headquarters, he reached Lieutenant Archie Braverman: "Hello, Lieutenant, I'm Dr. Arnold Banks — the person that you saw the other day at the Little Havana doll shop. You know, the place where the owner was found dead on the floor."

"Yeah, I remember, doc. What's on your mind?"

"Well, I think he was killed?"

"Killed? Why do you think so?"

"I'm almost certain I know who killed him."

"Who did it?"

"It's a doctor who works here at North Miami Beach General Hospital."

"Why do you think it's him?"

"I found him unconscious in his car a few blocks from Mazalo's doll shop. It was the same day I was going to see Mazalo. Because I had to take care of my colleague, I didn't go to the doll shop 'till the next day. That's when I called you, and we found Mazalo dead."

"What was the doctor doing in his car in Little Havana?"

"At the time, I didn't know, and I didn't care. I was only concerned with saving his life. But now I think he probably killed Ibu Mazalo."

"What makes you think so?"

"He checked out of the hospital and skipped town. Nobody knows where he went."

"Very interesting. Can I come over in a few minutes and get all the details, you know, name, age, position on the staff, and whatever else?"

"Sure, I'll be waiting."

* * * *

It was 9:32. Marilyn had been awake for three hours, but she wasn't able to do anything. She remembered coming out of a disturbed sleep, feeling woozy and weak. And then she heard a voice; it was smooth as velvet; she also couldn't avoid the eyes. The combination of the sound and the sight; it was inescapable; she was slowly and unalterably being drawn into an ethereal state, a state of tranquility and euphoria.

* * * *

Hank was in a completely different state. Yet he wasn't even aware of where he was or what had happened. He was captured by thoughts and visions that were inside him, beneath him, and hovering over him. He was in living Hell, in living death. His body, mind, and spirit were irrevocably trapped.

28

Wednesday, September 20

Wiping the dirt off his lips, he slowly got up and looked around. The moon's illumination allowed him to observe his surroundings.

Oh my God! I'm in a cemetery. Why am I so filthy? How the hell did I get here? Where's Marilyn and that priest, Pierre Mancion? Did he bring me here? Why? Is Mancion really a priest? Could he be a witch doctor?

While these thoughts were creating mental havoc, Hank took a few hesitating steps. The tombstones were in all sizes and shapes. He looked at the small headstones, the large crypts and mausoleums, and the in-between varieties. He was impressed with the beautifully decorated granite and marble structures. Some had crosses; others had snake emblems. A variety of nationalities were represented. Some were French; many were Africans; others were Spanish; and a few were either Americans or Europeans. A few of the deceased had been interred since the early 1800s; many were mid-20th century burials; and there were even some that had been laid to rest as recently as a week ago.

205

Marilyn would probably have found out the history of this God-forsaken place. I don't give a damn; it's just plain spooky.

Having unknowingly walked in a circle, he came to another headstone. It was a simple concrete slab. He looked at the inscription. It wasn't even engraved. The surface writing was in bright, bold, italicized, red letters.

Oh my God! It looks like blood. Let me see what it says.

Facing him in dark red lettering was: ***Hank Meltzer, an American, died unexpectantly of natural causes on September 20, 1989. He had no known relatives and no survivors.***

He was shocked but not paralyzed.

Died? Natural causes? What on earth does it mean? One thing is sure; I know I'm not dead. For now, I don't give a damn how and why I got here. All I know is I've gotta get away and fast.

Before he could make a move, it began. The first manifestations were subtle — sort of like the whispering wind signaling the start of a storm. Intensifying, it changed into an unholy blend of discordant sounds. The dissonant sounds materialized into living entities. The entities revealed themselves as a swarm of diversified creatures. Hank had been moving in the center of the cemetery. The chaotic living mass approached him from every direction — from the ground, in the air, and through the developing stream.

Hank looked out in amazement at the nightmarish assortment. Cackling, red hens marched in unison with bleating, horned, black goats.

What on earth are they doing here? This is no farm!

As they got closer to him, they became more daring. A jet-black snake slithered at his ankles. Hank jumped away only to land on a slippery iguana.

Picking himself up, he blurted out: "Crap! What's going on?"

As if to reply, two garishly colored toucans bellowed: "Waats go win on?"

Parrots, too? This is no zoo!

A pair of egrets swooped down and landed in the widening stream. They were quickly pushed asunder by the plodding crocodile.

Observing the sight, Hank quickly retreated and ran smack into a dozen prancing pink flamingos.

"Dammit;" he shouted, "I've gotta get out of here, somehow, someway."

It didn't appear that nature would be cooperative. At that moment, the advancing, expanding stream was right at his feet. Looking down to get a fix on the crocodile's location, he was met smack in the face by a leaping, ballooning puffer fish.

"Not another one of those poisonous sea beasts," he screamed as he jumped out of the path of the advancing stream.

Now the sounds were augmented as hordes of crickets, grasshoppers, frogs, and toads blended their voices with the previous diabolical assortment into an auditory barrage.

Then the insects attacked. First, it was the crawling centipedes and millipedes. Hank brushed them off only to have their place taken by an onslaught of furry tarantulas.

"Ouch!" he yelled as he felt the bite on his right forearm from the first creeping spider. Going into a shaking fit, he was able to get rid of the others. But the lowly creatures had formidable back-ups. Next in line were the leeches — the kind that thirsted for blood. They had a field day on the exterior of Hank's body, biting and sucking simultaneously. Hank was in pain and felt weak and woozy.

"What else can happen now?" he asked the assorted predators.

The answer didn't come from any one of them. It came from below. The ground beneath Hank began to shake.

"Holy crap! I can't believe it. Now I'm in the midst of an earthquake."

The earth shook, but it wasn't an earthquake. One by one, the headstones moved, lifted, and shattered as they fell to the ground.   Then the earth was displaced;   dirt flew in all directions. Further movement took place. First out were the hands, then the head, and the rest of the body followed. An army of hideously looking bodies came out of their graves. All sizes and shapes, men and women, each one unique. Yet, they all had the same kind of inhuman gait — a Frankenstinian shuffle — and their eyes were pupil-less and vacant.

Hank could only stare. All his life he had been brave — unafraid to tackle even the most fearless project. That was then; now, he was frozen in terror.

As if on cue, the birds, amphibians, reptiles, and insects suddenly turned around. It was as if they were merely the prologue to the main drama.

And like the parting of the Red Sea in reverse, the wide stream narrowed until it was no more than a seam in the earth. After a few minutes, even that filled in, and the ground was now as solid as before the animal rebellion had begun.

From every direction, the zombies advanced, slowly but incessantly. Their faces were emotionless — frozen without expression. All the previous external sounds cut off until the only thing that could be heard was the sound of the zombies' shoes as the now firm ground was touched.

As they came forward, their mouths opened. It was not for the ingestion of food or liquid or to bite in the style of a vampire. No! Their mouths were opened for vocalizations. They began to speak, but not sentences, not phrases — just one word: "Come." The tones and inflections were varied, but the word was the same: "Come." An incessant repetition of "Come, come, come, come." It started quietly; it increased gradually until it became a deafening roar: "**Come, come, come, come.**"

They had come to take Hank Meltzer, the private detective from Pompano Beach, Florida, away with them. They had come to have him join them as a member of their troupe — a company of mindless, soul-less zombies. All Hank could do was follow. In a matter of moments, his body blended into the unholy mass of sub-human protoplasm.

* * * *

Pierre Mancion was tired. It had been a long and grueling day, and he wasn't used to such arduous labor. True, he had the help of his two confederates, Jacques Cardinale and César Joliet, with Hank Meltzer's casket emplacement and subsequent burial. But he did most of the work. So, he decided to postpone any pleasurable activities with Marilyn Meltzer until tomorrow morning. Meanwhile, he would get a good night's sleep. She should sleep all night as well.

After all, he thought, *I placed her into a deep trance.*

* * * *

Bokors may be witch doctors, but even in that guise, they are still human. Like the rest of us, when they are tired, their attention slips a bit. When alert, Pierre Mancion was second to none in his ability to entrance or place a curse. He was also extremely egotistical and wouldn't admit when he wasn't up to par. So he didn't realize that because of fatigue, the hypnotic induction of Marilyn was somewhat hurried. As a result, she was not as deeply hypnotized as he had expected.

* * * *

It was an hour before midnight. Marilyn awoke with a start. She was still groggy, but her mind was clearing. *I haven't got the time or the energy to figure out why this Mancion guy did this to me and Hank. Oh my God, where is Hank? What did Mancion do to him? Was Hank poisoned or worse? Was he made a zombie? Please, someone help me.*

The panic attack lasted only a few minutes. With calmness restored, Marilyn had a silent conversation with herself. *Take it easy, Marilyn; be cool. You've got to find a way out of here. The first thing is to figure a means to get away from this bokor — yeah he's got to be a bokor. Then, you must find Hank. If you can't, get to see Mazalo, the priest. Oh, I pray I can trust him. If not him, whom? In this place, who can I trust? All right, Marilyn. First things first. Use your guile, get yourself free. Then you can worry about Hank and Mazalo. Meanwhile, try to sleep. You'll have a plan by morning.*

29

Thursday, September 21

Pierre Mancion was undoubtedly evil, but he wasn't a cold-blooded killer. True, he disposed of the two Cubans, but they had wronged him and, to his way of thinking, they deserved to die. Obviously the Meltzers had done something to displease Carlos Candiani, but the Americans had attributes that the bokor felt were sufficient to keep them alive. Marilyn was bright and beautiful; he intended her to become his love slave. Hank was strong and determined; once zombified, he was destined to be at the bokor's beck and call.

Implementing his plan now entailed disinterring Hank. At 6:45 A.M., leaving Jacques to watch over Marilyn, Pierre said to the subordinate: "She's still sleeping soundly, but keep an eye on her. I'm taking the Jeep. César and me are goin' to the cemetery. In a few minutes, we'll have Hank Meltzer dug up. We'll be back soon."

Pierre expected that in about an hour or less Hank would be tilling the fields in good zombie fashion while he and Marilyn would be having a leisurely breakfast.

* * * *

Yesterday afternoon at precisely 5:00, the rat-expert doctor made a decision. Plastic surgery was out; it would be too time consuming, and he wouldn't voluntarily go under general anesthesia. Driving to the airport, he made up his mind about his destination. This morning, as he gazed at the tropical sun, he was pleased at his choice.

* * * *

Dr. Ronald Fielding had an important meeting to start his day. The psychologist had an appointment with the hospital administrator, Joel Glick. Ronald's decision to resign didn't come as a complete shock. After all, he was in the retirement age bracket. Of course, no one expected that he would undertake plastic surgery and choose Phoenix to start a new career as an antiques dealer.

Isn't it paradoxical, he thought, *I'll be starting off with a rejuvenated face and outlook and deal with ancient objects.*

* * * *

Dr. Sidney Sargent also spoke to Joel Glick this morning. Calling on the telephone, he said that he was bedridden with a bad case of the flu and would be out until Monday. The latter part was true, but he wasn't sick, merely involved in a business deal in Chicago. He was flying there today to sign the papers. It was a venture with a national health foods organization. Sidney hoped it would be successful enough to allow him to close out his present physical therapist career.

* * * *

Dr. David Lavier couldn't have been more pleased this morning. Everything went just as he had planned. Lying out in the sun with nothing on but a pair of boxer shorts, the retired surgeon felt that the splendid tropical weather had to be a harbinger of a great new life.

* * * *

Dr. Ralph Blackmore was having breakfast on the sun deck of his villa. *You know,* he told himself, *it almost went too smoothly.*

Feeling the warmth of the tropical sun, his anxieties melted away, *I'm sure everything will be fine.*

* * * *

By late yesterday afternoon, Dr. Arnold Banks had completed his conversation with Lieutenant Archie Braverman of the Miami Police Department Headquarters. The doctor informed the lieutenant that retired surgeon and present hospital volunteer, Dr. David Lavier, was the individual he had found near Ibu Mazalo's shop, and that the same Dr. Lavier had skipped town, leaving no forwarding address.

Going to bed last evening, Arnold Banks was almost certain that Lavier was involved with the killing of Mazalo. This morning, he met pathologist, Ernest Goodman, for breakfast in the hospital cafeteria. The story about Lavier had spread like a raging fire throughout the hospital, and Dr. Goodman was extremely interested in finding out what Arnold Banks had to say.

After they sat down and placed their food containers on the table, Dr. Goodman said: "Arnie, you're probably not aware of this: there have been seven recent deaths of old timers that have had strange overtones."

"What do you mean?"

"Well, they were all sick and could have died from their disease, but the way they died did not appear to be directly related to the specific disease process involved in each particular case. During the last few weeks, I've checked out the family, friends, maids, and whatever of all the deceased.

Guess what? I found a West Indian or Caribbean-type doll at, or near, the bedside of each of the victims. Hank and Marilyn Meltzer — the private investigators — were working on these cases. But right now they're in Haiti investigating a so-called voodoo case. They believe the victim in that case was also exposed to a Caribbean-type doll."

"So you think there's some relationship with all of these things — you know, Mazalo's death, the recent death of the old folks, the zombified man's illness, and David Lavier's sudden departure?"

Getting up to give his corpulent body a little stretch, the pathologist said: "I'm not certain. There are other things, too. The toxicologist, Jonathan Milton, found that the doll at Conover's bedside — that was Marilyn Meltzer's deceased father — contained a very small amount of the highly potent neurotoxin, tetrodotoxin."

Putting down his cup of coffee, the rotund internist emoted: "Hey, this is getting intriguing."

"Not only that. I believe that it took more than that small amount of toxin to have killed Conover and the others — that is if those other dolls also contained the neurotoxin."

"What do you mean?"

"I think that they were shocked or stressed severely. They could even have been hypnotized."

"Wow, this is really beginning to fit together. David Lavier is an excellent hypnotist."

"Yeah, that's what I've heard."

"I suppose that if these hard-to-explain deaths now stop happening, you can assume that Lavier was behind the others."

"That's a good assumption. In fact, lately things on that score have been quiet."

Using the kind of logic that internists are trained to use to arrive at a correct diagnosis, Arnold Banks said: "So from what I gather, Lavier and Mazalo were working together using a combination of hypnosis and tetrodotoxin to kill sick, old people. But why would they want to do something like that?"

"To find that out we'll have to get a hold of Lavier."

"Yeah. He could be anywhere by now."

Sitting down again, Ernest Goodman said: "Lavier and Mazalo must've had some sort of a quarrel over money or something else. As a result, the old Haitian was killed, and Lavier was almost done in."

"That's right. But there was no sign of violence. You know, I bet you should do an autopsy on Mazalo. I wouldn't be surprised if old David hypnotized him into overdosing on his own toxin."

"Good idea. I'll arrange for an autopsy. There's no next of kin to worry about. How about David Lavier? Was he hurt bad?"

"When I saw Lavier in the car, he didn't appear to have suffered from any physical violence. He was bitten — probably by a tarantula. Maybe it was one of the toxic varieties used in voodoo magic."

"Could be, but most tarantulas are not poisonous enough to kill an adult."

"No, Ernie, it was an allergic reaction. I gave him a shot of 'epi' and saved his life."

Wiping his chin after finishing the last bite of a sugared donut, the pathologist remarked: "Maybe that was a mistake."

"Could've been. But that's water under the bridge. Now he's gotta be found."

"From what I've heard and what's happened recently, it won't be easy. He's a crafty codger."

Finishing their high cholesterol breakfasts, the two corpulent physicians parted company.

Arnold Banks was walking toward the administrator's office. As Joel Glick came out, he spotted Arnold Banks. Joel said: "By the way, Dr. Banks, have you seen Dr. Blackmore this morning?"

"No, can't say that I did."

"That's strange. He left a note yesterday afternoon canceling his cases for the rest of the week. I called his home and no one answered."

"I wonder where he is!"

"So do I. If you hear from him, let me know."

"I sure will. So long."

"So long, Dr. Banks."

As Arnold Banks was walking to his office, like a lightning bolt, a thought crashed to the surface. *Ralph Blackmore is not only a good anesthesiologist, he's also an excellent hypnotist. Could he have skipped town as well? Could he be the one involved with the strange deaths? Maybe Lavier was in Little Havana by chance or for a different reason than I guessed. Maybe he has merely taken off for a short vacation. Maybe he was just under stress and wanted to get away for a break. Wow! I'm not sure of anything now.*

* * * *

Pierre Mancion mistakenly thought that Marilyn was in a deep trance. She wasn't. The sound of his conversation with Jacques awakened her. Marilyn now knew about Hank's fate. To prevent herself from becoming stressed out, while keeping her eyes closed, she meditated. Twenty minutes later, feeling subdued and tranquilized, she slowly opened her eyes. Realizing that her opportunity for escape was probably limited to the next half-hour or so — before the bokor and his sidekick returned — Marilyn had to act decisively.

He's got a pistol in his lap. I've got to be quiet.

They were in Pierre Mancion's private room. It had an entrance from the back of the temple and a private outdoor exit on the opposite wall. Marilyn — fully clothed — had been sleeping in a semi-crumpled position on a small couch. The couch was situated to the left of the door leading to the sanctuary. Opposite her was Jacques. He was dozing while sitting on a hard, wooden chair. They were equidistant from the outside doorway — about three feet away. The door was closed. Marilyn hoped it wasn't locked.

Marilyn's meditation training had taught her how to move stealthily and breathe quietly. The only problem was the present situation made her heart feel as if it was about to leap out of her chest.

Quiet down Marilyn; say your mantra.

Following her own advice, she began the silent repetition. *Ha-reem; ha-reem; ha-reem.* In a few minutes, the effects were noticeable: muscles relaxed, quiet breathing, barely perceptible heart beat, low blood pressure. Surreptitiously, she slipped off the couch and began to crawl.

Jacques let out a snort. Marilyn immediately froze. His eyes reflexly opened; they closed without focusing. Marilyn was given a temporary reprieve.

A few seconds later, she reached the door. Effortlessly getting up, she turned the knob to the right and pushed. It didn't give way. She pulled; it still was secure.

Oh, no! Don't be locked, she screamed silently.

The Haitian began to toss and turn; the pistol moved precariously to the edge of his lap.

Marilyn turned the knob to the left. She pushed. Again, no movement occurred. Silently praying, *Please God,* she pulled. With a squeak from the rusty hinges, the door opened.

Fleeing outside with her only possession — her pocketbook — she heard a metallic clang.

The squealing door awakened Jacques from his reverie. As he twisted, the pistol fell to the floor. Picking it up, he looked around.

"Where did she go?" he cried in anger and anguish.

Ever since high school, Marilyn had been a fast runner. It started with the high school track team, progressed into the college lacrosse team, and culminated as a three-times-a week Florida jogger.

Running for her life, she reached the edge of the woods surrounding the bokor's temple. Tripping on a fallen branch, she fell to the ground — just as a bullet flew over her head.

* * * *

Looking into the parking area, and seeing the empty Buick, Jacques figured that she must have fled into the woods. Running in that direction, he fired several shots indiscriminantly. Waiting a few minutes and hearing nothing unusual, he proceeded cautiously toward the trees.

* * * *

Again meditating for inner quietude, Marilyn hid behind a large, bushy undergrowth. Looking out, she could see the Haitian advance. His gun was drawn; he was moving slowly.

* * * *

Pushing branches and leaves aside as he walked, Jacques could find no sign of Marilyn. After a few fruitless minutes, he reconsidered. *Maybe she went in the other direction.*

Turning around, he headed for the field at the back of the temple.

* * * *

Seeing the Haitian depart, Marilyn exhaled deeply. *Now I've got to make the most of it.*

As he walked in the field, Marilyn entered the car. Taking the other set of car keys from her pocketbook, she was thankful that Haiti — although backward in many ways — had a car rental agency that issued two sets of keys per car.

I haven't driven a shift car in years; I hope I remember how.

Shifting into first gear, she slowly let up on the clutch and gave it gas. But her timing was off, and the car's engine konked out. She tried it again with the same result. After the third failure, the engine backfired.

* * * *

Hearing the noise, Jacques quickly reversed his course. He saw the exhaust smoke.

"Stop lady!" he screamed as Marilyn finally got the car to move.

He fired the pistol. The car was in second gear and moving about ten miles an hour. The back windshield splattered. Shards of glass went into the visor — just missing Marilyn's left ear. The car was in third gear; the speed was up to 25 mph. Another bullet hit the rear bumper.

* * * *

Taking dead aim, Jacques had Marilyn's head directly in his visual field. He fired; nothing happened. The barrel was empty. Cursing, he walked back to the temple.

* * * *

Shaking with emotion, Marilyn drove away; she hoped to find the cemetery — the place where she knew Hank had been buried alive.

* * * *

The buried-alive Hank Meltzer opened his eyes. He could see nothing. Feeling around in all directions, he realized that he was lying down in some sort of enclosure.

Oh my God! he shouted to himself, *I've been buried alive. But I can think. I can't be a zombie. The antidote must've worked. How the hell am I gonna get out of here?*

On Monday evening when Hank got undressed, he took everything out of his pants pockets. Out of the right rear pocket came the packet containing a zombie antidote that Marilyn had placed there. Marilyn had acknowledged what she did. Together the two of them read the instructions — just in case.

Yesterday morning, when Hank got dressed, he placed the amulet and fetish in the left rear pocket of his gray Bermuda shorts. In the right rear pocket, he inserted the antidote packet. Later that afternoon, when he felt himself going "under," just before he collapsed, he opened the packet, generated a lot of saliva by chewing an imaginary meal rapidly (since no water was available), and swallowed the moistened contents. Obviously, it was enough to prevent zombification, but it did cause Hank to have a wild hallucinogenic nightmare.

This morning, in his anxiety over the current apparently hopeless situation, he temporarily forgot about the dream.

There must be some air pockets or tubes in here 'cause I'm still breathing.

Suddenly, he recalled the earlier events. *Holy shit, now I remember — the crazy animals, the zombies coming out of the graves, the surging stream. It was so real. I really thought it was the end. Gee, it was only a dream. The poison did it. I can't worry about that now. I've gotta get out of here.*

When Hank was a member of the Beaver Barbell Club, he was an excellent bench presser — pushing up 300 pounds off of his chest while in a supine position. The recent workout sessions with his old buddy and present employee, Eric Adler, had rejuvenated his triceps and pectoral muscles — those primarily responsible for bench pressing.

Mustering all of his strength, and aided by a copious release of anxiety-induced epinephrine, Hank pushed up on the lid. Slowly but surely, it began to move. However, the movement was minuscule. The lid couldn't be elevated because it was covered with many pounds of earth.

I'll have to unhinge it. Then maybe I'll be able to use it as a lever to push out the dirt.

With a tremendous surge of power, Hank unhinged the casket. Using every ounce of his strength, he was able to break apart the sides of the casket. Fortunately for Hank, it was a poorly constructed wooden framed box.

Now he had the arduous task of displacing the earth. Working in cramped quarters, he had little room for leverage. Another problem was the air tube connections became separated. Hank was having great difficulty in breathing.

Taking one of the broken slats, and using it as a shovel, he began digging his way upwards. For a weaker or less motivated individual, it would have been a hopeless situation. But Hank would not give up. After a few minutes of digging, there was only about six inches of earth to remove before he would reach the outside air.

Like a landslide, a sudden backlash of earth came crushing down, pushing Hank backward and filling his nose, mouth, ears, and eyes with dirt. Hank could neither see, hear nor speak. (Of course, there was no one he could talk to.) His mind, though, was still active. *Can't stop now, gotta get out, must find Marilyn, can't give up.*

With an unbelievable resiliency, he pushed aside the layers of dirt. Finally with a gasp, he moved away the last remnants of earth and reached the sunlight. Crawling up, he collapsed over the lip of the grave. He remained there for what seemed like forever.

* * * *

Pierre Mancion and César Joliet were only about a quarter mile away when Hank collapsed on the rim. Parking the Jeep (Mancion had now appropriated it as his own) on the gravel filled enclosure, they got out of the car and approached the rusted black wrought iron gate — the entrance to the cemetery. The sound of the clanking gate reverberated in the silent morning. It signaled the hour — exactly 7 A.M.

* * * *

The noise woke Hank out of his stupor. Wiping the dirt off his lips, he slowly got up and looked around. The sun's illumination allowed him to observe his surroundings. This time it was no dream. He saw two men about 300 yards away; they were advancing rapidly. Realizing that in his fatigued and somewhat toxic condition, he would be unable to make a rapid escape. So, he crawled on his belly until he was beside a large mausoleum. The Frenchman inside had perished over 150 years ago — obviously he had been quite wealthy to have afforded such a burial place with its wrought-iron railings and triple-tier construction. Hank wasn't concerned with the elegance of the marble edifice, but he was pleased that the extensive shrubbery placed around the gravesite afforded him concealment. Lying down inside a large bush, Hank dared not breathe audibly. Having been inside a casket for many hours had given him a lot of practice in shallow breathing.

* * * *

"That low-down bastard! How in hell did he get out?"

The normally calm and reserved, Pierre Mancion, was screaming uncontrollably. César Joliet was shivering in fear, hoping that the bokor's rage would not be displaced upon him.

"I can't believe it. Even if he wasn't given the zombie formula, he shouldn't have been able to get out of the casket. But he was given the poison, and it had to be effective. He was out cold when we brought him here yesterday. Wasn't he, César?"

"Yes, he certainly was," César meekly replied.

"Unless someone dug him out. Was it you?"

"Of course not! I wouldn't think of it."

"Well, the three of us were the only ones who knew that Meltzer was buried here. If it's not you, it has to be Jacques. In case Meltzer is still wandering around here, you stay and comb the area. If you find him, knock him out with your club. Don't kill him! I'm gonna go back and question Jacques. I should be back in about thirty minutes."

"Okay."

* * * *

Pierre opened the door. Jacques was sitting down; his hands were wrapped around his head.

Looking around, the bokor yelled: "Where's the lady?"

"She escaped."

"Escaped? You let her get away?"

"No! I closed my eyes for a second. The next thing I knew, she was gone."

"She didn't run out; you let her out. You also dug Hank Meltzer out of the ground and set him free. Now he's gone."

"No," the bokor's aide pleaded, "I didn't go to the cemetery."

"You're lying. I know; they paid you off. I will now close your eyes forever."

"No, not that. No! please! No! Look; search me. I have no money. I didn't let them get away. Why would I? I am loyal to you. To you only."

Mancion was deaf to the supplications. He had made up his mind. Once he made a decision, it was irrevocable.

Staring into his eyes, the bokor applied his curse. Using hypnotic techniques derived from ancient Congo lore, Mancion's gaze penetrated into the very depths of the native's eyes and soul. Pierre began a monotonous chant: "Rah-mah; mah-reem; rah-mah; mah-reem."

The native was trapped by the force of the bokor's implacable will power and his own unrelenting fear. The repetitive sound rapidly brought him into a deep somnambulistic stage. His cultural background primed his autonomic nervous system response — a curse by a bokor could only lead to death, unless the curse was lifted. The native realized that this curse was forever.

His body responded as expected: a racing heart beat; soaring blood pressure; rapid and shallow breaths; rigid muscles. Just when his heart was about to pulsate through his chest wall (at least that's how it felt to Jacques), the skids were turned on. His heart beat slowed down; his blood pressure decreased; his breathing quieted; his muscles slackened.

Were the gods relenting? No! It was merely a paradoxical response, a type that often happens to an apprehensive patient whose heart rate and blood pressure soar when faced with the sight of a needle, and then conditions reverse rapidly as the person swoons in a dead faint. But this was no fainting episode for Jacques Cardinale. Slower and slower — all of his functions retreated into silence — deathly silence. In a matter of minutes, the native fell down on the floor — the victim of the power of suggestion. The eye to eye contact triggered irreversible changes that ended as a horrendous death.

Pierre Mancion was so upset that he decided his underling did not deserve a proper burial. Considering this, he dragged the corpse into the woods, leaving it for the scavengers to devour. Returning to the car, he drove back to the cemetery. Spotting César sitting morosely by a small headstone, he knew that Hank Meltzer hadn't been found.

He shouted: "Get in the back, César. Jacques dug Meltzer out and he let the woman escape, too. I hope for your sake that you had nothing to do with any of that."

"I swear; I knew nothing, nothing at all. You can trust me. I will never betray you."

"We'll see. For now, we must try and find them. I don't care how long it takes."

* * * *

Turning a corner, Marilyn spotted the Jeep pulling out of the cemetery. Seeing it head in her direction, she drove the Buick into the adjoining woods.

* * * *

His mind preoccupied with finding the Meltzers, Pierre Mancion didn't notice the newly made clearing in the woods. Driving straight ahead, he began his search.

* * * *

Observing all that went on from his hidden perch, Hank spotted the Jeep pulling away. As it disappeared, he slowly got up, wondering what to do. He didn't have to reflect long. Sighting another car in the distance, he quickly fell down behind the mausoleum. Holding his breath, he carefully watched the car's movements.

* * * *

Meanwhile, Marilyn was in deep thought. *Now that I'm here, what makes me think that I'll find him. He probably was in the Jeep with the Haitians. I better turn around and try to follow them.*

* * * *

Spotting the Buick, Hank leaped from behind the crypt. Shouting as loud as he could, a weak sound was emitted: "Marilyn, Marilyn, here, Marilyn; here I am. It's Hank."
   Oh my God! I hope she hears me.

* * * *

Stress has many deleterious aspects to it, but one of its advantages is that its primes the senses. Hearing the faint sound as she was about to turn, Marilyn saw the bent-over figure. Getting closer, she realized it was Hank. "I'm coming, honey; I'm coming."

* * * *

There are many sources of happiness: money, prestige, power, health, friendships, family, religion, but for Marilyn and Hank, there could be no greater happiness in life than finding each other alive and well. The rest of the world didn't exist for the next few minutes while they held each other with loving embraces filled with tears of joy. Each had lost their first spouse and were overjoyed that a repetition of that occurrence did not take place. Finally when they were no longer overwhelmed with emotion, they put their collective minds to the forthcoming task of how to get out of Haiti alive.

30

Thursday, September 21

Marilyn was at the wheel; Hank wasn't up to driving. The trip back to Port-au-Prince took over seven hours including a stop-over at Gonaives for lunch. Hank was weak, tired, and sick from his ordeal. In bits and pieces, he told Marilyn the details of his entombment and escape. He also filled her in on his bizarre nightmare. In turn, Marilyn told Hank about her escapade and flight to freedom.

It was 5:15 as they approached the city. Having missed their return flight to Miami, they would have to stay another day in Haiti. Marilyn spoke out: "I think we should go see Ahram Mazalo. I don't think he was behind Mancion's attacks on us. But I really don't know what to think anymore."

"I'm not sure of anything, but I agree with you. I think we can trust Mazalo, but who knows? At any rate, someone let Mancion loose on us. You know, I'm beginning to think that the Cuban and his Japanese wife set us up. After all, if Mazalo is not involved, they're the only others who know we're down here."

"I think you're right. So, do we take a chance and go to Ahram?"

227

"Yeah, we'll do it. It's hard to believe he set me up. After all, he gave me the zombie antidote. This stuff saved my life. But this time we'll make sure we're well prepared."

With that, they altered course — destination Bizóton.

* * * *

Another course alteration was taking place. It was a sudden upward rush of air. The light, warm air was ascending while being displaced by denser and colder air on its borders. The air flowing in from the bottom was being deflected by the earth's rotation as the whirl was forming. The whirl rapidly increased in violence toward its center of low pressure. It started from the heated air of the Atlantic Ocean, the Caribbean Sea, and the Gulf of Gonâve. The violent whirl was several hundred miles in diameter. The tropical heat and the water vapor furnished the energy to maintain the vast, churning 75 mph winds.

Little did they know, but while Hank was entombed and Marilyn was imprisoned, a devastating hurricane was brewing. Now, as they were on their way to see Ahram Mazalo, the storm erupted.

* * * *

A non-metereological kind of violent eruption was taking place on a telephone line between Little Havana, Florida and Limbe, Haiti.

"What do you mean Gonzalez and Rodriguez fell into a waterfall and drowned? How the hell could that've happened?"

"I'm sorry, Carlos. I saw it coming, but I couldn't stop it. They were rushing to catch up with the Meltzers. They were side by side. Jorgé tripped on a rock and fell into Roberto. They were right at the edge of the fall. I called out. It was too late. They fell in, and I couldn't look for them and still keep an eye on the Meltzers."

"So, what happened to the Americans?"

Mixing lies with the truth, the bokor replied: "I followed them, met them at the Citadelle. I turned on the charm and convinced them I was a friend of Ahram Mazalo. Then, I invited them to my sanctuary. After that, I poisoned them. They are now in my possession."

"Well, don't kill them yet. Haruo and me want that pleasure for ourselves. We'll be down on the next plane."

"I would be pleased to see both you and Haruo, but it will not be possible now. We are in the midst of a strong hurricane. No planes will be flying for a few days, I'm certain. Meanwhile, I'll keep them drugged."

Calming down, Carlos replied: "Okay, just keep them zonked out. We'll be down as soon as we can take off."

Now realizing that in spite of its intensity, the storm gave him at least a couple of days to find the Meltzers, Pierre Mancion concluded: "That will be fine. I'll take good care of them."

But for the time being, Mancion and his aide, César Joliet, were also grounded.

* * * *

When the winds started, Hank knew trouble lie ahead.

"Marilyn, this gotta be a hurricane or at least a real powerful storm. I remember the last hurricane we had back in Florida. We don't want to get caught in something like that."

"That's for sure. We're not too far from our hotel. I'll drive as fast as I can."

"Don't worry about speed, just get us there. The winds 'll blow for a few hours before the rain starts. At least that's the way it was back home."

"You're right. I'll be careful."

Hank remembered the last time he was caught in a storm. It was last year in Florida when he had been poisoned with tetrodotoxin — the puffer fish poison. He nearly didn't make it to Dr. Epstein's office. But that storm lasted just a few minutes. He was certain that this one would be much worse. His cockiness about the delayed onset of the torrential rain was pure masculine bravado. Silently, he prayed he was right.

* * * *

Actually, the hurricane had been brewing for several hours. While they were driving, the Meltzers had been so taken up with each other and so concerned with getting back to Port-au-Prince that they didn't notice the increasing velocity of the winds. By the time they became aware of the change in the weather pattern, gale force winds were already starting.

It was now 6:15. Under normal conditions, they would have been at the hotel twenty minutes ago. Frantically, the wiper blades moved back and forth, trying to bring some clarity to the windshield. The liquid streaks pelted the glass with unrelenting force, and the worn-out blades were helpless against the onslaught. Internally from the defroster, hot air gushed upward, but the volume was insufficient to bring clarity to the inside windshield.

The wind played havoc with the Buick — rolling it from side to side. In addition to everything else, Hank and Marilyn were getting nauseous.

"Hank; I can't see any more. I don't know what to do. I - - - "

Just as she was about to give up in desperation, Hank screamed: "I can't believe it; it's there; I see the sign; it's the hotel; we've made it."

They were only fifteen feet from the circular driveway. The Hotel Vodun had saved the Meltzers and the petered out Buick.

In a few minutes, they were resting comfortably in their quarters awaiting a room service hot meal. Before that, the front desk clerk gladly accommodated them by extending their stay for three more days — the time when the hurricane was predicted to become another page in history. Fortunately, the Meltzers' history was still in the making.

31

Monday, September 25

The Express Mail letter arrived at the hospital administrator's office at exactly 9:15 this morning. In this age of instant communication, it was not unusual to get next day mail or faxed materials, especially for a hospital administrator. However, Joel Glick was intrigued when he saw the sender's name.

With great anticipation, he opened the envelope, and read the letter:

Dear Joel:

It must have come as a shock to have found out that I canceled my patients and left without saying a proper goodbye. I didn't do it out of ingratitude or to be antagonistic. I've been very pleased with the staff, administration, and my colleagues at North Miami Beach. However, I'm getting on in years, and I felt the need for a drastic change. Although this sounds like a last minute decision, I have been planning it for several years. For a long time now, I have taken my vacations in the Caribbean.

My favorite destination was St. Maarten. Rather than just retire down here, I decided that I still like my specialty, but I wanted to practice at my own pace and continue my research in a thoroughly relaxed environment. Therefore, last year I took the examination to be able to practice down here in St. Maarten. I recently found out that I passed. I am practicing once a week and am enjoying my life thoroughly.

I now realize that I have too many friends and acquaintances in Florida to just leave without any further word. So, I shall return shortly, stay for about a month, and make the appropriate farewells.

Sorry for any inconvenience I may have caused.

Sincerely,

Ralph Blackmore

* * * *

The violent rains subsided a day and a half ago. Today, it was relatively calm, but it was still a wet and drab looking day. Hank and Marilyn had to extend their stay for two more nights. The airport was a mess with wrecked planes, fallen debris, and torn up runways. If the clean-up crew could rectify things, they would be leaving for Miami Thursday morning. This morning, they were finally able to communicate with Ahram Mazalo. Filling him in with the bare bones of what had happened, an appointment was arranged for 3:00. It was to be in his *hounfor.*

* * * *

"Well, Haruo, I finally got a go ahead from Pan Am. Our flight to Haiti is on for Wednesday afternoon. That is unless there's a last minute glitch."

"That's great, Carlos. We finally will be able to gain revenge for our comrades back in Tokyo."

* * * *

By noon, Drs. Banks and Goodman had seen the letter anesthesiologist Blackmore wrote to administrator Glick. The two obese physicians discussed the implications at lunch.

Internist Arnold Banks began: "Ernie, now we know for certain: Lavier has to be Ibu Mazalo's killer."

"It sure looks that way, Arnie," the pathologist replied.

"Yeah, it would make no sense if Ralph was the killer for him to have written a letter giving a return address and telling Glick that he'd be back soon."

"You're right — unless he's the killer but believes that nobody suspects him."

"That's a possibility. Using that logic, he would come back just to make us think he's got nothing to hide."

Nevertheless the pathologist wasn't convinced about this alternate possibility saying: "It certainly seems that Lavier is the more logical candidate. After all, he disappeared; he was close to the scene of the crime; and he left no forwarding address."

"Right! He also hasn't tried to communicate with any of us."

"So now all we have to do is find Lavier."

"A tall order. By the way, did that toxicologist find puffer fish poison in the other dolls — the ones associated with the other victims?"

"Yes. Milton found traces of tetrodotoxin in all the dolls. After our last conversation, I told Lieutenant Braverman about our speculation with respect to Lavier. Over the weekend, Braverman's men got a search warrant and went through Lavier's house. As far as I know, they didn't find anything unusual. They also have no idea where he's at."

"Well, at least that's a good start."

"Not only that, I've also started the paperwork to get the bodies of the victims exhumed. I don't think we'll be successful with that approach. Milton said that he's certain that they're was too little toxin used. After all, as far as we know, none of the victims showed serious signs of puffer fish poisoning. Not only that, Milton said that the trace amounts that could've been present, by now most likely would've been broken down by the body."

"You're going ahead with it anyway?"

"Right! We're not going to leave any stone unturned."

* * * *

Ahram Mazalo was amazed: "You're lucky you weren't rich or prestigious enough to have been buried in a crypt. As strong as you are, you wouldn't have been able to break out of stone and marble."

Hank and Marilyn had found their way to Mazalo's *hounfor* a few minutes after 3:00. It was fortunate that the houngan had recently renovated his temple. The prior building would have been destroyed by the storm. Minor damage had occurred, but the structure was intact.

Marilyn had spoken first and gave a detailed description of her capture and escape. Hank had just finished revealing his own harrowing experience. The priest's reply brought a wry smile to his haggard features.

Marilyn then spoke up: "So Ahram, what can you tell us about Pierre Mancion?"

"He's small but powerful; he's very wicked. He's got strong political connections with the government and especially the *tonton macoute* —that's the secret police. Not only that, he's probably the most skilled practitioner of black magic — an ultimate bokor. We've got our hands full in trying to deal with him. But he brainwashed my brother. As much as I am angered and disappointed in Ibu, I realize that he came under the influence of this evil man. If you want me to, I will do all I can to wipe him off the face of the earth, and send his soul to infinite damnation."

Hank and Marilyn looked at each other. As much as they wanted to return to Florida, they still wanted to gain a measure of revenge. They also wanted to be able to find out if Mancion had any connection to the Candianis.

Speaking for the two of them, Marilyn said: "We want your help."

"There's one stipulation, however."

"What's that," asked Hank.

"The method I have in mind to deal with Mancion may be quite repulsive to you, but I have to insist that it be done that way."

Hank looked at Marilyn; she nodded in return.

"Okay," Hank said, "do it your way; we don't have to watch."

* * * *

No one was watching David Lavier. That was because he wasn't doing anything in particular. In fact, he was bored. He couldn't help but recall George Bernard Shaw's immortal lines: *"But a lifetime of happiness! No man alive could bear it: It would be Hell on earth."*

The first couple of days of sun, relaxation, sightseeing, and shows were fine. But as Shaw reminded him, too much of a good thing was just that — too much. *Cancun is great for a vacation, but it's not forever. I miss my friends and colleagues. I want to get back to the hypnosis meetings; I want to continue my research. I've gotta go back — at least for a little while.*

* * * *

This evening, two jets arrived at Miami International Airport. They landed within twenty minutes of each other. Both had left from southern warm weather resort areas. The plane that departed from St. Maarten came to a shuddering halt in front of gate 5 at 6:20 PM. The one that left Cancun taxied in a few minutes later. On each plane was a doctor returning for a short stay, a doctor associated with the North Miami Beach General Hospital.

The plane from St. Maarten had a baggage unloading delay. The plane from Cancun had prompt baggage release. The baggage pick-up sections for the two flights were adjacent to each other.

Picking up his suitcase, Dr. Ralph Blackmore headed for the exit. As the anesthesiologist was about to leave, someone accidentally knocked into him. Turning around, he spotted the retired surgeon, David Lavier.

"What are you doing here, Dave?"

"I just got back from Cancun. How about yourself?"

"I just returned from St. Maarten."

"Great! Let's share a cab goin' back."

Riding back to Miami, they talked about hypnosis. But it went deeper than that. Realizing that the chance meeting could have dangerous implications, the rat-expert doctor used a subtle hypnotic technique on his knowledgeable colleague. It was subtle but powerful — powerful enough to lead his associate to an insidious death.

32

Wednesday, September 27

Today, after two fruitless days of searching, Ahram, Hank, and Marilyn finally tracked down Pierre Mancion. They had been to his temple on both previous days and found it deserted. Yesterday, a decision was made to intervene, and then wait for the bokor's arrival. Hence, using Ahram's tools, and under his direction, Hank drilled a small opening near the outside foundation of the building. It led directly into Mancion's private room. After the aperture was completed, Hank covered it with leaves and dirt, giving the site a normal appearance to the casual glance. Hank and Marilyn had no idea for what the opening was to be used. Nevertheless, true to their word, they didn't question Ahram about his intent.

Ever since he unknowingly passed Marilyn on the road, Pierre Mancion had been combing the countryside looking for her and Hank. Two hours ago, exhausted, he returned to his sanctuary. César Joliet was not with him. The bokor dropped him off at his broken down shack. Joliet, considering himself lucky to be alive, packed some belongings, had a small meal, and promptly took off as fast as he could. He had no idea where he was going. His only goal was to get as far away from Mancion as he could. Knowing what happened to Jacques Cardinale, whom he was certain was innocent, he wanted no part of a voodoo curse.

Mancion was in no condition to curse anyone. He just wanted to get some rest. After that, he would decide whether it would make any sense to continue his pursuit of the Meltzers. At this moment, it appeared fruitless. So what he would have to do is figure out a way to deal with the Candianis. They were due here later this afternoon.

When they find out that the Meltzers escaped, they'll be after my head. I'll have to figure out a way to get rid of them before they get me. First, I need a short nap to renew my energy.

It was now 4:00 P.M. Ahram Mazalo and the Meltzers were in the rejuvenated Buick. It was parked in a partially cleared section of the woods, out of sight from the returning Mancion. Two days ago, the Buick had been given a new lease on life by the car rental's service station. Although, the Meltzers could have rented another car, they figured the Buick — in spite of its problems — hadn't deserted them when they needed it most. So, with a tune-up, a lube, and a cleaning, the car was in tip-top shape (or at any rate as good as it would ever be).

Ahram, holding a large, black satchel, spoke to the Meltzers: "I'll be gone for a few minutes. Just stay in the car and relax. Remember, I'm doing it my way."

Hank and Marilyn had accepted Ahram's authority in this mission; therefore, they remained quiet. The houngan left the car and walked toward the house. In a few minutes, he had reached his destination.

Pierre Mancion was resting comfortably in his bed. The crickets, frogs, and grasshoppers had quieted down, and all was now silent and peaceful. Yet unbeknown to him, a beehive of activity was going on.

* * * *

At that moment, while sitting on a park bench across the street from the hospital, the rat-expert doctor was feeling truly sorry about his latest victim. After all, he didn't ever want to end the life of someone who was not seriously ill. He certainly didn't want to terminate a colleague, and of all people he never would have wanted to get rid of a fellow member of the Greater Miami Society of Clinical Hypnosis, especially someone he had known for years.

I had no choice, he told himself. *That unfortunate meeting at the airport would undoubtedly have led the authorities to me. There's one consolation; he lived a long and successful life. But now I know I made a mistake. I should never have come back. Now that I'm back, I'll have to get plastic surgery. There's no way, though, that I'm going to have general anesthesia They'll just have to do it under "local." It won't be so bad. I'll use self-hypnosis, too. So, it's plastic surgery. And then I'll move somewhere else and get started again. Maybe I'll become a stage hypnotist. It's got to be better than just sitting in the sun; it might even be fun.*

Just then, an idea crashed to the forefront. The implications were startling. *Wow! What a strange twist. I won't have to do anything. Ralph Blackmore was away in St. Maarten. He told me about his sudden departure and his decision to return to say his farewells. I'll just go back to the hospital and tell them I was on a short vacation, too. If they ask me about my being in Little Havana, I'll tell them, from my interest in hypnosis, I went to a shop to purchase voodoo dolls — just for fun, of course. With me returning and Blackmore not coming back, they have to figure he was the killer — that his letter about returning was just a ploy. Since I've come back of my own free will, they'll never suspect me. Then I can go back to doing everything I had done before. I'll just have to forget about helping sick old people out of their misery — at least for awhile.*

* * * *

The Lord created the Heaven and the Earth and populated the
Earth with living creatures. Judging by the Biblical version
of the Garden of Eden, the ecological relationships among the
various plants and animals was originally intended to be
harmonious. Apparently when Eve ate the apple, disharmony
set in. Not only did it eventually lead to Cain killing his
brother Abel, it also set in motion a whole host of inter-and
intra-species conflicts. Thus was born the predator-prey
relationships.

This afternoon, three groups of predators were competing
with each other for their prey — a member of the species,
Homo sapiens.   One of the predators was an Insectivora
representive, the second was a member of the Annelid
worms, the third came from the Class of Reptilia.

Pierre Mancion got out of bed. Going to the sink, he
washed his face and hands. Feeling the need for fresh air, he
headed for the exit. Opening the back door, he walked
around the temple, and headed for the dense forest. Entering
the woods, he spotted two individuals. They were about fifty
feet ahead of him.

Who can they be ? he wondered.

As he got closer, it was evident to him that one was a man,
the other a woman.

They're Caucasian. What can they be doing here ? he
asked himself.

A few seconds later, he was almost upon them. Now he
was certain; it was the Meltzers.

*Subtle methods are a thing of the past. I'm gonna get rid
of them for keeps*, he told himself.

Taking out a Colt .45, he pulled the trigger twice in rapid
succession. His vision was perfect; he had scored a double
bulls-eye. The Meltzers went down screaming. The sound
of their dying moans reverberated in his head. But suddenly
he wasn't happy; just the opposite, he was in agony.

Waking up, he realized it was him screaming, the rest had been a dream. He was being attacked on all fronts. The creepy, crawling tarantulas were inflicting their painful wounds on his back and legs. Although he worked with spiders for his various formulae, they disgusted and frightened him. Now, they were tearing him apart.

Others joined in the foray. Scores of leeches mounted a frontal assault, sucking the blood from his chest and arms. Pain and fear mounted as the worms dug in deeper and deeper.

The most treacherous attack of all came from the slimy ones. From the snakes' tubular fangs, the toxin-modified saliva was ejected into his face, mouth, and neck. Writhing in pain, Pierre tried to dislodge the various creatures. As each one was flung off, two or three others came on as replacements.

* * * *

Ahram walked into the house of evil. Hearing the bokor scream brought a smile to his face.

"Why did you try to make Hank Meltzer a zombie? Why did you have his wife terrorized?"

"Get these monsters off me. Then, I'll tell you everything."

"You have no choice, my friend."

"All right; it was Carlos Candiani; he's working with Haruo Maruoka. They wanted me to take care of the Meltzers. It was for revenge for those Japanese terrorists, the JRA. Candiani and Maruoka work for them. Obviously, Hank Meltzer was in Japan and did something to members of their gang. Now, please, get them off me. Carlos and Haruo will be here soon. You can take care of them yourself."

"Okay, Pierre, I'll save your life, but only if you help us trap the Cuban and the Japanese lady."

"Of course, anything."

"Now, close your mouth and eyes, put these plugs in your ears, and hold your nose."

Ahram Mazalo then delivered a strong spray to the entire exterior of Pierre Mancion's body. Falling like flies, the locusts and tarantulas hit the ground; the snakes uncoiled and writhed away aimlessly. In spite of being covered, enough of the fumes got to Mancion to temporarily cause him to lose consciousness.

Knowing that he had a few minutes to spare, Ahram went out to the car. He told Hank and Marilyn about all that had occurred and the imminent arrival of Carlos and Haruo. They would be well prepared.

33

Wednesday, September 27

When Carlos and Haruo left earlier today to fly to Haiti, they left Carlos's zombified father, José, with Carlos's friend, Ronaldo Colofron. During the last few days, José had been quieter than usual — not that he could make any kind of conversation anyway. His frequent nasal utterances had almost stopped. He just sat around and stared into space.

It was 4:15 P.M. The Pan Am jet with Carlos and Haruo on board had pulled up to the gate at Port-au-Prince International Airport. At that very moment, José Candiani let out a piercing shriek.

"What the hell was that?" yelled Ronaldo to no one in particular.

Rushing into the bedroom, he saw the old man slumped forward on his bed. Listening to his chest, he could hear nothing. He put two fingers on his wrist; he felt nothing. Placing a water glass in front of his nose and mouth, he waited for fogging to occur. Nothing happened.

"Holy shit! The old man is dead. I better call the hospital. I don't want Carlos to think I had anything to do with it."

243

* * * *

At exactly 5:15, Carlos got behind the wheel of a rented blue 1980 Plymouth Valiant. Seated next to him was Haruo. They were on their way to visit Pierre Mancion in Limbe. This trip was all business. Once they had taken care of the Meltzers, they would check in at a hotel.

"Because of the damn airport security, we couldn't take any guns. No matter, we'll get something from Mancion."

"That will be fine, Carlos. I am certain he has a method that would appeal to our needs."

"Yeah, the weirder, the better."

* * * *

By this time, they were all inside Pierre Mancion's private room. The bokor was being extremely cooperative. He told them everything he knew about the Cuban man and the Japanese woman. In turn, Hank filled in Ahram Mazalo and Pierre Mancion about the doll relationships of the recent Florida deaths and the zombie, José Candiani.

"Ahram," said the bokor, "I am very sorry to tell you something that will dishearten you greatly, but your brother, and my pupil, Ibu, has been killed."

"What!" shouted the three others simultaneously.

Pierre then gave the details as far as he knew them about Carlos Candiani coming into the doll shop and finding Ibu Mazalo dead on the floor with one of his dolls nearby.

"I am greatly saddened. Although I disapproved completely with what my brother was doing as well as your methods, Pierre, I could never have wished for his death."

"Well, now we can't question your brother about the zombification of José Candiani. What the hell, that was just a set-up as we've now found out."

"You're right, Hank," Marilyn interjected, " I think there's even something else involved. All of those mysterious deaths of the sick old men, including my father, seemed to have resulted from the toxin released from those dolls. Didn't you also tell me, Hank, that Dr. Goodman, the pathologist suspected that suggestion or mind control was part of the picture?"

"Yeah, I see what you're getting at. Maybe, some knowledgeable guy — even a hypnotist — was working with Ibu to get rid of the old people."

"And if I'm correct," added Marilyn, "they probably had some sort of argument, and the hypnotist or whoever he was, killed Ibu — perhaps with the same lethal combination."

"One other thing," said Hank. "As far as I can remember from my talks with Dr. Goodman, all of the victims had recently been hospitalized at the same hospital, you know, North Miami Beach General."

"I got it," interjected Marilyn, "it probably was a doctor who was the killer — or maybe some health-care worker."

"That's just what I was gonna say," Hank said sarcastically, "But I think it was a doctor. I don't think it was just some hospital worker."

The slightly perturbed Marilyn asked: "What makes you think so?"

"When I was a detective back in Philadelphia, we sometimes used hypnosis to help solve crimes. I was invited to attend a couple of the meetings of the Greater Philadelphia Society of Clinical Hypnosis. At one of those meetings, I asked the society's president about their membership. He told me that they were limited to physicians, dentists, and psychologists. In other words, they were all doctors. So, if the Miami hypnosis society operates the same way, and if the killer is a hypnotist, then I bet he's a doctor."

"All of this sounds like good reasoning," said Ahram, "but let us wait. I am sure that Carlos Candiani can fill us in on the details."

Fearing for his life, Pierre Mancion remained silent.

During the next few minutes, a plan unfolded. All that was required was the arrival of the JRA terrorists.

* * * *

A few days ago, the rains had ceased; since then the weather had been blisteringly hot.

As they entered the town of Limbe, the heat was getting to Carlos Candiani: "This is worse than Florida. And the damn car doesn't even have air conditioning."

"This is a poor country, Carlos. They can't afford luxury items. Don't worry, we won't be here long. As soon as we complete our mission, we'll check into the hotel — it has air conditioning — and tomorrow we'll be on our way home."

"All right, Haruo. Anyway, according to the directions, we should be at Mancion's place any minute now."

"That's it," shouted the Japanese terrorist, as she spotted the horse's skull across the crossbar. It denoted the entrance to the bokor's sanctuary.

"Wait a minute! Don't get out yet. Somethin's 'fishy' here."

Carlos noticed the Jeep in the parking enclosure and further back in the woods, he spotted the parked Buick.

"Why are there two cars here? Yeah, and why are they far apart?"

Haruo shrugged her shoulders.

"You stay in the car. I'll look around. Keep the car locked and lie down. I'll be back in a couple of minutes."

Stealthily, he surveyed the building. Peering through the large side window, he saw that the sorcerer's ritual room was empty. Moving toward the back, he looked through the rear window. Two people were seated. They appeared to be having an animated conversation. No weapons were in sight.

Returning to the car, he signaled to Haruo. She unlocked the door.

"I think it's safe. We'll just be careful."

They approached the front door. Carlos turned the knob. As it gave way, the two of them entered. The odor was overpowering.

* * * *

Hearing the front door close, Pierre left his private room and entered the inner sanctum.

"Carlos, I presume?" Having never met him in person, Pierre assumed correctly that the male opposite him was the Cuban, Carlos Candiani.

"And this beautiful woman must be Haruo."

"Correct on both scores. You gotta be Mancion, right?"

"Yes, my friend, I am Pierre Mancion."

"Nice place yah got here. But the stink is somethin' awful."

"I'm sorry that you disapprove of the odors, but in time you will hardly even notice them."

"The hell with the smells. Just show me where you're keeping the Meltzers."

"Fine. They're in my private chamber. I'll take you to them."

"All right. No games, yah hear me?"

"Why of course not. Why would I do something like that? After all you pay me well. I'm no fool."

"Carlos, don't over react. Pierre seems like a very nice and trustworthy person."

"Thank you, Haruo. Oh by the way. I was talking to my deputy, Franchot Bleuer when you came in. He's in the back. He was just about to leave."

"Okay. Just get rid of him. Then, it's down to business."

As he heard the cue, Ahram, in the guise of Franchot, entered the bokor's nefarious sanctum.

After the introductions were made, Ahram turned to leave. At that very moment, he grabbed Haruo while Pierre kneed Carlos.

As the JRA terrorists let out resounding screams, both were given intramuscular injections of a dilute dosage of zombie poison. Pierre Mancion had supplied the concoction, and Hank and Marilyn, coming out of their hiding place behind the bamboo curtains, delivered the injections.

* * * *

At first, César Joliet was happy just to be able to get away from Pierre Mancion. He was lucky to be alive considering what the bokor had done to his other helper, Jacques Cardinale. After César had run for about a half hour, he changed his mind.

Running away will solve nothing. With Mancion's tontons macoute connections, eventually he'll be able to track me down. No, I've gotta take my chances. I will go back to his place; I know how to get rid of him for good.

* * * *

The knockout dose was such that it would keep Carlos and Haruo unconscious for at least one hour. While they were drugged, Ahram tied the two of them up. For good measure, he also tied up Pierre.

"So, my American friends, what do we do now? Do you want me to take care of all three of them native style? Do you want to bring them to America? Or do you want to take care of them yourselves?"

While Hank and Marilyn were considering the options, nature was insidiously at work. It wasn't a spontaneous act of nature. As with most of the deleterious manifestations attributed to either an act of God or nature, this one was initiated by man. In this instance, the man was César Joliet.

* * * *

César had prepared himself well. Pierre Mancion's temple wasn't in the kind of condition as was Ahram Mazalo's *hounfor*. In fact, the hurricane had weakened it considerably. Aware of this, César went around to all four corners of the building. He placed the necessary materials in the required positions. Energizing the reaction, he quickly left the premises.

* * * *

They were so involved with coming to an equitable solution that they didn't recognize the change. Part of their lack of awareness was related to the pungent odors. They were so strong that even with the passage of time, the foul emanations were still present. True, olfactory accommodation had lessened the strength of the penetrating odors, but there were still enough present to mask the new smell.

Since they were concentrating on each other, their field of vision was also narrowed. As such, they didn't notice the enveloping grayness.

By the time they were aware of the roaring flames and the choking smoke, the entire building was on the verge of collapse.

Chaos filled the air. It was every man for himself. There was no time to untie the bokor and the JRA terrorists and still get out alive. Nevertheless, Hank and Marilyn went to their aid and tried to undo their knots.

Ahram screamed out: "Get out quickly; you'll be burned alive." With that, he left.

Just then, the altar came crashing down. The snakes and goats — mere statues — roared with the fire as if they were alive.

"We can't save them, Marilyn. If we don't get out this second, we're goners."

Dragging the reluctant Marilyn to the back door, he was just about to open it went the roof collapsed and the boards and cinders completely blocked the exit.

Ahram, who was outside, had witnessed the crash. Fearlessly, he leaped through the window of the back private room. While the smoke was suffocating him and the Meltzers, he pulled each in turn through the window. Marilyn became unconscious from oxygen lack. Hank was barely conscious. Ahram carried Marilyn to safety a few hundred feet away. Hank, although in a semi-conscious state, was able to crawl to them.

Inside the sorcerer's sanctuary, the flames and smoke combined with the noxious voodoo and zombie chemicals. As the temperature mounted, the reactions became more violent. Suddenly, nature brought forth one of its most ferocious kind of reactions, and the building disappeared with a frightening explosion.

34

Monday, October 2

At 2:00 P.M., an informal conference was taking place in the doctors' lounge at the North Miami Beach General Hospital. Unrelated to any recent deaths, its purpose was to address the current situation with respect to Drs. David Lavier and Ralph Blackmore. In attendance were: the hospital administrator, Joel Glick; the pathologist, Ernest Goodman; the internist, Arnold Banks; the psychologist, Ronald Fielding; and the physical therapist, Sidney Sargent.

In spite of his plans, Ronald Fielding still had his old face; the plastic surgery was scheduled for next week. Following recovery, he planned on taking off for Phoenix to begin his new career as an antiques dealer.

Before the conference began, he was musing: *This is probably the last time these guys will see me like I am now. Boy, would they be shocked with the new me. Hell, who cares! I'm doing it for myself.*

Sidney Sargent's health food organization deal wasn't due to begin for two months. At that moment, he was thinking about it as well as the current situation. *Once things get started, I'll announce my resignation. Right now, I really*

251

want to know what happened to Ralph Blackmore and whether Dave Lavier is innocent or guilty.

Because of circumstances, Arnold Bank's retirement had to be put on hold. First of all, in trying to arrive at a decision, he didn't get any help from the voodoo gods. At this moment, he was reflecting about it. *Judging from what happened to Ibu Mazalo, I don't think I want their blessing. Anyway, I can't even consider retiring now. I really want to help solve the mystery surrounding the bokor's death and those of the other old-timers. The culprit's got to be either Lavier or Blackmore. Whoever it is, as dastardly as the deeds were, I'm intrigued about how they were done. Once we solve the crimes, then I can think about retiring.*

Everyone present knew that, so far, Ralph Blackmore had not returned to say his farewells, even though one week ago, he promised to return shortly. No one present knew he had been murdered.

Everyone present knew that David Lavier had returned, but only Arnold Banks knew why — or at least Lavier's purported reason for returning.

The meeting this afternoon was organized by Drs. Goodman and Banks along with hospital administrator, Glick. They hoped that with the counsel of the other invited doctors, some plan of action would come forth.

Ernest Goodman was the first to speak: "I asked Jonathan Milton, the toxicologist from the University of Miami, to help in the investigation of the rash of recent deaths of old-timers. Although we spent a lot of time and effort to get the victims exhumed, as Milton had expected, no evidence of tetrodotoxin was found. However, he did find a trace of the neurotoxin in each of the dolls found near the victims' bodies."

"So, we've only got circumstantial evidence that foul play has been committed," chimed in Arnold Banks. He added, "However, I found David Lavier unconscious in his car in a section of Little Havana near where the sorcerer, Ibu Mazalo, had died. One of the tetrodotoxin-laced dolls was found close to Mazalo's body."

"That's also circumstantial evidence," interjected Sidney Sargent.

"Right," answered Dr. Banks," and Dave recently admitted to me that he had been to see Mazalo because he was interested in voodoo dolls. In case any of you don't know it, Lavier is heavily involved with hypnosis. And there's some evidence that voodoo is related to hypnosis.

Ernie Goodman has a hypothesis that voodoo, or some form of hypnosis or mind control, could be involved in the killings. The reason he thinks that is because the trace amount of tetrodotoxin that might've been in the victims' bodies was probably too little to have been the cause of their deaths. Am I right about that, Ernie?"

"I couldn't have said it better."

"That doesn't matter," added Dr. Sargent forcefully, "that's even weaker than circumstantial evidence."

"I've got to admit you're right," said Arnold Banks. "One other thing, Dave also told me that he believed that he had been bitten when he was in the bokor's doll shop. He had no idea he was bitten by a spider, and at the time, he didn't realize he had an anaphylactic reaction from the bite."

"One thing I don't get," spoke out Ronald Fielding. "If Lavier is guilty, why would he take a chance on getting caught by returning to Florida? For that matter, Arnie, did he tell you why he left here so quickly?"

"He did; he told me that he was under a great deal of stress and needed to get away in a hurry. He apologized for not letting anyone know about it. *'But after all,'* he said, *I'm only a volunteer and can be replaced.'* He then said, *'Being down in Cancun was great in the beginning, but then I got bored and decided to return.'* That was basically the reasons he gave me for leaving and then returning."

The men buzzed amongst themselves for a few minutes, and when things quieted down, Joel Glick gave his summary statement: "The important thing is that all we have against Lavier is, at best, circumstantial evidence, and his explanation, although a little far-fetched, is definitely plausible. On the other hand, Dr. Blackmore, who was also well-versed in hypnosis, has not returned. What I suggest is that we re-instate Dr. Lavier but keep a sharp eye on him. Meanwhile, we should ask the police to check out Dr. Blackmore. I'm sure we'd all like to know his whereabouts. Is he still in St. Maarten? Who knows? Anything could have happened."

"You're right," added Arnold Banks. "By the way, the police have been involved with these deaths as have been private investigators, Hank and Marilyn Meltzer, who just got back from Haiti. Ernie and I will be talking to them later. I'll let you know what we find out. Meanwhile, Lieutenant Archie Braverman of the Miami Police Force, got a court order and searched Dave Lavier's premises. They did an extensive investigation — at least, that's what he told me — and found nothing irregular. So until we find out something to contradict what Lavier has told us, I think we should just take him at his word."

The rest of the group murmured their assent and the conference concluded.

* * * *

It was two weeks since they left Eric Adler to watch over the private investigative practice. Today was their first day back at the office. Eric told them how he managed the two new cases — a cheating husband and a double-crossing business partner. He was pleased when they praised him for his handling of the cases. When he heard about their exploits in Haiti, he was floored.

"So, Eric, it was a good thing that Marilyn and me kept in shape. Marilyn's speed and reflexes saved her life. Maybe, my little bit of strength helped me dig out of the grave. You better stay in shape. You never know when you'll need strength and endurance."

"You guys are great. I don't think I ever could've done what you did."

"If you had to, you would have found the way."

"Thanks, Marilyn, but I'm glad I didn't have to try and find out. By the way, I did find out something that will interest you guys quite a lot. Last week, I was checking in with a friend of mine who is a receptionist at the North Miami Beach General Hospital. Knowing that it's your personal project, I wanted to find out if lately there were any unusual deaths of old folks. This receptionist — Julie's her name — made some discrete inquiries and said there had been nothing unusual except that an old man who looked like a ghost came into the Emergency Room. He was dead when they saw him — probably had a heart attack. As weird as he looked, the most interesting part was his name. It was José Candiani."

"Holy shit! That's the guy who was the zombie."

"Right, Hank, but please watch your tongue."

"Sorry, Marilyn. Thanks for your help, Eric. Wow, this means that our first investigative case is over. How about that! All the participants are dead."

"It wasn't a total loss, Hank. We did get paid, but the whole thing, obviously, was a set-up. What do you think the JRA will do now? Do you think they'll send any one else after us?"

"If they have any sense, they'll forget the whole thing and create chaos somewhere else."

"If they had any sense, they wouldn't be terrorists."

"You're right, Marilyn, but we can't stay up nights worrying about them."

"Meanwhile, Eric," Marilyn added, "later today we have an appointment with Drs. Goodman and Banks. We'll be discussing the voodoo doll cases."

"One other thing, Eric," Hank interjected, "Ahram Mazalo, as we told you, saved our lives. He said he would be pleased to come to Florida if we needed his help in solving the bizarre voodoo doll-related deaths. So, we may call on him. If we do, you'll get a chance to meet one hell of a guy."

"That's great; he sounds like some character."

"He sure is. Anyway, buddy, watch the office. We'll let you know how things turn out."

"No problem. Watch out for yourselves."

* * * *

As was customary for the dinner trade, the place was filled to the brim. The customers were gorging themselves on assorted delicacies such as pasta primevara, veal scallopine, chicken cacciatore, and fetuccine alfredo. Two rather obese, well-dressed men had not yet started to eat. While they waited for a couple to join them, they were engaging in polite conversation.

"We're both intelligent people, right?"

"I hope so."

"We know we can't live forever, right?"

"That's for sure."

"So why are we committing slow suicide?"

"We are?"

"Sure we are, Ernie. Just look at the two of us."

"Well, we are a little overweight. Is that what you mean, Arnie?"

"Don't use fancy talk; we're just plain fat. Our coronaries are probably clogged already."

"Okay, what's on your mind?"

"Starting tonight, we should cut out fats and sweets, and no more late night snacks. Tomorrow, we begin a regular exercise program."

"You know, I've been thinking about that myself for years. I just never had the gumption to do anything about it."

"Look, I'll tell you what; we'll reinforce each other. Let's arrange our schedules so we can work out together. We can also supervise each other's diets. So, what d'ya say?"

"It's a deal."

Just then, Hank and Marilyn walked into the lavish Italian restaurant. After an exchange of introductions and greetings, everyone ordered a low-fat, low-cholesterol, high-starch meal. Salads and pasta would soon be on their way. Before the arrival of the main course, everyone had a glass of white wine.

While sipping the wine and tasting the greens, the stories unfolded. Once the preliminaries were over, they were ready to discuss a course of action.

Dr. Goodman spoke first: "Hank, Marilyn: since the police have no evidence to go on, they can't do any follow-ups on Dave Lavier. Meanwhile, they're trying to find where on earth is Ralph Blackmore. I've been selected by the hospital's Board of Directors to offer your firm a fee of $3,000 if you would take on the investigation of this matter. They especially want you to check out Dr. Lavier's actions and activities. Now I know it's not a great deal of money that - - - - "

Before he could continue, Hank interrupted: "I'm sure Marilyn would agree with me. We wanna find out what caused her father's death. We're also interested in the deaths of the other old-timers. The $3,000 is a little low, but we'll take on the case."

"Thank you, folks."

Dr. Banks then spoke out: "Try to be as circumspect as possible. We really want to find out if he's up to anything unusual."

"We know what you want, doctors. Between the three of us, we'll never let him out of our sight. If he's the one behind these strange deaths, we'll nab him."

"There's one major problem," Marilyn said. "Even if he's the guilty party, he may change his tactics. He may decide to turn a new leaf."

"Then again," interjected Dr. Goodman, "Ralph Blackmore may be the culprit. I'm sure we'll soon find out about him from the police."

The business having been concluded, the two in-shape and the two soon to be in some-kind-of-shape individuals enjoyed their "healthy" meals. For the first time in years, the doctors

had no dessert. Hank, not being a dessert eater, had no
problem. Marilyn — the chocoholic — was strongly tempted
to order the chocolate fudge-filled canoli. When she saw
everyone else refuse the waiter's suggestions, she suppressed
her desire. She knew about the chocolate brownie in her
"fridg."

* * * *

Dr. David Lavier was at home resting comfortably. Although
so far things were working out well — after all, they
apparently "bought" his explanations, and he got his job
back — he was concerned about two contingencies. The first
one revolved around the whereabouts of Ralph Blackmore.
*Eventually they're going to find out that he took a plane
back to the States. I don't think they'll find his body, and
even if they do, I can't see how they'll be able to identify it.*
Last week, during the cab ride from the airport, the
surreptitious hypnotic technique worked well. Dave Lavier
was able to get his hypnotic colleague into a deep
somnambulistic trance. The conversation in the back seat
was quiet — quiet enough that the driver would have heard
very little of what went on. Even if he did hear something, it
would have made no sense to him. The confusion technique
used by Lavier would have been indecipherable to the cabbie.
Knowing that he couldn't complete the technique for
his own diabolical purpose — the attainment of a
hypnotically-induced death — while still inside the cab,
Lavier gave Blackmore a post-hypnotic suggestion to ask to
come into Lavier's house and request a drink. It worked as
planned, and the initial outcome was perfect.
As far as the cabbie recognizing his or Blackmore's
appearances, he wasn't too concerned about that. They
didn't face him either when they got in or out of the cab. He
also had the cabbie let them out two blocks from his house.
Once they were inside his house, the rat-expert doctor
worked on his colleague's mind for 45 minutes, but the

anesthesiologist was neither a rat nor an average human. His own hypnotic training enabled him to be able to fight the ultimate depression of his bodily functions that would have eventually led to his death. Exasperated from trying to cause a hypnotically-induced death, Lavier decided he would have to end his associate's life using the same techniques as were successful on previous occasions. Going down to the basement, he extricated the last toxin-laced doll from its hiding place; it had been placed in one of the sections of the basement's dropped ceiling. (During their examination of the house, the police never bothered to look there.)

The anesthesiologist was tough, but he was no match for the crafty old villain. In another hour, Ralph Blackmore was in the first stage of decomposition.

Knowing that it was still too early to do anything with the body, Lavier fortified himself for the long ordeal with a few glasses of white wine. Finally, at about 2:00 A.M., he figured it was late enough that the chances were good that no one would be around. First, he went down to the basement and retrieved all the cages with their albino rat inhabitants.

Carrying them up to the first floor, he addressed his furry friends: "My little pets, I have no further need for your services. I'm going to give you freedom, but in return, I expect you to do me a favor."

Putting the cages in the back seat of the distinctive Honda, he left the garage and returned to the house for his decomposing colleague. Carting the corpse into the car's trunk, he headed for a deserted section of Miami. Finding a secluded street, and making certain that no one was watching, he lifted a manhole cover and quickly dumped the body into the sewer. Opening the cages, he dropped the dozens of white rats on top of the corpse. Bidding them farewell, he whispered: "Goodbye, my lovely friends. You can now join your filthy sewer cousins. Enjoy the feast." He hoped the rodents would compete with each other and take good care of the body. Leaving for home, he was certain that no one had seen him.

Lavier's other current problem was more pressing. His laboratory assistant, Jack Albus — the guy who helped him with his recent rat experiments — was no genius, but Albus knew a lot about the doctor's rat experiments. Lavier was positive that Albus was aware that the rats' deaths were somewhat like hypnotically-induced deaths.

Thinking aloud, the doctor said: "I've got to get rid of Albus before someone associates him with me and starts asking questions. Who knows? The cops might even get to him. But I've got to finish Albus off without leaving any evidence. How should I do it?"

Getting out of his recliner, he walked to the window. Staring out, he saw nothing, but his mind was racing. Suddenly he had the solution. *Wow! I know how. Yeah, I'm sure he'll be a good subject. Not only that, he'll be the first one who'll die by suggestions alone. I don't like getting rid of young people, but I can't afford to take any chances. I'm sorry, Jack; you've had it. Your number's up.*

35

Wednesday, October 11

With the surgeon's scalpel, he had dissected the last of the human remains. Actually, there was practically nothing left to dissect. The rodents had performed exquisite surgery of their own. The grisly cartilage and tendon was a little too much for the rats' digestive system, but what they left over was useless for identification. Miami County Coroner, Dr. Bill Barth, was in a quandary about who the hell he was looking at. That's why he had called in Dr. Jeff Duben, a forensic dentist from Ft. Lauderdale.

Walking into the stark-white, brightly-lit hall of death, Jeff Duben remarked: "Every time I come here, Bill, the formaldehyde stench reminds me of the gross anatomy lab back in dental school. How can you take the smell?"

"You get used to everything, Jeff. I even eat lunch here."

"Judging by how thin you are, you're not eating enough."

"Judging by that pot of yours, I suggest that you join me for meals."

"You're one up on me. So, what've you got there?"

"It was brought in this morning from the sewer system. The rats did a number on him; they devoured everything but

261

some cartilage."

"How can you be sure it's a man?"

"I can't be certain, but from the size of the pelvis and the length of the femurs, I think it's a male."

"That's interesting. So, what kind of jaws does he have?"

"Well, he's missing about half a dozen teeth, but he's got bridge work. You've got enough to work with, I'm sure."

"Good, let me take a look."

After about a half-hour, Dr. Duben had done a complete examination of the intact jaws. In the adjoining room, a full series of periapical radiographs were taken. They were developed and fixed in the automatic processor.

Coming back into the morgue's main dissecting room, Jeff Duben announced his findings: "I think you're right about the sex. The roots are long and the posterior crowns are large and bulky — both of which suggest that the specimens came from a male. As far as the age is concerned, this was an older man, probably in his late 60s or early 70s."

"That's something; you told me that newer research is helping you guys tell age from the teeth. Refresh me about that."

"If we look at teeth that don't have cavities, fillings, fractures, or evidence of grinding — in other words, intact teeth — we can examine the size of the root canals from x-rays. You know, the root canals calcify with age, just like joints. Well, research has shown that there are typical rates of calcification dependent upon age. From the size of this guy's root canals, I can judge his approximate age. Another clue is the amount of bone support. The bone loss around his teeth — indicative of periodontitis — is that of an older individual. One other thing: the amount of wear on his lower incisors also indicates a man in his late 60s or early 70s."

"That's great. Now, how about identification? Who was this guy?"

"I don't think that'll be much of a problem. He's got two three-unit fixed bridges, two gold inlays, and five root canal fillings. By the way, the type of restorations and root canal fillings also gives me a clue as to his age."

"How's that?"

"The guy had three silver cone root canal fillings. Now, these were prevalent in the late 40s and 50s, but starting with the late 60s, most dentists did their root canal jobs with gutta-percha — a softer material that shows up much less radiopaque on radiographs than does silver cones. As far as the restorations are concerned, gold inlays were quite popular during the same years as the silver cones. Now, most dentists make either composite fillings or full porcelain-type crowns. So, if these were done about 40 or 50 years ago, as I suspect, the guy couldn't have been a youngster."

"You're quite the detective."

"Thanks. So, now I'll have to make up a dental diagrammatic representation of this guy's jaws and teeth. We'll circularize it to the precincts and media. Since he had good dentistry done, he obviously had gone to reputable dentists. If his recent dentistry was done in south Florida, we'll be able to identify him in a few days."

"Super! It never ceases to amaze me that teeth are the hardest objects in the body. If it wasn't for you guys, we'd be lost. Fingerprints and DNA processing are great, but they're useless in a case like this."

"Have a great day. Oh by the way, I was only kidding; your belly is not really big."

"Right, Bill, and you're not really a living skeleton."

Flashing a broad smile, Dr. Duben left the room, happy to have escaped the formaldehyde fumes.

* * * *

For the last nine days, Dr. David Lavier was an exemplary senior citizen. He was caring with the sick and dying patients and friendly to the hospital staff and employees. He kept regular hours and didn't stray from the immediate environment. He made no long-distance calls, and the most exciting thing he did was to see a reissue of the movie, "The Godfather II." (He missed it the first time around.) He found it exceptionally well done, but he deplored the violence.

This morning, he set in motion the seeds of destruction. He called his part-time lab assistant, Jack Albus. Jack had been taking assorted part-time day jobs while he went to electrician school in the evenings. One of his jobs was working with Dr. Lavier on his various rat experiments.

"Hi, Jack. This is Dr. Lavier. How are you doing?"

"I'm fine, doc; what's up?"

"How's your schedule?"

"I'm still goin' to school at nights. You know, I'm gonna be an electrician. I just finished a part-time job as a lab tech. I've gotta another one startin' next week — next Monday to be exact. Why? What d'ya have in mind?"

"I'm giving a lecture at next week's meeting of the Greater Miami Society of Clinical Hypnosis. It's on animal hypnosis. I want to use my cat as a subject. I could use your help. It won't involve too much. It's a lot easier than working with rats. Basically, I just want you to attract the cat's attention while I use the meditative word technique of hypnosis."

"That sounds weird, doc: hypnotizing animals. How much is the pay?"

"Actually, hypnotizing animals is not that strange. We use a combination of monotonous sounds and touch. You'll see. As far as the compensation is concerned, I think you'll be pleased. It'll only take about an hour of your time, and I'll pay you $100."

"Just like a lawyer: a hundred bucks an hour. Can't complain about that. When do you need me?"

"I was thinking about this Saturday morning at 10:00."

"Well, the truth is I've an appointment then with Dan Marino. He wants to discuss strategy for Sunday's game. He needs my expertise."

"Who's Dan Marino?"

"Who's Dan Marino? He's only the star quarterback for the Miami Dolphins. One of the best passers ever; that's who he is."

Waiting a few seconds for this information to be digested, with a twinkle in his voice he said: "Relax, doc, I was only pullin' your leg. What I said is true about Marino, but he's no friend of mine. Wish he was! Saturday is fine; I'm free. No problem. I'll be over to your place at 10 on Saturday. Thanks for thinkin' of me."

"You're quite welcome. Oh, by the way; you haven't discussed our previous rat experiments with anyone, have you?"

"Hey, doc, I told you, mums the word. My lips were sealed — still are."

"Good! See you on Saturday."

* * * *

"Hello, Hank Meltzer?"

"Yeah; who's this?"

"It's Jack, Jack Albus. He called me. You know the doctor; Dr. Lavier called. He wants me to come over Saturday morning at 10:00. Somethin' about animal hypnosis practice. I'm supposed to help him hypnotize his cat, help him prepare for a talk to his hypnosis society."

"Sounds fishy to me."

"Sounds that way to me, too."

"Okay, you keep the appointment. Don't worry, we won't let anything happen to you."

"Why? Do you think he's violent?"

"No, but as I said, if I'm right, his mind is a very potent weapon."

"Wow! Just make sure I'm safe."

"No problem."

But Hank wasn't so sure. During the last nine days, Marilyn and he had been busy investigating all of Dr. David Lavier's contacts. Most of them were associated with the hospital and nothing unusual came out of the various inquiries. Then, they found out about his employing Jack Albus. When Marilyn contacted Jack and told him of their suspicions, he readily came to their office and told them everything he could remember about the experiments. That was three days ago. At that time, Hank had told Jack if the doctor contacted him to let them know. And that's what he just did.

"Marilyn, I think we should call Ahram Mazalo. Ask him if he can come over as soon as possible. I mean, I can handle it if the guy uses a gun or a knife, but if it's his mind that's doing it, I can't deal with that. I won't even know what he's doing."

"You're right. Why don't you call up Dr. Banks and tell him what we think. If he agrees with our suspicions, I'm sure the hospital will pay Ahram's expenses. And if they don't, we can take care of it."

"Well, we don't have to lose money on the case. But I'm with you. If they get cold feet, we'll bring him over ourselves."

A call with a detailed message to Arnold Banks was returned one hour later later by hospital administrator Glick. Because the police had informed him that Ralph Blackmore had been on a flight to Florida from St. Maarten over two weeks ago, and no one had heard from him since, foul play was suspected. Hence, the Board of Directors readily agreed to pay for Mazalo's expenses.

* * * *

"Hank, of course I will come over. I'll take a flight out tomorrow morning, and by mid-day I'll be back in Miami, again. This time I'll know with whom I'm dealing. My last trip to Miami perturbed me greatly. I was saddened at how my brother lived, but I'm especially upset at how he died. If this Dr. Lavier was the man responsible for his death, as well as the death of Marilyn's father and those other old people, it will be my pleasure to make sure he gets what he deserves."

"That's great, Ahram. I really appreciate your help."
"It's my pleasure."

* * * *

The rat-expert doctor had just taken a refreshing swim in his climate-controlled indoor pool. He dried off, slipped on a white terry cloth bathrobe, and sat down on the inclined lounge chair in his private study. He called Whiskey, and the white, Persian cat, leaped onto his lap where she nestled comfortably. Once again, the doctor was in a contemplative mood. This time he wasn't going to talk to Whiskey about euthanasia or mercy killings. Tonight, more profound thoughts were about to be expressed: "Here I am close to 70; that's almost seven decades of life. I've accomplished a lot, but the one thing that I wanted the world to remember me for — the psychological control of life and death — will never be achieved. I can never lecture about it; I can never demonstrate it; I can never discuss it with my colleagues. Yet, I know that in a few days, I will be able to accomplish it. The spark of life can be ignited or extinguished, and Saturday, Jack Albus will be snuffed out forever. And nobody will know how I did it.

Wait a minute! Now I know how I can show it to the world without any fear of reprisal. I'll set up the camcorder on a tripod from the boiler room. I'll see to it that Jack faces the opposite way. Of course, just like with the rat experiments, it will permanently record my fantastic achievement. I will go down in history."

The one-sided conversation having concluded, David and Whiskey closed their eyes and rested.

* * * *

What started out as a noble gesture — at least as far as David Lavier was concerned — to help sick, dying people leave this earth peacefully, now had turned into the ravings of a crazed killer. What David Lavier failed to realize was that the recording of his act of mental murder would be the proof needed to get him arrested for murder. Without that, the authorities would have nothing concrete to get a conviction for murder. If Hank, Marilyn, and Ahram succeed in preventing Jack Albus's murder, they would also be taking away the one piece of evidence they would need in order to have him put away for good. This was to become a dilemma, of which no one was presently aware.

36

Friday, October 13

It was 9:22 A.M.; Dr. Allison Macrea was upset.

"If there's anything that bugs me it's people breaking appointments. I always keep my appointments. I must be some sort of a nut because so many others just have no respect for obligations.

"Please calm down, Dr. Macrea. I'm sure he just forgot," said receptionist, Joan Kramer. "He's never broken an appointment before. I might've guessed it, though. There was no one home when I called to confirm yesterday — all I got was his machine."

"How about the hospital? Did you try calling him there?"

"I certainly did. I left a message with a secretary or receptionist, but with all that hospital bureaucracy, who knows if he ever got it."

"All right, I'm sorry I lost my temper. Rather than just sit around and read the paper to kill time 'till the next patient shows up, why don't you give me that identification handout — you know, the one with the dental chart of the guy who was dragged out of the sewer."

"Oh, wasn't that revolting?"

In about a minute, Joan returned with the paper.

"Here it is, Dr. Macrea."

Picking up the photocopy sheet, the doctor's eyes scanned the chart, but her mind was somewhere else. Allison was thinking about the tremendous expense of setting up a dental practice and how many years she'd have to work just to pay back the loans. *I count on these patients showing up; I need every cent. Yeah, but I love the location — right in the heart of North Miami Beach. It's everything I've always wanted. I'll just have to grin and bear it. Who knows? Maybe soon I'll get some lucrative bridgework or even an implant or two.*

Coming back to reality, she started to read the chart. Suddenly, something on the sheet struck her. *Silver cone root canals and gold inlays.* "Joan, quick, bring me Dr. Ralph Blackmore's chart."

Since he was the patient who had just broken the appointment, the chart was readily available.

"Here it is, doctor."

The dentist only needed a glance.

"Oh my God!" screamed the normally dignified Allison Macrea. "The dead guy in the sewer was Ralph Blackmore. Get me the police."

* * * *

Typical for Friday, the 13th, the news was devastating. Dr. Ralph Blackmore was dead: the dental forensic evidence was infallible. Without a doubt, he had been murdered, but who did it and how? No one suspected ghosts or goblins, but the way he looked when he was brought out of the sewer made his death appear ghoulish. Although there was no clear-cut evidence, everything pointed to Dr. David Lavier as being the killer. Not only that, everyone present at the hastily called, late afternoon meeting was certain that he had also murdered Ibu Mazalo, James Conover, and the several other recently deceased old-timers. The odds were that tomorrow morning, Dr. Lavier would attempt to do away with Jack Albus, his part-time lab assistant.

The meeting was taking place in a private room at the Miami Police Department Headquarters on Biscayne Boulevard in Miami. Present were: Lieutenant Archie Braverman; Sergeant Chubby Corcoran; hospital administrator, Joel Glick; internist, Arnold Banks; psychologist, Ronald Fielding; pathologist, Ernest Goodman; private investigators, Hank and Marilyn Meltzer; and houngan, Ahram Mazalo.

The lieutenant was the first to speak: "The most frustrating thing about this case is we all know that there's a killer out there, but our hands are just about tied. Why couldn't he have used a gun or a knife or drugs or even a baseball bat? At least, we'd have a weapon to deal with. But if you guys are right, this nut is killing people with his mind. How the hell are we gonna nail him?"

"Maybe, if we catch him in the act, we can shock him into confessing," suggested Dr. Banks.

"That's not so easy," replied Dr. Fielding. "How can we be sure that Dave is trying to kill Albus? He could always claim he was only trying to hypnotize the young man."

"Even if he was attempting to end the guy's life, and you were able to get some kind of confession, he could later claim he was under duress — that it was a forced confession. I don't think that would work," the lieutenant stated.

"It's going to be a tough proposition," Dr. Goodman added. "Let's consider the prior evidence or should I say lack of evidence. None of the voodoo dolls had Lavier's fingerprints. No toxin was found in the bodies of any of the victims. He even covered his tracks at Ibu Mazalo's shop. There was no evidence that Lavier touched either the bokor or the doll. Am I right, lieutenant?"

"You sure are!"

"But we know he did it," chimed in Joel Glick.

"Knowing it and proving it are two different things," emphasized Dr. Banks.

"You're right, but look at the evidence," countered Joel Glick. "There have been no unusual deaths of old-timers recently. Dr. Lavier is probably keeping a low profile since he's not certain if we suspect him. We think he will try to kill Jack Albus tomorrow. I think it's because he wants to get rid of any evidence that could relate his activities to mind control and death."

"That's true,' interjected Hank. "Jack Albus told Marilyn and me all about the rat experiments that he worked on."

"Yes," added Marilyn, "It was clear to me from our discussion with Jack that Dr. Lavier was attempting to prove that fear and stress can cause death."

"Yeah," stated Sergeant Corcoran, "but that still doesn't tell us how we're gonna nab the guy — does it?"

"That is the principal question, isn't it," spoke out Ahram Mazalo. Here is my suggestion. Tomorrow morning at about 9:45, we drive to the vicinity of the doctor's home. Lieutenant Braverman and Sergeant Corcoran wait in an unmarked police car — you have one of those, don't you?"

"We certainly do," the lieutenant stated forcefully.

Ahram continued: "The car should be parked a reasonable distance from Dr. Lavier's home. You wire me up with a miniature tape recorder that is capable of being received in your car."

He looked at the policemen as if to question them about whether or not they had that kind of equipment. The lieutenant looked at him and gave the houngan an affirmative, sarcastic nod.

The plan continued to be unfolded: "Marilyn, Hank, and I will have driven to the site in their Oldsmobile. If the rest of you also want to be in the vicinity, you can all come together in another car. However, you men should remain in the

background. Now at exactly 10:08, I will ring the front
doorbell. This should give Dr. Lavier enough time to have
started his death-inducing experiment but not enough time to
have terminated Jack Albus. By the way, I do not believe that
Westerners know how to utilize the power of the mind to the
extent that death will ensue. I know how to do it, but, of
course, I have never performed that horrendous act.
However, bokors are fully capable of committing mental
murder.

I'm sorry if I got off the track. Let me get back to my plan
of action.   When Dr. Lavier answers the doorbell, I will
announce that I am Ibu Mazalo. Knowing my brother's
idiosyncrasies and bearing a strong family resemblance to
him, Dr. Lavier will be shocked by — what he will believe is
— Ibu's reappearance from the dead. Before he knows what
has happened, I will shake his hand and consequently bend
his soul. Seeing me and feeling my firm handshake should
so shock him that I will be able to come inside the house and
hypnotize him immediately. Meanwhile, I will leave the front
door open so that Hank and Marilyn can follow me a few
minutes later. They will then be able to listen and observe all
that is occurring. Once I get Dr. Lavier to lie down
comfortably, I will extract a confession out of him."

Looking again in the direction of Lieutenant Braverman
and Sergeant Corcoran, Ahram said: "I realize that this can
be considered a confession obtained under duress.
However, I believe that when he wakes up and hears the tape
of his own voice admitting to the various murders, he will
realize that he has no defense. Then he will confess again —
this time wide awake and under no duress.   There you have
it Mrs. Meltzer and gentlemen; that is my plan."

"It sounds like a gamble," said Lieutenant Braverman.

"True," added Marilyn Meltzer, "but it's worth trying.
Isn't it?"

"I agree," said Dr. Banks. "I've known Dave Lavier for
many years; he's a proud man.   If he finds out that we all

know about him, he'll confess. I'm also sure he'll want to tell us why he committed those murders. I'm certainly curious."

Looking around, Dr. Goodman commented: "I think we all are."

"Okay," said Lieutenant Braverman, "let's do it, but remember Mr. Mazalo, you can't force your way in; he has to let you in voluntarily."

"Of course, lieutenant, I don't believe in violence."

With that statement, everything was finalized.

* * * *

Thousands of miles away, another drama was unfolding. An unusual early morning meeting was taking place in a small nondescript building in the Kiba district of Tokyo. The building was the secret home of the mainland branch of the Japanese Red Army. The 25 left-wing guerrillas were there to discuss, among other things, the fate of Haruo Maruoka and her Cuban colleague, Carlos Candiani. Actually, they had received no communication from the two of them in almost a month. A decision was about to be made whether or not to pursue the matter any further.

Yasuhiro Fujio, the pudgy, local leader, speaking in Japanese, was reporting the negative findings to the rest of the group. "Haruo Maruoka is one of our finest members. I am determined to find out just what happened to her. If anything unfortunate occurred, we cannot let that American, Hank Meltzer, get away with it. So, I believe we should use every means possible to - - - - "

Metal smashed, glass shattered, wood crashed, sparks scattered. The auditory/visual explosive disturbance was deafening and completely unexpected. It caught the JRA leader in mid-sentence. Acting on a tip from a paid informant, fifty members of the Tokyo police force stormed the hideout. Hearing the violent commotion, the JRA terrorists grabbed their weapons and fired indiscriminately at the invaders. The police, wearing bullet-proof jackets, answered the fire with a barrage from their automatic weapons. In a matter of minutes, the carnage was complete. The mainland branch of the Japanese Red Army was decimated. The police attack force escaped with few casualties: one dead, six injured. For the time being, depending on one's viewpoint, either a terrorist group or a band of freedom fighters, was wiped out. Whether or not the group would rise from the ashes — like a Phoenix — was anybody's guess.

* * * *

Back in south Florida in a small apartment in Miami Beach, a thin, scrawny, 22-year old part-time lab assistant was very much alive. However, he was having trouble sleeping. He wasn't the kind of a guy who shared his problems, and any way, who could he talk to? His girlfriend, Barbara, was home fast asleep. So, he was left to his own resources. Lying down in bed, thinking about the next day's events left him anxious and frightened. Of course, he didn't have to go along with the plan. He could back out. If he did, he was certain he'd be alive for at least another day. If he followed the plan, there was the chance it would be his final day on earth. But he felt confident that he would wind up the day still healthy and $200 richer — $100 from the doctor and $100 from the Meltzers. The psychologist and the Haitian priest had assured him, he'd be perfectly safe. Then, there was another side to it. If he did as expected, he could help them convict the crazy doctor. Sure, they couldn't bring the victims back to life, but it would be some measure of revenge for the families.

Yeah, Jack Albus thought, *I'll do it and become a hero to boot.*

* * * *

The rat-expert doctor also had trouble sleeping this night. He was restless, not out of fear, but out of anticipation. *Tomorrow,* David Lavier thought, *I'll go down in history.*

* * * *

By a little past 10:30 A.M., two Miami Beach residents would have had their fates sealed. One was a student; one was a doctor. One would have died, and one would have walked away scot-free.

37

Saturday, October 14

The room was pitch black. It was 3:00 A.M. He awoke with a start. His mind was racing feverishly. *Of course! Why didn't I think of it before? If I can use my mind to end life, if I can shut down the immune system, if I can re-program the autonomic nervous system, then why can't I do the reverse? Why can't I use my mental prowess to activate the immune system and stimulate the autonomic nervous system? Why can't I prolong life? Why not? Of course, I would only do it for the strong, for the healthy, for those with good genes. There are enough sick, weak people around. I know how to deal with them. Unfortunately, it looks like I won't be "helping" those kinds anymore. But people like me, folks with active minds, healthy bodies, why should we be shut off forever at age 70, 80, or 90? We should live longer, to 100, 110, 120. Why stop there? I know I can do it. I will dedicate myself to the prolongation of life. Great!*

Wait a minute! Now I remember. There was an article on this subject. I read it recently. Where was it? Yeah, it was in some hypnosis journal. I've got to find it.

277

Jumping out of bed, he walked to the bathroom, relieved himself, washed up, and headed for the study — the room where he kept all his scientific journals. Thumbing through title pages of this year's issues of *the American Journal of Clinical Hypnosis, International Hypnosis Journal, Psychosomatic Medicine, Psychosomatics, International Journal of Psychosomatics,* and *Psychotherapy and Psychosomatics,* he could find no title related to the subject of mental prolongation of life.

Closing his eyes, he tried to relax his mind and let the thoughts flow. After a few minutes he was successful.

Now, I remember; it was a foreign journal. Was it from England? Canada? Ireland? Was it from - - - ? Yes, of course; it was from Australia.

Finding the appropriate journal, he hit it right with the first issue he picked up. There it was right in the September 1989 issue of *the Australian Journal of Clinical Hypnotherapy and Hypnosis.* It was the lead-off article: "The Effects of Hypnosis on Reducing Premature Mortality and Enhancing Vigorous Longevity." It was by Dr. Donald R. Morse from Temple University in Philadelphia.

For the next hour, he critically examined the article. The doctor then concluded: *The guy gave a good review and some hypothetical insights into how hypnosis can prolong life. Yeah, but he didn't really show just how hypnosis could do it, and there were no studies to prove that mental effects could prolong life. That's because no one really knows how to use the mind to add years to life and life to years. I do. I know I do, and I'm going to prove it.*

* * * *

Lying on the animal board, having its paws tied tightly, it was in a helpless, hopeless position. The 30-gauge needle was about to deliver 0.5 cc of sodium brevital. As if it knew what was coming, the rat let out an eerie shriek.

Aiming for the heart, he pushed   the plunger. A strange
thing happened. Instead of penetrating through the skin
and deeper tissues, the needle bent, and the solution splashed
back in his face. Immediately, he was aware that something
was wrong. He was right. Amazingly, the cords holding the
rat's extremities snapped. With incredible speed, the rodent
leaped on him. Its claws dug into his hairy chest; the rat's
incisors pierced the skin of the front of his neck. The vessels
burst open; the scarlet red blood spurt out and splattered
everywhere. His heart beat fast and intensely; it felt like it
was coming right out of his chest. He was breathing faster
and faster, trying to catch his breath. He just couldn't get
enough air. He gasped. He screamed just as his heart flew
out of his chest and crashed against the wall.

With the sweat pouring out of every pore in his body, he
woke up. Jack Albus was scared. He had every right to be
frightened. The nightmare was so real, so foreboding.
Using the bedspread, he wiped the sweat off his forehead.
Sitting up in the bed, now wide awake, he thought and
worried some more. Turning on the light, he looked at his
watch. It was 8:15 A.M.

*I wish it was 10:00 already. I wanna get this over with. I
can't stand waiting any more.*

* * * *

He must have been reading his mind, because just then, he
decided to make a phone call.

"Hello, Jack? (The tone was slow and drawn-out.) I hope
I didn't wake you up. This is Dr. Lavier, Dave Lavier."

"Oh! Hi, doc. No, you didn't wake me. I've been up a
few minutes. I didn't sleep too well. I had a bad dream. It
was worse than that; it was a nightmare."

"I'm sorry about the nightmare, but I'm glad I didn't wake
you up out of a sound sleep. It probably would have been
better if I called you a few minutes before, though. We could
have nipped that nightmare in the bud. But a bad dream is
nothing more than a means of letting out stress. The fact

that you're wide awake now, that's good; that's fine; that's excellent. (Again, every syllable was accentuated in a careful and precise manner.) The reason I called is I wanted to know if it would be at all possible for you to come over a little earlier — say 9:30 instead of 10:00. The earlier start would help me out; that is, if it wouldn't be too inconvenient for you; if you didn't have something else you had to do."

"No problem. In fact, I was just thinking about that myself. You know, that it would be good to start earlier."

"Terrific, wonderful, Jack. I can't thank you enough. (The words were dragged out even slower than before.) I'll see you in a little over an hour."

"You bet, doc."

* * * *

In the airy kitchen of their Pompano Beach home, Hank and Marilyn Meltzer were in the midst of a wholesome breakfast. Now that they were into "health" foods, bacon, sausages, and eggs were a thing of the past. Not completely, though, Hank and Marilyn still had eggs once a week and every so often, they'd splurge with ham or bacon and eggs. Today, however, it was the usual fare: orange juice, mixed bran cereal with skim milk, decaffeinated coffee, and a muffin.

Sitting around the breakfast table, they were going over the upcoming events.

"Do you think this is gonna be the end of it? Will the guy crack? Can Ahram's plan work?"

"Whoa, Hank, one question at a time. It is going to be tough, really tough. Even so, I think our time has finally come. Yes, I really do believe that things will work out, but maybe not just the way it's been planned."

"You're probably right; things rarely work out as planned."

* * * *

Ahram Mazalo had just finished his ritualistic prayer session. Although the Meltzers offered him use of their home, he preferred the privacy of a hotel room. At this moment, he was ready for reflection.

Now that I've just communicated with Ibu's soul; I've decided to forgive him. Yet, his soul is still not free. For him to have everlasting peace, his death must be revenged. I really want to do it myself, but I am a non-violent person. So I'll not take away the doctor's life and soul. But I will make his mind reveal his wrongdoings. Then the police can take over.

* * * *

By 8:30, Lieutenant Archie Braverman and Sergeant Chubby Corcoran were by themselves in a small alcove at the station house. They were drinking coffee while talking strategy.

The tall, thin, middle-aged officer spoke first: "As you can tell, sergeant, this is not an ordinary case. We're just gonna have to sit tight and listen. I really don't know what the hell will happen."

The rotund, Lou Costello look-alike put down his cup and responded: "Yeah, lieutenant, I don't trust that witch doctor from Haiti. Do you think he's gonna cast a spell on the old doctor?"

"I really don't know, sarge. One thing, though, this guy is not supposed to be a sorcerer. They tell me he's one of the good kind of priests. If you want to, you can ask him about it; he'll be here soon. You know, we have to wire him up. So, we'll be listening to anything he does or says. I don't think he'll stick his neck out."

"You're probably right. This still is gonna be one for the books."

* * * *

Meeting in the doctors' lounge were hospital administrator, Joel Glick, psychologist, Ronald Fielding, pathologist, Ernest Goodman, and internist, Arnold Banks. It was 9:15. In a few minutes, the four of them would get in Glick's 1989 Cadillac Coup de Ville and drive to the vicinity of Dr. David Lavier's Miami Beach home. Theirs was merely a back-up role in the case. They were not supposed to even get close to the house; nevertheless, their interest was peaked.

"I really wish I could be there with Ahram Mazalo. I've done some reading in voodoo and mind control, but I've never witnessed it first-hand. Of course, some of my patients think I'm a witch doctor. How about you, Arnie? Do you know much about voodoo?"

"I don't know much about the psychological aspects, Ron, but I am quite interested in the sociological and religious aspects. You know, I've got a collection of icons, statues, and assorted paraphernalia from many religions and cults. I never did get to check out voodoo. Did I tell you that I was about to meet the bokor, Ibu Mazalo, when I found Dave Lavier slumped out unconscious in his car?"

"No, I wasn't aware of that."

"As you know I only deal with concrete things," interjected Dr. Ernest Goodman. "Still, I'm convinced that mind control was a strong part of the picture in these deaths."

"It probably was," added Ronald Fielding. "Hey, Joel, let's get you into this conversation. What thoughts do you have on the subject?"

"Of course, speaking for the hospital administration, we are pleased that apparently it's coming to a head. Deaths that directly or indirectly implicate the hospital are bad news for our reputation. So as far as that's concerned, I'll be happy when it's all over. In another vein, as you remarked yesterday, Dr. Banks, - - - -"

"Hey! Hold it, Joel. Cut out the formalities. We're in this together. Just call me Arnie, and I'm sure Drs. Fielding and Goodman will agree that first names are right for them, too."

Drs. Ronald Fielding and Ernest Goodman immediately nodded their assents.

Joel Glick promptly got back to what he was saying: "Fine, guys. What I was about to say was that I am really intrigued by the possible motives that Doctor — the hell with it — that Lavier had for committing murder. Have you guys got any ideas?"

"I know him fairly well," replied Dr. Banks. "His wife died a few years ago from Alzheimer's, and I know he was very upset before she passed on. It bugged him that nobody would put her out of her misery. I think, under similar circumstances today, things might've been different. At any rate, maybe he had a breakdown of sorts at that time. Possibly, he decided he would not let a similar thing happen to other people. After all, until very recently, he got rid of only sick, old people. Isn't that true, Ernie?"

"Yes, everyone of them was either on the verge of dying from his disease or was chronically ill with a serious or fatal disease."

Dr. Fielding then joined in: "I really do think that Dave became psychotic, but with his twisted reasoning, he probably felt he was helping these people out of their misery. However, with the more recent killings like those of Ibu Mazalo and Ralph Blackmore, and the possible one today, I think he was just trying to save his own life by getting rid of anyone who might have suspected him or could have implicated him. There's no doubt, though, his mind snapped."

"Yeah, Ron, but do you really think," questioned Joel Glick, "that he could mentally cause someone to die?"

"The way I look at it, we've been able to control the autonomic nervous system and the immune system to some extent by psychological means, but to actually cause death, **no way.**"

* * * *

Dr. Ronald Fielding had a probing, penetrating mind, and his analytical skills were excellent, but in about thirty minutes, his conjecture about psychosomatic death would have been proven wrong — dead wrong.

38

Saturday, October 14

After hanging up on Jack Albus, the rat-expert doctor began his preparatory work for his most important human experiment. Using his Craftsman power drill, he made a large enough opening in the boiler room door to accommodate the tubular portion of the Panasonic Camcorder. He set up the tripod in the boiler room, and attached the camcorder to it. He was now angling the tube portion so that it would focus directly on him and Jack Albus. He wanted the view to show both of them from the waist up as they would be seated opposite each other. The camera's view would show their profiles which was just what he wanted. A few minutes later, he tested the microphone; the sound was perfect. He next programmed the timer to go on at 9:30 and go off at 11:00. However, he was certain it would be over way before that time.

I figure that in about 45 minutes Jack will have taken his last breath.

Calling Whiskey, he gave her her chow. Watching her carefully eat it, he was satisfied that she would be content and cooperative.

Dr. David Lavier glanced at his watch. It was 9:25.

He'll be here in five minutes. I must get upstairs to greet him.

* * * *

Driving a red, 1981 Honda Civic, Jack Albus pulled into the driveway. *Someday, I'd like to be rich and afford a house like this. But if that means in order to get it, I have to be crazy like Dr. Lavier, forget the whole thing.*

Ringing the front door bell, he was still nervous.

"Is that you, Jack?"

"Yes, doctor." The anxiety had made him formal.

Opening the door, the doctor escorted him inside. They exchanged pleasantries as they walked down into the basement to the elaborate laboratory.

Positioning Jack in the correct chair, the doctor began: "Jack, since you have been here several times, Whiskey is comfortable with you. You'll have no trouble holding her."

"I hope so; I don't like cat scratches."

"I guarantee it; she will not bother you. In fact, I'm certain that she will be hypnotized rapidly and deeply. All you have to do is hold her on your lap."

"Sounds great to me."

With that, the doctor placed the white, Persian cat on Jack's lap. As he predicted, the cat purred contentedly.

"By the way, if you want to, you can close your eyes and relax as well. It would be boring for you to just watch and listen, because basically there will be nothing to see. If all goes well, the cat will just close her eyes and go limp — nothing dramatic."

"Okay, doc."

It started strangely. Instead of speaking in sentences, he sang.

I never heard the doc sing before. What on earth is he singing? makes no sense to me — none at all.

It was a Creole song; the doctor learned it from Ibu Mazalo. The words made no sense to Jack or the cat; then again, they didn't have to. In fact, that was the whole purpose. Confusion was the method. Dave Lavier had become an expert in the art of confusion. Sending mixed signals, creating a dilemma, generating a catch-22, evoking a double bind; that's what it was all about. Dr. Milton Erickson, a major figure in medical hypnosis was a pioneer in the confusion technique of hypnosis, and Dr. David Lavier became an expert in its use.

* * * *

Earlier this morning when Jack Albus agreed to come over to Dr. Lavier's home a half hour prior to his original appointment, he completely forgot that the entire plan of action was based on exact timing. Stress causes people to become forgetful. It becomes difficult to think logically when anxiety is overwhelming. Jack had been fearful when he went to sleep. The nightmare increased his apprehension. Upon waking, his anxiety intensified. The closer he got to the time of his appointment, the more intense the stress became. The truth is that Jack was not unique in that regard. Studies have shown that the closer, in time and position, that a person comes to a feared object or situation, the greater is the attendant anxiety and stress. By the time Jack had rung the front door, he was in the throes of a panic attack. Yet, he still had to go along with the appointment. If he didn't know better, he would have thought that Dr. Lavier had hypnotized him this morning during the telephone call.

As far-out as that concept was — hypnosis via telephone — it really happened. Dr. David Lavier was aware that susceptible people can be hypnotized by a variety of methods. There have been authenticated cases where individuals have been hypnotized by touch, by music, by odors, by words spoken in a foreign language, and even by telegram. For Dr. Lavier, the use of the phone, with the possibility of using a persuasive, monotonous tone, was child's play compared to hypnosis via the written word. He used a subtle post-hypnotic suggestion that would not allow Jack to fail to show up at the appointed time.

* * * *

The rhythmic sounds continued in a slow, monotonous pattern. Along with the incomprehensible words, meaningful sentences and phrases were interspaced. "You are getting very sleepy, very tired, so relaxed, so peaceful, so calm. It is so wonderful to just let go, to let yourself go. Your heart is slowing down; your breathing is getting so quiet, so calm, so relaxed, so peaceful, so tranquil. Every nerve, every muscle, every organ, every tissue, every cell is quiet, is calm is relaxed, is turning off, is shutting down. Peace lies ahead, eternal peace, everlasting peace."

Then the doctor returned to the rhythmic chanting. The sounds flowed effortlessly.

By this time — 9:45 — the cat was either fast asleep or deeply hypnotized. It was immobile; its eyes were closed; its breathing barely perceptible.

Jack Albus was in the deepest state of hypnosis — the somnambulistic stage. To test the depth, Dr. Lavier gave an analgesia suggestion: "Your hands are falling asleep; it is as if they were in a bucket of ice cold water. The finger-tips, the fingers, the hands, the wrist — they are all getting ice cold, frozen, numb. Your hands are completely numb, without any kind of feeling."

Testing this suggestion, the doctor took a safety pin, unlocked it, and jabbed it repeatedly into Jack's hands. Jack didn't flinch at all and remained absolutely silent.

The doctor tried another suggestion: "I am attaching a large, pink, helium-filled balloon to your right wrist. I let it go. It is rising higher and higher. As it rises, you feel a tug on your wrist. You feel your fingers moving. Now your hand is moving. Now your arm is lifting. Your whole right arm is moving upward as the balloon goes higher and higher.

Watching the arm slowly move upward without any apparent effort gave the doctor further evidence that he had achieved a very deep stage of hypnosis.

Great! He's ready for the final suggestions — the fatal suggestions.

* * * *

Right on schedule came the Cadillac bearing the three doctors and the hospital administrator, the Oldsmobile bearing the Meltzers and Ahram Mazalo, and the unmarked Plymouth bearing Lieutenant Braverman and Sergeant Corcoran. Mazalo had been wired up and everything tested out perfectly.

Even the weather had cooperated. It was a beautiful fall day, warm but not too humid, and no rain in sight or even in the forecast.

* * * *

The camcorder was meticulously recording all that had transpired. A perfect demonstration of combined human and animal hypnosis was captured on the tape. It showed a textbook version of the confusion method of hypnotic induction.

With humans and animals, it is possible to go directly from deep hypnosis into sleep. The cat was fast asleep. Jack Albus didn't know where he was. He heard sounds, he felt sensations. His body felt as if it was floating. It almost felt as if he had no body at all. He had no feeling in his arms. His eyes were closed; he couldn't open them. Were he able to open them and look at his elevated right arm, he probably would not have considered it strange. It would have felt "normal" to be in that unusual position.

After awhile, the sounds got more distant. Jack no longer had any idea of where he was, of what time it was, or of even who he was. Feelings of joy and tranquility became the very essence of his existence. He no longer felt like an independent individual. A spiritual embodiment of serenity, that's what he had become. It was an elixir of ethereal bliss, unlike any drug-induced high he'd ever experienced. Jack lost all control, and he didn't even care. He was in a state of complete surrender.

39

Saturday, October 14

He rang the bell. It was exactly 10:08. A minute passed; no response. He rang again; this time he kept his finger on the bell for at least twenty seconds. Still, no response. He knocked on the door; no response again. He pounded on the door; no one inside had stirred. Now it was 10:11, and Ahram Mazalo was getting perturbed. He turned the doorknob.

"Incredible! It's open," he said loudly.

Then quickly realizing the necessity of silence, he kept his mouth shut and walked through the vestibule.

* * * *

Hank and Marilyn had gotten out of the car when Ahram knocked for the first time. When he finally entered, they were only ten feet behind him, being concealed by a bushy hydrangea.

"As usual, Marilyn, you were right; things never go as planned. I hope Ahram's not too late."

"I've still got a gut feeling that everything will work out."
"I hope you're right. Anyway, it's time for us to go in."

* * * *

Down in the basement, two levels below the foyer through
which the houngan was just passing, David Lavier was
oblivious to outside disturbances. When one is deeply
involved in inducing a hypnotic trance, at times, the hypnotist
himself enters an altered state of consciousness. That was
now happening to the doctor. So even if he had heard the
external sounds, it would have become part of the
background and would have been ignored.

For Jack Albus, at this very moment, it would have taken
the sound of a thunderstorm or an earth-shattering explosion
to have roused him from the depths of consciousness to
which he had sunk. Even then, he might have been too far
gone. At least, he was alive — barely.

* * * *

In the Plymouth, the lieutenant and sergeant were aware of
the problems. They knew that Ahram Mazalo was three
minutes behind schedule. However, they had no idea that Dr.
Lavier had been working on Jack Albus since 9:30.

"What do we do, lieutenant?"

"For the time being, we'll just sit back and listen. It won't
be long now."

"Okay."

* * * *

Passing through the vestibule, he entered a double set of
stairs. The wider stairway went upstairs to the bedrooms and
bathrooms. The narrower stairways went downstairs to the
family room, the private study, and a third bathroom.
Hearing nothing from either direction, Ahram, aware of the

doctor's private laboratory, assumed that it was downstairs. Grasping the handrail, he walked gingerly on the fluffy beige carpeted floor. As he reached the lower level, he walked directly into the ornamental family room with its large picture window facing Biscayne Bay. To the left was the doctor's private study. Glancing in, Ahram noticed the fully-filled bookcase, the large walnut desk, assorted tropical plants, and an aquarium that was conveniently situated in the wall between the family room and the private study.

Where is the lab? he asked himself.

Although he didn't know too much about Florida construction, he was aware that because of the water level in tropical climates, it is the general rule that homes are ranch-type without a basement.

Obviously, this is not a typical home. There must be a basement.

He was right. Years ago, when he began his animal research, Dr. Lavier wanted privacy to conduct his experiments. Therefore, he hired a contractor to build him a unique house on a raised plot that would allow for the construction of a split-level home having a full basement.

Coming back into the family room, Ahram turned around. Then, he noticed two doors. Carefully, opening the one on the right, he was met with shoes, sneakers, clothes, and hats.

Closing the closet door, he opened the adjacent door. This one had a narrow staircase leading to a lower level.

Aha, I've found the basement.

The downstairs was dark but not pitch black. A soft yellow light was on somewhere in a back corner. Holding onto the rail, he slowly and carefully descended into the basement. To the right, he saw the laboratory bench, the assorted animal cages, the variety of lab equipment, and the numerous supplies. To the extreme left was the closed boiler room. Directly ahead, he saw two people seated opposite each other. On one man's lap was a cat; it appeared to be sleeping. The man holding the cat was immobile. The other individual, undoubtedly Dr. David Lavier, had his eyes closed and was saying something in a rhythmic tone. It was so soft that he couldn't make out the words. It almost sounded as if he was chanting in a French dialect.

Ahram decided, to achieve maximum effect, he would walk directly in front of Lavier and then announce his presence.

* * * *

Following in his footsteps, Marilyn and Hank entered the family room. They, too, would have been puzzled about the location of the laboratory, but Ahram had left the door to the basement open. Walking down the staircase, they stopped before they entered the main room. Observing everything that Ahram had seen, they saw him approach the two seated individuals.

Whispering, Hank said: "We'll go back up to the foot of the stairs and remain out of sight until we get Ahram's signal."

"Fine," she responded while slowly tiptoeing up the staircase.

* * * *

The three doctors and the hospital administrator were restless. It was now 10:17. Getting out of the Caddy, they advanced in the direction of the house.

"Let's just walk slowly toward the house," suggested Dr. Goodman. "By the time we get there, I'm sure something will have happened. What do you say?"

"Sounds fine with me," answered Dr. Banks.

Dr. Fielding nodded in agreement and Joel Glick said, yes. With that, the four of them began their slow advance toward the house.

* * * *

Watching them move, the police were not pleased that they
didn't follow the plan.

"What they hell are they doing?" asked Lieutenant
Braverman to no one in particular.

Being the only one around, Sergeant Chubby Corcoran,
answered: "Damned if I know."

"Listen, you go outside and stop them. You can let them
stay out of their car, but don't let them go inside the house.
Got it?"

"Yes, lieutenant."

* * * *

Speaking in deep, mellifluous tones, he said: "Good
morning, doctor. It's so good to see you again. Am I
interrupting something?"

* * * *

For the moment, he had no idea where he was or what he had
been doing, but the voice was so familiar. Reflexly opening
his eyes, David Lavier saw an apparition, a ghost, a satanistic
vision. Not believing his eyes, he closed them again, tried to
breathe quietly, and he did nothing.

* * * *

"Have you forgotten your good friend, Ibu so soon? Was
our friendship so short-lived? Was it merely a financial
arrangement? Did you think that something as trivial as death
could set asunder our permanent bonds?"

* * * *

Now, David Lavier knew he hadn't been dreaming. This was
real, but it couldn't be real. Ibu Mazalo was dead and buried.
He couldn't have come back. Opening his eyes again, once
again his gaze met the old bokor. Temporarily losing control,
the retired doctor screamed: "Oh my God, it's the devil?"

40

Saturday, October 14

From their perch on the top of the steps, they had listened to everything.

The moment of revelation is at hand, thought Marilyn.

Hank wondered whether Mazalo's ploy would work.

Slowly walking down the steps, they anxiously awaited the outcome.

* * * *

The voice was deep; the tone was firm and authoritative: "Now that I have returned from the other world, you must confess all. You must tell me whose lives you ended and why you did those dastardly deeds."

* * * *

Hearing those words, the lieutenant and the sergeant left the car and headed rapidly toward the house. Observing their accelerated movement, the doctors and the hospital administrator took off right behind them.

* * * *

I don't know what's going on. He looks like Ibu Mazalo; he sounds like him. But unless, I'm crazy, it can't be him. Who else could it be? What am I going to do?

* * * *

As he entered the house, Lieutenant Braverman looked at his watch; it was exactly 10:20. By the time the police had reached the basement, the other four were in the upstairs foyer.

* * * *

With everything that had happened during the last few minutes, it might have been expected that the stuporous subjects would have recovered — or at least regained consciousness. Reality was quite different. The cat was still fast asleep or in a somnambulistic trance. Without an EEG, it would be impossible to differentiate the states of consciousness. Had Jack Albus been hooked up, his brain wave patterns would have shown theta waves, signifying a profound meditative state. His heart rate was down to 30 beats per minute; his breathing rate had slowed to 6 respirations per minute. His mind was completely blank.

* * * *

It was 10:22. Ahram Mazalo continued to speak in a monotonous, but convincing, tone. By now, everyone was in the basement. The houngan, the rat-expert doctor, the part-time lab assistant, and the cat were together opposite the boiler room door. All the others were congregated in the center of the room.

* * * *

Opening his eyes again, he spotted the group in the distance. Focusing, he recognized Arnold Banks, Ronald Fielding, and Joel Glick. The woman and three other men were unfamiliar to him. He now realized that this was no supernatural appearance, no hallucinatory apparition. This was reality, and it was apparent that they had uncovered his crimes.

* * * *

Arnold Banks had seen the look of recognition and despair; he sensed that David Lavier was ready to confess, to admit to the murders, to reveal his motives.

* * * *

At 10:24, the final scene began.

Silently, he repeated the sound, *aum*.

Aum, aum, aum, aum.

The sound was attuned to his heart rate, then his respiratory rate, then his brain wave patterns. It waxed and waned; accelerating and decelerating, but never stopping. It soon became distorted. After awhile, it seemed to take on a life of its own; integrating itself into his brain, nerves, muscles, tissues, and cells.

The parasympathetic division of the autonomic nervous system took over control of his body. The heart rate was down to 40 beats per minute, then 30, then 20. The respirations decreased from 14 per minute to 12, to 10, to 6, to 3. The brain wave patterns went from the fast moving, beta to the slower, alpha to the even slower, theta to the very slow, delta.

And then they were flat. The heart stopped beating; the lungs exchanged gases one more time and collapsed.

In the end, he proved his point. It was his own death that substantiated his hypothesis: the power of the mind can induce death. He would go down in history: the entire episode that concluded at 10:31 was recorded on video tape. The Panasonic Camcorder was the most important piece of equipment Dr. David Lavier ever used.

41

Saturday, October 14

The next few minutes were chaotic. The only one who realized what was happening was Ahram Mazalo. Sensing that the doctor was going into a self-induced trance, he tried to disrupt his concentration. First, he tried to do it verbally. When that proved futile, he resorted to physical action. Shaking also was fruitless.

"Hey!" screamed Hank, "What about Albus? How is he?"

Hearing Hank, disrupted Ahram from his resuscitative efforts with the doctor. Quickly moving to the apparently comatose young man, he was about to intervene with some lifesaving measures.

While that was happening, David Lavier was taking his last breath. Instantaneously, Jack Albus opened his eyes:

"Where am I? What happened?"

All present were amazed at this sudden turn of events. Yet individuals knowledgeable about hypnosis are aware that a firm basis for the hypnotic trance is the strong bond of rapport between the hypnotist and the subject. Once that bond is broken, the trance is weakened and eventually unraveled.

301

Experience has shown that if a subject was in a deep
somnambulistic state, and the hypnotist suddenly died from a
heart attack, or any other method, the subject would come out
of the trance. The awakening often would be preceded by a
few hours of normal sleep. For Jack Albus, it was different;
his recovery was spontaneous.

When Jack sat up and awakened, the cat also returned to
consciousness as she leaped to the ground. She was the first
one to her master. Purring and licking, she failed to bring the
old doctor back to life. Next to try was Dr. Arnold Banks.

Putting the stethoscope to David's chest, he listened.

"My God; he's dead — absolutely dead!"

"He must've had a heart attack," suggested Dr. Ronald
Fielding.

"No, my friends; it was no heart attack," said Ahram
Mazalo. "The doctor didn't want to face us; he willed himself
to death."

The lieutenant and sergeant were skeptical; Drs. Banks and
Fielding were uncertain. But the houngan and his friends,
Marilyn and Hank Meltzer, were positive: the old doctor
proved his point; the mind can kill.

Epilogue

Over a year had passed since the death of Dr. David Lavier. Dr. Arnold Banks had retired to Mexico — Cancun, of all places. He lost 35 pounds, never felt better, and became enthralled with the country's Mayan archaeological treasures. Dr. Ronald Fielding had his plastic surgery. His associates were pleased with his appearance, and he was just plain ecstatic. The antiques business wound up being a happy and profitable diversion. Dr. Sidney Sargent had also relocated to a new place and a new field: health foods. It was a prosperous and satisfying undertaking. Another doctor lost a great deal of weight. It was Ernest Goodman: he did even better than Arnold Banks, having taken off 42 pounds, and keeping it off. He couldn't have been more pleased. Ahram Mazalo went back to Haiti. Continuing life as a houngan, he also became politically active, trying to help democratize his country.

Hank and Marilyn Meltzer were home this beautiful winter day: low 80s, moderate humidity, cloudless sky, not a chance of rain.

303

The practice had been going well. The private investigative agency was now well-established. Since last year's bizarre episode, all of their cases had been relatively routine.

Eric Adler decided to stay on as a permanent employee, and they were more than pleased with his efforts.

Hank and Marilyn were outside on the sun deck, resting comfortably on lounge chairs. They were thinking back to that incredible Saturday.

Marilyn was the first to speak: "If the police hadn't found Dr. Lavier's diary — the record of all his experiments — we would've never been certain of his motives."

"Yeah, he must've had the diary with him when he went down to Cancun. That"s why the cops didn't pick it up the first time they searched his home."

"It's hard to fathom. Here he was: a brilliant and quite likeable man. If his wife hadn't come down with Alzheimer's, he might have spent the rest of his life doing charitable work and having been recognized as a renowned surgeon, hypnotist and animal experimentalist."

"It's true, but he became a horrible man with a distorted sense of morals."

"Many people were greatly saddened because of him. I certainly was. Yet in his death, he might have done something that eventually might prove beneficial to all mankind."

"What's that?"

"The last entries in his diary detailed his ideas and techniques for using psychological means to prolong life. As a result of his death, he may have paved the way for all of us to have longer and healthier lives."

"Incredible!"

* * * *

Not incredible but certainly coincidental: at that very moment, two long-time friends — retired doctors — who hadn't seen each other for over a year and a half, ever since they left their Pompano Beach practices, were both vacationing at the Hawaii Big Island Tennis Resort. Avid players, they both signed up for a seniors tournament. Getting each other as first round opponents was a pleasant surprise. Before warming up, they chatted for a few minutes.

After catching up on each other's activities, the ex-podiatrist, Charles Heuer, said: "Al, it's too bad about our buddy, Mitch. He might not've been too keen on practicing dentistry. But it sure beats his present circumstances. Looks like he'll be locked up for the rest of his life."

The ex-physician, Alfred Laturno, countered: "That was tough luck for old Mitch. Now if I wanted to get revenge, I'd have been a little smarter."

"How about that! I was thinking the same thing."

Here's What Reviewers Have Said About Don Morse's "Deadly Reaction" — The First Hank Meltzer Medical Mystery/Thriller

"*Deadly Reaction,* a medical mystery-thriller, weaves together scientific knowledge and a gripping plot. - - - The means the killer uses to introduce the toxin into the body is diabolically clever. - - - The book is unique in terms of the nature of the murderer, his modus operandii and the scientific information divulged." — **The Philadelphia Inquirer**

"Don Morse's first work of fiction (*Deadly Reaction*) is a combination of medicine and murder. - - - (an) entertaining and educational thriller." — **South New Jersey Courier Post**

"In his first mystery novel, *Deadly Reaction*, which has brought him national media attention, Dr. Morse painted a psychological history of the psychopathic killer." — **The Pennsylvania Psychologist**

"The suspense is murderous. Don Morse's new murder mystery novel, *Deadly Reaction*, should find favor among those who like to read a *Quincy-* style story line. Floridians should also enjoy the book's significant setting — Pompano Beach. Call it a fine scientific whodunit." — **South Florida Newspaper Network: Monday Paper**

"Dr. Morse has found a perfect way to intertwine every piece of his background (degrees in dentistry, microbiology, psychology, and nutrition) to come up with the medical mystery/thriller, *Deadly Reaction*. - - - A really great book." — **WTRK-FM-Philadelphia**

"*Deadly Reaction*, a medical mystery thriller, is laden with information on rectal exams, foot doctoring, toxicology, Japanese culture, and Morse's own specialties of dentistry, microbiology, psychology and nutrition." — **Atlantic City Press**

"*Deadly Reaction* is a red-hot murder mystery thriller." — **Joe Franklin — WWOR-TV-New York**

"*Deadly Reaction* is quite a fascinating book. - - - If you want to find out how to commit the perfect crime, read this book." — **WUSL-FM-Philadelphia**

"Dr. Don Morse's medical mystery/thriller, *Deadly Reaction*, is really quite an interesting story.- - - It is an interesting and fascinating novel." — **WIP-AM-Philadelphia**

"In Dr. Don Morse's *Deadly Reaction*, there is a very dramatic and surprising ending. - - - The price of the book is $17.95. That's a pretty good bargain, I would say." — **WFPG-AM-Atlantic City**

"Whodunit? That answer can only be found in the thrilling new medical murder mystery, *Deadly Reaction.* - - - This compelling novel combines suspense, intrigue and medical information into a fascinating adventure that takes the reader from Philadelphia, New Jersey and Florida to faraway Hawaii and Japan. - - - highly successful in providing a story that is both a mystery and educational." — **Cherry Hill News**

"I consumed that book (*Deadly Reaction*) in one weekend. - - - you're going to have an awfully hard time putting it down to have dinner. - - - a book well worth getting your hands on. - - - a fantastic and interesting book. - - - I can recommend it highly. - - - I found it particularly fascinating because it's really an educational book and it's entertaining. - - - Go out and buy it today." — **WWZD-AM-Vineland**

"Dr. Morse, a versatile endodontist, decided to draw upon his background in nutrition to create a thriller (*Deadly Reaction*) about a psychopath who kills his victims with the neurotoxin found in the Japanese puffer fish, which is a delicacy in many Japanese restaurants." — **American Dental Association News**

"Don Morse's *Deadly Reaction* has food and mystery: what a good combination." — **WBUX-Doylestown**

"*Deadly Reaction* is a wonderful murder mystery, a really excellent thriller. It's a whodunit with a very complex story line. It is a very detailed and intense book. It requires a full amount of concentration to fully enjoy and savor its flavor. - - - One of the things I liked about the book was the fact that while you're reading it you realize that the author, because of his background, can give us details and play cat and mouse tricks with us that an average writer couldn't do. Others would had have taken a hell of a lot of research on their part, and they still would have missed some of the subtleties. - - - One thing that is really fascinating is the author's way of teasing the reader in terms of the themes and sub-plots. I had no idea who did it. I did not figure out the end at all. - - - There were some characters in the book that I really like a lot. One of them was the former Philadelphia cop, Hank Meltzer; he was an interesting character. - - - I really see it as a possible TV mini-series — the book lends itself to that style. If you like a really good whodunit, check it out. I strongly recommend the book." — **WSBR-AM-Boca Raton**

"A new murder mystery story, *Deadly Reaction*, by Dr. Don Morse, is an interesting book. He gives a travelogue of Japan and Hawaii, with a history of toxic substances thrown in. - - - it is a fun novel. The method of destruction is unique." — **American Endodontic Society Newsletter**

"Don Morse's medical mystery/thriller, *Deadly Reaction,* is very good. It is very well written and easily read. - - - The characters are very interesting. I can identify with the cop. I found him particularly appealing. - - - The plot is held together very well. Just when you think you have it figured out, a little twist. It's very well done." **WKSZ-FM-Philadelphia**

"The unique quality of this book is that Dr. Morse has taken his medical and scientific knowledge and put them into a murder mystery. - - - Not only is it a perfect read and a good murder mystery, but it is health educational material in its own way." — **WMMR-FM-Philadelphia**

"The medical mystery thriller *Deadly Reaction* is about a near perfect murder that involves a unique nerve toxin that is difficult to detect. The toxin, found only in fugu fish of Japan, could have been used by any of three suspects, all doctors. Dr. Morse uses his background in microbiology, immunology, psychology, toxicology and nutrition to take the reader step by step through the investigations - - - In his book, he shows how naturally occurring toxins in foods can be more dangerous than additives that many people worry about." — **Temple Times**